Molly Moynahan teaches Creative Writing at Rutgers College in New Brunswick, New Jersey and privately in Manhattan. She was born in Princeton, New Jersey and attended Rutgers University and Trinity College, Dublin. She lives in Manhattan.

D1344028

Parting Is

All We Know

of Heaven

Molly Moynahan

BANTAM · NEW FICTION

PARTING IS ALL WE KNOW OF HEAVEN

This is a work of fiction. Names, characters, and incidents are the product of the authors' imagination. Any resemblance to actual events or persons, living or dead, is entirely coincidental

A BANTAM NEW FICTION BOOK 0 553 40366 4

First publication in Great Britain

PRINTING HISTORY
Bantam New Fiction edition published 1991

Bantam Books are published by Transworld Publishers Ltd., 61–63 Uxbridge Road, Ealing, London W5 5SA, in Australia by Transworld Publishers (Australia) Pty. Ltd., 15–23 Helles Avenue, Moorebank, NSW 2170, and in New Zealand by Transworld Publishers (N.Z.) Ltd., Cnr. Moselle and Waipareira Avenues, Henderson, Auckland.

Printed and bound in Great Britain by
Cox & Wyman Ltd., Reading, Berks.

This book is dedicated to my sister, Catherine Moynahan-Rich and her son, Henry Moynahan-Rich. And to my other sister, Brigid Moynahan-Brizzi.

. . . accept the things I cannot change . . .

My life closed twice before its close;
It yet remains to see
If Immortality unveil
A third event to me,

So huge, so hopeless to conceive,
As these that twice befell.
Parting is all we know of heaven,
And all we need of hell.

Emily Dickinson

Parting Is
All We Know
of Heaven

CHAPTER

1

WHEN THE PHONE RANG SHE HAD BEEN EATING SESAME chicken in bed, reading an article about how to microwave fresh vegetables so that they retained their flavor and vitamins. It was a Wednesday, the day food columns appeared in all the newspapers. Despite her own failure to produce anything resembling the creatively planned small dinner parties featured in these articles, such as the *déjeuner sur l'herbe* suggested for a spring event, hope died hard. Just as she kept believing that somewhere there was a man who did not feel it was his duty to inform her he was incapable of commitment, she believed there was hope that someday she might orchestrate a perfectly cooked, color-coordinated, wonderfully simple dinner for five on her stove, which featured a single working burner and a broken oven thermostat.

It was late September, unseasonably cold. The pre–Labor Day freeze had killed a large number of late-blooming flowers. Apples had frozen on the branches in upstate New York. The Korean fruit stands supplied very expensive brands imported from Israel. The heat had not been turned on. She was under the quilt, dressed in long underwear, two pairs of socks, and a large sweater knitted by an ex-boyfriend's mother.

The thing that upset her most about trying to plan a dinner

party was the fact that she owned no silverware. She had managed to accumulate enough forks and knives from her college cafeteria, but these were not the sort of utensils you wanted to give your guests. Chopsticks seemed a logical solution. This was why people got married, she thought, finishing off the sesame chicken, to get silverware. And china. She thought she might consider such a project: register at Bloomingdale's, find a cooperative male pal, and collect some table settings.

She answered the phone expecting to be reminded of a rehearsal for her latest acting scene. Instead she was told by her brother-in-law, Michael, to go immediately to Columbia Presbyterian Hospital.

"Why?" she asked, her stomach already beginning to turn, her teeth grinding together, her skin crawling with cold shivers, fingers of dread. She held the receiver so tightly against her ear she could barely hear. Michael was married to her sister Amelia. He was a very calm man. His voice sounded like a controlled scream.

"Cynthia's been hurt. Very badly. We'll be there as soon as we can."

Michael and Amelia lived in New Jersey with their son, Tom. Cynthia was her eldest sister. As she replaced the receiver, the phone rang again.

"Oh my God, Cordelia!" It was her mother. "They don't expect her to live!"

Running. She fell over the vacuum cleaner and mop, which had been left in the doorway as a gentle reminder to clean. Pulling on her jeans and sneakers, she thought her mother must be confused. If her sister was hurt she would be taken care of until she was better. Living was not the issue. Healing was the important point. It seemed strangely remiss of her mother, a doctor, to confuse the issue. But then her mind began to clear, and she realized that what was happening at that moment was history, like when JFK was shot and her mother was repotting an avocado plant and sat down on the couch and began to wail about John. Cordelia could still remember the checked shirt she was wearing, her mother's face smudged with dirt and tears. Then Martin Luther King, Bobby Kennedy, John Lennon. Each time, she had thought: *This is what I did while So-and-so died.* She imagined herself at a party, leaning forward to accept a celery stick, leaning back and saying:

"Oh, yes, I remember that. That's the night my sister died in Columbia Presbyterian."

She ran from Sixty-ninth to Eighty-sixth before she could find a cab. At one point, having tripped and fallen on a cracked piece of sidewalk, she stayed on her knees, her lungs bursting, and prayed to God to spare her sister. She thought she might reach the hospital in time to perform some sort of miracle.

Cynthia had been stabbed eighteen times. The nurse would not allow Cordelia through the swinging doors that led to the room where all the people were trying to keep her sister's heart from stopping. She could just see Cynthia's hands: long, slender fingers, the rings missing, the skin very white. Someone handed her a knapsack. Inside were a medical textbook, an apple, Cynthia's house keys, and a whistle. A policeman took it away from her.

"I'm sorry, honey," he said. "We need this for evidence."

"That's not my sister," she said to him. He shook his head. "That's not my sister," she screamed. "Her rings aren't on her fingers, and my sister isn't going to die."

Then she shut up. The other people waiting outside the emergency room nodded approvingly when she sat down. She'd allow the mistake to continue for a little while. Soon the family of the unlucky girl dying on the table would arrive, and everything would be the way it was. The way it had to be. She would take Cynthia out for lunch, and they'd talk about their lives.

By the time her mother arrived, Cordelia was perfectly calm.

"Hi, Mom," she said.

"The car." Her mother's voice sounded strange, flat and lacking rhythm.

"What about the car?" Cordelia asked quietly, trying to block her mother's view of the emergency room.

"It's parked illegally," her mother said, her voice rising an octave on each word. "I'm blocking a fire hydrant. I didn't know where to go." She held Cordelia's shoulders and stared into her

3

youngest daughter's eyes. "Where is she?" she whispered. "I'm a doctor."

"Mom," Cordelia said, trying to find something to tell her.

"She's-not-going-to-die," her mother said, shaking Cordelia hard with each word. "You tell me she's not going to die!"

"No," Cordelia said flatly. "They made a mistake."

The doctor came out from between the swinging doors, shaking his head. His white coat was covered with blood.

"I'm so sorry," he said, addressing Cordelia. "We tried everything."

Cordelia's mother screamed. She started toward the swinging doors, stumbled and fell. Two nurses rushed over to pick her up.

The doctor turned back to Cordelia. "I'm very sorry," he said. "She lost so much blood. . . ."

Cordelia shook his hand. "Thank you for trying so hard," she answered brightly. "We really appreciate it."

The doctor would not let go of her hand. The moment became awkward. Cordelia felt sorry for his discomfort.

"You should talk to my mother," she suggested helpfully, removing her fingers from his grasp. "She's a doctor."

Each of the nurses was holding one of Dr. Cavanagh's hands. She was staring at the doors that separated her from her dead child. Cordelia could not stand to look at her.

"Cordelia," she whispered.

Cordelia pretended not to hear. She could not possibly comfort anyone. There was something wrong with everything. It was difficult to breathe.

She walked outside, expecting to see spirits rising from their graves like at the end of *Poltergeist*, the moon spinning toward earth, the city shaking with the beginnings of an earthquake. She thought she'd find people frozen in their tracks, as in her favorite episode of *Twilight Zone*, when time stopped and someone was able to change the future.

The city was quiet. It was very cold. Her eldest sister was dead, and her blood was being scrubbed off the floor of the emergency room by an orderly. The impact of Cordelia's knuckles against the stone came as a relief to the numbness, the silence. A car pulled up to the curb, and her sister Amelia flew out of the door. When she saw Cordelia standing there holding her smashed hand, waiting for some sign that the world was not going to survive this loss, she stopped.

"Oh my God, Cordelia," she said. "Is she going to live?"

Cordelia shook her head. Michael got out of the cab and Amelia sagged into his arms, moaning, her face completely crumpled, like that of a small child whose worst nightmare has come true.

"Where's Mommy?"

"Inside," Cordelia, whispered. "She's got to do something with . . ."

That person inside was not their sister. She had seen Cynthia slip quietly out through the swinging doors, naked and silent; she had put her fingers to her lips in a signal to her youngest sister not to betray her. It was right that she should leave—her body wasn't of any use—but Cordelia wanted to follow.

"What are we going to do?" Amelia asked, looking from her husband to her sister, trembling so violently that her hair fell out of its clip, down to her shoulders.

Cordelia shrugged. For a moment she had the idea that nothing had happened. It was possibly a terrible dream. She closed her eyes for a second, willing herself to wake up. When she opened them again, Amelia still stood there, staring at her, pale and shaking, clutching her husband.

"We can all die," Cordelia said, laughing slightly. "It wouldn't be so bad if we all died."

Amelia shook her head slowly and, leaning on Michael, stepped on the pressure-sensitive mat that opened the hospital door and was swallowed up by the light. Cordelia stood staring at the moon.

"Fuck you, God." she said. "Fuck you all."

CHAPTER

2

O N HER TWENTY-NINTH BIRTHDAY SHE TOOK A FREE YOGA class she had seen advertised on the wall of a bus shelter on West Seventy-second Street.

That morning she had opened her eyes and thought that while T. S. Eliot was undoubtedly a brilliant poet, he was completely mistaken about April. "February is the cruelest month," she muttered to her ashy reflection as she washed her face. "I will show you fear in a handful of dust," she murmured to herself as she shut the door of her apartment.

They had managed Thanksgiving and survived Christmas by ignoring what was still too incredible to accept. Her sister's place at the table remained empty. The chestnuts disappeared from the stuffing, as it had always been Cynthia's chore to peel them, and no one thought to volunteer as a replacement. At Christmas they had drunk themselves sober and then separated to wait for the sun to rise and then again to wait for the darkness.

Cordelia thought she would spend New Year's Eve locked in an empty room, but instead she found herself at a huge party given by someone she didn't know in a downtown loft. She had become increasingly drunk, morbidly depressed, and incapable of doing anything but hanging on to a strange man, who kindly took her outside at midnight to throw up in the gutter.

6

On New Year's Day she woke at dawn and ran until her strength gave out. She sat in Riverside Park and then went to two movies until the holidays were over and there was nothing left to celebrate.

The yoga class was held in a renovated loft on Seventeenth Street. The teacher was a tall, thin man with a beard and strange green eyes. Cordelia suspected that he wore tinted contacts, as they were so emerald-like in their brilliance. When he answered the door he placed his hands on either side of Cordelia's face and stared into her eyes.

"I have known you before in a previous life. I loved you thousands of years before Christ," he said.

His hands were damp, and it was creepy to be touched so intimately by a complete stranger. Still, he had a soothing voice, and the yoga coaxed the tension from her upper back and neck. The room was cool, dimly lit, and quiet. After forty-five minutes of stretching, everyone lay flat on the carpet while the teacher chanted a number of relaxation mantras. Cordelia felt strong fingers pressing into her shoulders.

"Let go," he whispered. "Let go of all that grief, and you will accept the truth."

She didn't know what he meant, but his hands, a stranger's hands, somehow promised safety. So she let go and wept flat on her back in the quiet room. Her sobs echoed against the bare white walls. Tears rolled from her eyes into her mouth and ears. Afterward the entire class chanted until the room vibrated with the sound of their voices.

"Want a cup of tea?" The yogi had removed his turban, to reveal a headful of brown curls. Cordelia disapproved of holy men behaving like human beings.

"No, thank you," she said, unfastening the bolt of the steel door. She was eager to escape his scrutiny, ashamed of her behavior.

"Come back soon," he called after her. "The process must continue."

As soon as she reached the street, Cordelia found a deli and bought a large container of coffee and a Hershey almond bar.

7

"Happy Birthday," she said, her face turned toward the bitter February wind. "Happy birthday to me."

The previous night she had been wakened from a deep sleep by the phone ringing in the kitchen. She had flung her alarm clock under the bed and turned over, but the sound continued. Half asleep, she stumbled into the kitchen, stubbing her toe on a chair.

"What?"

"Did I wake you?"

"Hello?"

"I must have. I'm very sorry, Cordelia."

"Yes?"

"It's Harrison."

"Who?"

"Harrison. Harrison Bishop. Cordelia?"

"Harrison?"

"This is Cordelia, isn't it? Cordelia Cavanagh?"

"Harrison?"

"Yes."

"Oh my God! Oh my God . . . Harrison."

She'd known he would call someday. Despite hearing next to nothing from him in nearly eight years, she'd known it was only a matter of time before his voice would once again dissolve her bones, weaken her to the point where she could barely stand.

"I've left my wife."

"Oh."

"Well, I suppose she more or less left me."

"How sad."

"I've lost custody of Sam."

Sam was Harrison's son. A photograph of a baby had arrived in her mail one day with no letter. She had heard that Harrison had married an American and that his wife was expecting a child. The name "Sam" and a date was penciled on the back of the picture, which was of a baby with a high forehead, piercing blue eyes, and the expression of a future lord. She had stuck the photo next to one of her nephew Tom.

"I'm very sorry, Harrison."

8

It was extremely cold in the kitchen, and Cordelia had been naked under the down quilt. At first the pain of her toe had blocked out everything. Now the receiver rested on her shoulder, while she hopped up and down, trying to raise her body temperature.

"May I come and see you?"

The question hung unanswered for a moment. She thought to say no. No, he could not arrive at her door and turn a not particularly wonderful existence into a living hell. She stalled.

"God, it's freezing in my kitchen!"

"Cordelia?"

"Yes?"

"May I come?"

"I'm thinking."

"What of?"

"Of whether it's a wise idea."

"Of course it is! It's a bloody marvelous idea!"

"When were you planning this . . . junket?"

"Tomorrow."

"Tomorrow's my birthday! In fact, today's my birthday." She had actually wailed.

"Happy birthday."

"Harrison. . . ."

"It's perfect. We'll have a wonderful time. I know the address. I'll try to get out of Washington by noon. I'll call and tell you. I can't wait to see you! It's the big three-oh, right? Sweet dreams, Delia."

He hung up before she could correct him. "I'm only twenty-nine," she whispered to her bread box. She wandered back into the bedroom and turned on the television. Mary Tyler Moore was in the middle of telling Murray about her latest date disaster. Her lower lip was trembling, while Murray made sympathetic clucking noises. It was two in the morning.

She pulled the quilt off the bed and trailed back into the kitchen to check the inventory of the fridge. The shelves contained the following:

a box of baking soda (very old)

9

a jar of blackberry jam (Christmas)

a mysterious carton of Chinese take-out (either duck or shrimp, probably deadly)

a jar of Grey Poupon mustard (old boyfriend)

The freezer was slightly better, producing a half-eaten pint of fudge ripple ice cream. For the first time in her life she didn't need to diet, and there was nothing good to eat. Waves of self-pity engulfed her. She tasted the ice cream; it had been in the freezer too long.

She opened the shades and watched as the couple across the air shaft laid down shelf paper. It was an odd chore to perform in the middle of the night. When the ice cream was gone, Cordelia briefly considered emptying her cupboards and sorting out their contents. But the idea of setting up some sort of triage unit to deal with the unused coriander was depressing. Her cabinets reflected her failure to do anything but dabble in culinary trends. One year it was Thai, then Indian, then sushi. Now she cooked nothing except grilled cheese sandwiches, unless she was responsible for feeding someone else.

"I don't want you to come." It was not a convincing whisper. *"I don't want you to come, you stupid prick!"*

There was a thud from the apartment below. It was Mr. Stetzler. She grabbed a broom, intending to retaliate hard enough to make Mr. Stetzler fear for the end of the world.

Until she saw Harrison Bishop she had feared her decision to come to Ireland for her junior year had been a mistake. She had first noticed his height, then the sculptured perfection of his body. The proportions were those of a Renaissance sculpture, David if he'd played center for the L.A. Lakers. She had been having a dull time at the cast party for *The Milk Train Doesn't Stop Here Anymore*, in which she was cast as one of the fattest and sexiest of Tennessee Williams's southern belles. The only people who had spoken to her so far had said they didn't understand what it was Williams had been trying to prove. The Irish attitude toward Americans was condescending and indulgent.

"Fuck the Irish," she muttered under her breath. "They think we spend all our time paying psychiatrists and shooting each other. The only drama they appreciate is one where everyone drowns or drinks himself to death." She had been living in Dublin for nearly six months now, and she was tired of the subtle disapproval she felt was based upon misconceptions about American behavior. Her professors at Trinity explained things to her very simply: "American students need plenty to write in their notebooks," they said. They didn't think she was capable of reasoning or simple thought.

For the party, she had changed into an "American" outfit, a tight sweater and a leather miniskirt. Now she felt awkward, wishing she had chosen a less conspicuous way to prove herself indifferent to their attitudes.

"Hello, there. You were very good."

He had to bend nearly in half to speak to her. She thought he did it out of pity, since she was standing alone, stuffing herself with unripe Brie.

"Thank you." She tried to tug the hem of her skirt closer to her kneecaps.

"You've managed to shed about eight stone."

"She's meant to be very fat. They strapped pillows around my waist."

"Absolutely. Anyway, I'm partial to large women."

"I'm not large!"

She said it without thinking how silly it sounded and then felt ready to burst into tears and beg this beautiful stranger to forgive her, to just allow her to stand near him for a little while. Her insecurity regarding the play's reception had increased her sense of social failure. She looked up and saw that his eyes were filled with something that resembled compassion. Of course, she thought; women probably always fell to bits in his presence. The idea that she was not unique infuriated her. She stubbed out her cigarette in a cucumber sandwich and tossed back a glass of champagne.

"Are you South African?" she asked.

"Yes."

"You practice and support apartheid?"

"No. Do you practice and support limited nuclear warfare? Funding the overthrow of governments unpalatable to the American taste?"

"No," she muttered stupidly. "I'm sorry." She was surprised at the sharpness of his reply. He was too handsome to be smart.

"Do you like acting?" He was smiling now, and his eyes twinkled.

"Actually, I think it's pretty fucking pointless." Cordelia stood on tiptoe, lowering her voice, her mouth by his ear. "I feel like curling up under a table somewhere. Why are you talking to me? You don't have to."

"Because I think you're the most beautiful woman in the room. You may curl up under my table." He had stooped again and whispered this into Cordelia's ear. He smelled lovely, like spices and some sort of almond soap. She opened her mouth, but he put his fingers gently against her lips.

"What shall we do now, babe?" he said in a bad American accent. "I think something's gonna happen."

"Take me home," Cordelia answered, putting down her drink and picking up her bag.

They rode his bicycle through the empty Dublin streets. She sat astride the crossbar, very high above the ground, his arms around her, holding the handlebars. Every once in a while, he buried his face in her neck and then raised his chin to howl at the moon. It was snowing lightly. Cordelia's hair was covered by a lacy white veil. The city looked clean and lovely, sparkling in the moonlight.

His flat was in Rathmines, a section of Dublin favored by Trinity students for its proximity to campus and the inexpensive rents. They made a sharp left turn down a lane and nearly went over. The house was small and built of gray stone. The garden had been allowed to run wild, and the front was nearly covered by winter roses. His flat was in the basement; it shared a kitchen and a bathroom with two other tenants. The landlady lived upstairs in one room and never slept during the night. She didn't care what people did as long as they dropped in for a chat from time to time.

While Cordelia put the kettle on, Harrison fed silver into the hot-water meter and filled the massive claw-footed tub. He poured in almond oil and told her to get in. When she had finally managed to submerge herself in the scalding water, her entire body beet red, he burst into the bathroom singing, a rose stuck between his teeth. He washed her hair and scrubbed her back and massaged her feet. They soaked, her head upon his chest, until she almost fell asleep.

The bedroom was cruelly cold. He lent her a large cotton T-shirt and left her with a hot-water bottle while he tidied the kitchen. When she woke, he was slipping under the down quilt next to her. It was dawn; red streaks slashed across the brightening sky, and a thin winter light sneaked through the curtains. Harrison pulled her against him, his body fitting hers perfectly. She fell back asleep and dreamed of wild zebras galloping across the Liffey and up Grafton Street.

She didn't go home for a week. Harrison lent her sweat pants and pullovers, which she belted and wore happily. They took walks and baked bread and read books sitting in front of his small coal fire, separate yet still touching. When she woke in the morning it was to roll over and bury her head in his chest, to have his hand stroke her head, to hear his voice murmur "dearest" or "darling," to feel herself absolutely safe and taken care of.

It should have been enough, but it wasn't. She wanted him to tell her that he loved her but he didn't. She wanted him to say it first. When she gave up and said it one night after they had made love on the rug, their bodies shiny with sweat in the firelight, he had remained silent, and that silence was so painful she had risen gasping from the floor, unable to breathe.

"I'm sorry," she had whispered, sitting hunched over in his chair, her arms shielding her nakedness from his eyes. "I shouldn't have said that."

"No," he whispered, not looking at her. "Don't be sorry."

But she was.

She was convinced a man capable of such tenderness could be

13

worn down, gradually altered to fit, like a shoe bought too tight. She went back to her house thinking that he would miss her and tell her that he wanted her to move in, but instead they went on as before, except she sometimes stayed in her own house and there was now a part of herself she could not show to him for fear he would laugh or turn away. She became afraid of his leaving her, and that fear destroyed much of what was good. It took her a little while to observe that Harrison treated others, including children and small furry animals, with the same indiscriminate kindness he accorded her.

One night she drank a great deal in a good restaurant and became enraged at Harrison's easy solicitude toward their waitress. She called him a "silver-tongued fascist" and a "pathological ass-licker." Harrison tried to keep smiling at the other diners, but finally he took her outside, where she got down on her knees and begged him to hit her.

"Do something to show me that I'm special," she shrieked. "Kick me in the stomach so I can feel something!"

He left her kneeling on Grafton Street. Harrison hated public indiscretion.

On her final night in Ireland he had arrived on his bicycle with a knapsack full of wine, cheese, and fruit. They had not seen each other for nearly a month. She had found another lover and rarely allowed herself to frequent the places on campus where she was likely to see Harrison. The other lover hadn't lasted. It wasn't until she opened the door and saw him standing there, his head level with the frame and his arms full of gifts, that she realized how much she had missed him.

In the garden, they lay naked in the moonlight. She sat astride him and, looking down, saw the love in his eyes.

"My beauty," he murmured, pulling her down so that her breasts were tight against his chest and he was deeper still inside her. "My flower gatherer."

They said nothing about their arguments or their failure to reach a compromise. Sleepless, she held him in her arms and wished they had fought harder for each other. When her taxi arrived the next morning to take her to the airport, he was doing yoga in the garden, standing on his head. She tried to make him stop, but he would not open his eyes.

"Harrison," she said, "I'm going home now."

But he was like a little boy refusing to say goodbye to his parents. The last view she had of him was from the back of the taxi. He was upside down, his body impossibly long and graceful, the toes pointed toward the sky.

CHAPTER

3

SHE FINISHED THE HERSHEY BAR AND BOUGHT A COPY OF *Variety* at the newsstand outside the health club where she worked part time. The audition notices catered mostly to nineteen-year-old girls willing to star in "adult-oriented" horror movies. She had gone to one of these auditions and was asked by the director if she objected to being cast as the victim of a rapist-murderer-necrophiliac. The plot revolved around the sufferings of a deranged telephone installer who had a chemical imbalance that made him impotent with nice girls but caused him to lust after sluts, whom he raped, murdered, and then raped again. His job afforded him plenty of opportunities to find victims. She was cast as a nice girl, whom he mistook for a slut, who wanted to have a telephone jack installed in her bedroom. The finale involved the use of nearly every garden tool one could imagine, including hedge clippers and a lawn mower. She was required to say the same thing over and over with varying degrees of anxiety and distress: "Oh, no! God help me! Oh, God!"

She was asked to remove her shirt during the audition, and after a moment she did. The director looked her right in the eye and said something about breast implants. It seemed a bit tactless, and when the makeup person approached her with a powder puff as if he intended to dust the offending objects, Cordelia stood in stunned silence, her arms crossed against her bare chest, resembling a rather tawdry Joan of Arc.

"She's much too flat," the director said. "But we can use a body double."

She was paid well, and the movie was released on the southern chainsaw-murderer circuit, where it played on a drive-in double bill with *Motel Hell*. Some guy Cordelia had gone to high school with called her in the middle of the night after the film was released to ask her where she'd got her new tits. The noise in the background indicated a bar. Her mother thought her facial expressions were wonderful, and Amelia informed her she had sunk to a new low of degradation and that her betrayal of the female sex would haunt her for the rest of her natural life. When she tried to tell her father the news, he interrupted her to explain the plot of a miniseries he had four lines in, and she decided that since the movie would never play in L.A., she might as well not tell him. Cynthia had thrown a party, using a still from the film as an invitation. The picture was of Cordelia staring with unnatural intensity at her telephone. She was introduced to the guests as "My brainless, doomed, too-dumb-to-be-a-slut sister."

Cordelia had met her last boyfriend at that party. A beautiful Hungarian musician with long blond hair and the moral integrity of Fritz the Cat, he had asked Cynthia to go to bed with him one night while Cordelia was in the kitchen attempting to make them blini. Cynthia had picked up a pair of scissors and threatened to cut off all his hair. Yuri's hair was the most precious thing he owned. When Cordelia emerged, he had gone, and Cynthia and she ate all the blini, while Cynthia told her how many women Yuri had abused. Cordelia had already begun to worry about her weight, because she and Yuri were spending large amounts of time in Hungarian pastry shops, consuming Linzer torte with *schlag*.

"My squash ball's dead."

Cordelia looked up from reading *The Seagull*, to meet the lopsided grin of Joshua Benson.

"You like Chekhov?"

"You just want one ball?" Cordelia unlocked the door to the pro shop and pulled down a new can of balls.

"Ah, go ahead and sell me a whole can! What the heck, you only live once! I think you'd make a great Nina, Cordelia."

"Nina? Really?"

"Sure. She's passionate and full of energy and dreams."

"But she complains so much. She just goes on and on about the past. . . ."

"Nah. She's the kind of woman men would die for." Joshua had turned bright red, and sweat was forming on his upper lip.

"How's the acting biz anyway, Cordelia?" He was leaning over the counter, staring into her eyes.

"Okay. A little slow."

"You going to be on Broadway soon?"

"I hope so. You want to charge the balls, Joshua?"

"Sure. Can you go to dinner with me? Anytime."

"Oh, thanks. I really can't."

"Ever?" His face had gotten all crumpled, and he looked as if he was about to cry.

"Oh, no! I mean, I can't tonight or tomorrow or next week."

"But sometime?"

"Sometime. Sure."

Joshua was bouncing nervously on the balls of his feet, and she feared he might suddenly spring over the counter and lay his worldly possessions (which included a condo in Forest Hills, season tickets to the Mets, and a Jaguar) in front of her. His nervous smile was infectious. She felt her lips stretching across her teeth until her jaw began to ache. She remembered that he was a periodontist.

"How's your business?" she asked, trying to change the subject.

"Booming. Yuppies hate to floss. I'll collect on our dinner in two weeks."

She tried to look noncommittal, but he bounced off, waving his squash racket, content that he would probably be savagely defeated by his latest squash partner.

She was nervous and tired, and it was all Harrison's fault. After his middle-of-the-night phone call she had slept only three hours, rising at five-thirty to transform her apartment. The morning was spent cleaning, shaking out rugs, pruning plants, folding clothes, dusting books, washing the floor, the tub, the refrigerator, and, in a final fit of self-abasement, the oven. She had dripped lye on her hand and burned the skin off three knuckles. The oven gleamed. After that she had bleached the hair on her upper lip, plucked her eyebrows, shaved her legs, and applied a cucumber mask to her face, while she conditioned her hair with hot oil and tried in vain to remove the calluses on her feet with a pumice stone.

Her final attempt at transformation had been achieved by attending the morning yoga class. Now she sat behind the front desk of the Garden Squash Club, handing out towels and pretending to read Chekhov while, in actuality, she planned how impressively detached she would appear that evening; free of all unsightly hair but, more important, self-possessed and mysteriously serene.

"You read too much. How are you ever gonna be discovered, with your face buried in a book?"

She opened the refrigerator and put down Philip Syrianos's bottle of Perrier in front of him, without looking up. Usually she flirted with him, but her entire mind was filled with the prospect of seeing Harrison, and she didn't have the energy to act charming.

"Hey? Whatsa matter? Not talking to me?" His solid-gold Rolex appeared on the counter in front of her. She looked up to meet his stare, the deep-set eyes that always startled her with their almost feminine beauty.

"Put that on, babe. You're my good-luck charm."

The watch made her wrist feel delicate and insubstantial. He could have stored it in the safe, but he always said he preferred her to wear it. The entire exchange reminded her of the way a boy would give a girl his jacket to hold while he fought with another kid on the school playground. It was childish but very sexy. He walked into the glass-walled front court and began warming up, his long legs moving him without effort to each corner of the court. The next time she looked up, Philip was serving, his body coiled like a leopard about to spring, yet relaxed as only a powerful player could afford to be. The serve was so powerful the ball was difficult to follow. As the players switched sides, he looked over at her and winked.

At three, she changed into a lavender Lycra bodysuit, black shorts, and running shoes. She set the treadmill's incline to steep and began to warm up her legs. Her Walkman played a Talking Heads song about waking up a baby, as if to remind Cordelia that every other woman she saw on the Upper West Side was pregnant or pushing a stroller. Her stride shortened as she increased the speed of the machine, her breath caught in her throat. She envied those women so much she could barely stand to look at them, hated their air of self-satisfaction as they whispered to the children or held their own protruding bellies. She was tired of smiling at other people's babies and nodding sympathetically when a pregnant woman talked about how exhausted she was.

Pushing again on the button that increased the speed, Cordelia was eager to reach the state where she no longer felt the strain on her body, that place somewhere between agony and nirvana where she could run for hours, her body moving like a well-oiled machine. The voices in her head were difficult to silence. She used exercise as a drug without considering the consequences. After her sister's murder she had stopped eating, and she had now lost most of her body fat. She had spent the winter in a state of semistarvation, consuming enough to avoid collapsing but always on the edge of hunger, embracing deprivation like a secret lover. Her periods stopped, and she viewed her body as something close to a weapon, sharp and clean, angular and cruel. On the nights when she could not black out the picture of her sister lying on the emergency room table and her mother down on her knees, screaming at God, Cordelia pulled out her running shoes and ran in circles from Sixty-ninth Street to 102nd. On her fifth or sixth loop, her mind would empty, and her sole aim would be to lengthen her stride or locate a steep hill to sprint up. At this stage she would no longer feel the tears running down her face, nor was she conscious of talking to herself, an inner singing mantra that basically consisted of her chanting: "I'm okay. I'm fine. Things are better, I promise."

She wasn't okay. She had stopped eating for long enough to be called anorexic, and still the voice kept promising the same thing: "If you get thin enough, no one can hurt you." Sometimes she ran past people returning from a dinner out or from the theater, and they would stare at her and shake their heads. She knew the furies she was running from were invisible to most people. The Korean grocer had patted her arm one night and winced at how bony she had become.

"You not well," he said, trying to make her buy something more substantial than an apple and a bottle of seltzer.

"I'm just fine," she had told him. "How's your wife?"

But he had shaken his head at her, his finger pointing at his mouth.

When forty minutes had elapsed, she realized Philip was standing next to her, stretching his hamstrings, his racket held high and his heels flat. Cordelia pulled off her headphones and slowed down the machine.

"Pretty healthy pace at that incline." He leaned over to touch his toes. The muscles in his legs were very defined. His shirt slid down his back, exposing several inches of tanned skin.

"Yeah, well, I could lose some more weight." Slowing down made her realize how hard she'd been running. It was difficult to speak.

"Nah." Philip eyed her critically, his eyes lingering on her legs. "Well, maybe an inch or two on the thighs."

Cordelia had always been proud of her thighs. An ex-lover had once compared their texture to silk.

"Here's your watch," she said curtly, unfastening it from her wrist and holding it out. "I have to go."

Philip turned off the treadmill and took her hand. "What should we do about us?" he asked quietly, turning over her palm as if the answer were written there.

Cordelia looked down. Her socks didn't match, and she needed a new pair of shoes, a really good brand, like Tiger Asics, but she was too poor. When she looked back at him, her expression was blank.

"Don't give me that airhead stare, you little bitch!" he whispered. "We've been flirting with each other for months. Every time I walk into this place you give me some sort of signal."

"I give you a towel," Cordelia said. "That's my job."

He grabbed her arm just above the elbow and squeezed until she screamed.

"I like my women completely honest, Cordelia. If we're playing cat and mouse, I want you to admit it. It's your job to tell the truth."

Pulling her arm out of his grasp, she got off the treadmill and walked past him without a word or a look.

"I'm going to get what I want," he whispered as she passed. "You won't get away from me."

In the women's dressing room, she pulled off her soaked running clothes and stood naked in front of a full-length mirror. The bruise was already visible on the inside of her elbow. He was very strong. She pushed down hard on the purple spot, and tears sprang to her eyes with the pain of it. She noticed that her ribs were growing less visible and her hips were no longer hollow. From the back, her spinal column was still prominent. She looked at her thighs and wondered what sort of exercise would be most effective.

As she turned onto Sixty-ninth Street, she noticed a man standing in front of her building, a very tall man with a great mane of thick black hair. It was Harrison. Cordelia ducked behind a small tree and then scuttled back across Broadway. It was not yet six. She had expected Harrison to call her sometime after seven. She was wearing a dirty sweatshirt with a sleeveless, ripped, T-shirt layered over it, sweat-pants, shorts, tights, and over it all, a down jacket. Her hair was plastered to her scalp by sweat and pulled back with a piece of the electrical tape used to wrap the handles of squash rackets. In all her layers, she bore a remarkable resemblance to the rotund Michelin tire man. It occurred to her to walk into a store and buy new clothes, but she still needed a bath. How long would Harrison stand in the cold, waiting?

"You low-life bastard," she muttered under her breath as she crossed the street, waving and smiling. He appeared overjoyed to see her; running toward her with arms outstretched, he swept her off her feet, kissing her eyes, her lips, and her hair. Cordelia stiffened. She felt the scene lacked dignity.

"My God," he whispered dramatically. "I had forgotten how beautiful you are."

She felt stupid and uncomfortable being held so tightly by him, especially with several of her neighbors staring out their windows. She dropped her gym bag on his foot, and he put her down. Holding her shoulders, he smiled into her face.

"You are so lovely," he said.

"You've been married," she replied, pushing him up the steps to her apartment. "You aren't responsible for hysterical blindness."

While she removed the first layer of clothing, Harrison prowled around her small apartment, opening drawers and cabinets, smelling her coffee beans, examining the contents of her closets, looking under the bed, picking up the clothes she had hoped to be wearing on his arrival. He looked at a script that was lying on her desk, stared at her head shots and read her résumé, and then began to read a letter she had just received from a friend in Ireland.

"Stop it!" Cordelia screamed, snatching the paper from his hand. "Don't read my mail."

"I'm sorry. I'm acting like a fool. It's . . . I can't believe I'm really here. That this is where you actually live." Harrison's hand was on his coat; he turned toward the door. "Should I leave?"

"No! Don't leave." Cordelia put her hand on the wall to balance herself. She tried to remember how long she had slept. The day had been endless. "Just sit down and stop searching my apartment for clues! Act like a guest. Watch television or something. I need to take a shower."

"Could I make some tea?"

"Please. The teapot's on the fridge."

Above the sound of the shower, she could hear him humming "Eleanor Rigby" and rattling cups. His face had hardly changed. She allowed the water to pound against her neck, trying to will the tension from her muscles. She was crying and wished she could remain under that curtain of steam forever.

When she came out of the bathroom he was sitting on her bed, reading her journal.

"Harrison!"

"What's wrong?"

"That's private."

"Who's Philip?"

"Nobody!" Cordelia grabbed the notebook from him and turned toward her closet.

"Why are you so thin, Cordelia?"

"Acting." She picked up her clothes, shoved the journal into her sock drawer, and walked back to the bathroom.

"Is Philip your lover?"

Cordelia shook her head. The bruise on her elbow had turned violet.

"You shouldn't lose any more weight, Delia. Your shoulder blades look like angel wings."

She faced him and smiled. "I won't."

"Can I see you naked?" His beautiful blue eyes were blank, as flat as glass.

"No." She assumed his wife's desertion was causing him to behave strangely.

"I used to see you naked all the time."

"Harrison . . . we haven't spoken to each other for eight years."

"So what? It's just like it used to be. We're fighting. I'm sitting here overwhelmed by your beauty, waiting for you to finish dressing, making tea, wishing we could go to bed."

"Harrison . . ."

"We used to be naked around each other constantly."

"And I used to love you," she snapped.

"Don't you still? Even a little bit?" Harrison's voice cracked.

She stared at him, expecting to catch a smile, but instead he put his face in his hands as if she had hit him.

"Look . . ." She wanted to cross the room to stroke his head, but she could not move.

"I'm okay." His voice was thick with tears.

"What did she do to you?"

"Oh, not much. Slept with my best friend. Destroyed my business. Stole my son. The usual thing."

"I'm very sorry." Yet she resented his assumption that she was capable of providing some sort of comfort, as if she were a shrine he could return to once every eight years or so for solace. It was incredible in the face of her own tragedy. Her indifference to living felt more pronounced, the distance between them immense. She knew he expected her to cross the room, to drop her towel, to take him in her arms and make him feel better. There was no reserve, no compassion in her heart for anyone. She locked the door of the bathroom and ran the water to drown out the sound of his sobs.

They rode the subway downtown to Chinatown, where they ate sesame chicken and dim sum at a Formica table. Harrison picked up the last dumpling and put it against Cordelia's lips.

"Eat this," he said, smiling. "You've lost all your lovely curves."

Before she could speak, he was kissing her. Their lips parted, and Harrison's tongue was all over her face, while the waiter stood patiently, waiting for them to vacate the table. On every corner in SoHo he bent her backward from the waist, so low her hair swept the sidewalk in a dramatic fall. He kissed her throat, and where his lips touched she felt heat. When they were quiet again they walked all the way back up to her apartment, and Cordelia imagined her other hand being held by a small blond boy who looked just like Harrison.

She lit the candles on her night table, and then Harrison undressed her slowly, kissing each section of bare skin as it was revealed to him. In the soft light she saw the lines of his body, the familiar carved-marble perfection of his torso. He held her in his arms like a child, gathered her against him, and the sound of his heart beating was like waves on a beach. He smiled down at her, but she saw the fear in his eyes, the fear that she would turn from him and not provide the comfort he had come for.

She tasted copper, the sour taste of pennies in her mouth, a taste she recognized from the night her sister had bled to death in the hospital. It was the flavor of defeat. She pulled out of his arms and walked to the window to see if Cynthia's star had risen yet. When she looked back, Harrison's head was bowed, and his nakedness had become sad.

She crossed back to the bed and stood in the circle of his arms, his head heavy against her breasts. From him escaped a deep sigh, the sound made by a lost child who has finally found his mother, or a tired dog about to fall asleep.

"Cordelia," he said, "I've made so many mistakes."

They did not make love but stroked and touched so that the other's body became something known and trusted. She lay awake thinking about the night they had pedaled so happily through the snowy Dublin streets. Harrison held both her hands, his head on her shoulder. It had been better before they both understood what it meant to suffer.

CHAPTER

4

WHEN CORDELIA STUMBLED INTO THE KITCHEN THE NEXT morning, bleating for a cup of coffee, she was greeted by the smell of fresh yeast and garlic. Her sister Amelia and her nephew, Tom, were coming to lunch. Harrison was playing what sounded like "Ruby Tuesday" on the counter with the garlic press and a wooden spoon while he read the list of food she was preparing for the meal.

"Chicken breasts," he said, beaming at her. "Homemade mayonnaise and French mustard." He stirred something with his finger, and the odor of fresh yeast rose from the bowl.

"I'm baking bread," he said cheerfully. "What shall we do about a sweet? Tarte Tatin? Chocolate mousse?"

Cordelia put a filter into the Melitta and filled it with French roast. The sight of Harrison in her apron was difficult to absorb.

"This is *my* lunch," she snapped. "I'm making the food."

"Of course you are," Harrison replied, tasting his mayonnaise, mashing the garlic. "I assume Amelia likes dill?"

It wasn't her lunch at all. Cordelia felt herself to be completely eclipsed by Harrison's energetic and effortless charm. His chicken salad was delicious, and Tom was mesmerized by the huge, funny man who made him real swords from newspapers. Amelia was terribly impressed.

27

"Where did you find him?" she whispered, while Harrison was giving Tom a ride in the bedroom. "He is the most perfect man."

Cordelia was too furious to speak, so she nodded, picked up her coat and dark glasses, and left the apartment. She stood in an icy breeze in Riverside Park, watching the cars zoom up the west side. Harrison's effect on people had always been extreme. In the Dublin pubs the patrons would send drinks over and women would pass him their phone numbers. She hated the way he pretended not to notice the attention and would act surprised when she pointed out a woman smiling at him from across the room.

"I picked you," he'd say irritably. "Let it go."

But he hadn't really picked her. She had just stayed and made it impossible for anyone else to take her place. Not being chosen had made her furious. Her Irish friends had never understood this anger. After she returned to America they wrote her letters pointing out how inappropriate a match it had been and suggested she find a nice American oil billionaire or rock idol rather than pining away for a confused and alienated Afrikaner.

Harrison appeared at the edge of the park. "I walked Amelia to her car," he said. "She asked me to thank you for lunch."

"Oh. Well, I didn't have much to do with that, did I? It was your lunch, your audience—my sister and my nephew."

"He's a great little boy," Harrison said quietly. "Sam would like him."

"He's *my* nephew!" Cordelia shouted, her eyes filling with tears caused by recognition of her own petty immaturity.

"Yes," Harrison said, "he's your nephew. I'm sorry I spoiled everything. I'm going now."

"You just make me feel completely inadequate."

Cordelia watched a heavily laden Dodge Dart with rusted-out sides cut off a bright-red BMW. The BMW owner gave the Dodge the finger, and the passengers in the Dodge leaned from every window to shout: "Fuck you, motherfucker!"

"How can you think of yourself that way? Last night was the best time I've had in years."

Cordelia turned around to face him. He pushed her dark glasses off her face and touched her cheek. She kept her hands behind her back, afraid to touch him. He was holding his knapsack, ready to leave. As usual, their timing was wrong.

"I still want you to want me more than anything," she said, "after eight years. I don't understand why."

"I can't love anyone properly, Delia. That's why my wife left me. She said she felt like she was married to an uncle."

"Your wife left you because she's a fucked-up bitch. I don't know how to love anyone either. My last boyfriend said I was incurably neurotic. And not in an interesting way. Not something fashionable or trendy. Just unstable and inconsistent and neurotic."

"Someone should worship the ground you walk on, Cordelia." Harrison kneaded the tense muscles of her upper back. "I'm too afraid of failing you."

Fail me, she wanted to scream. *Fail me completely, but don't leave!* He bent low to kiss her. For a moment she traced the extraordinary bones of his face with her fingers.

"Someday I'll come to Africa," she whispered. "You can build me a hut on the edge of the jungle and visit on Sundays."

"Goodbye, flower gatherer." Harrison ran across West End Avenue and disappeared around the corner. When she opened the door, her phone was ringing.

"Hello?"

"Delia?" It was her sister.

"Hi."

"Nice disappearing act."

"Sorry." She stuck her fingers in the bowl of chocolate mousse and put a huge dollop in her mouth.

"Why are you so hostile in the company of perfect men? Isn't he the one you were seeing in Dublin?"

"Sort of."

"He's left his wife."

"She left him."

"I doubt it. I don't think many women would walk away from

that man. He's probably just being kind. Why don't you get back together with him? He's so charming, and you've had these horrible boyfriends. . . ."

"That's surface, Amelia. He's not what he seems to be." She put her fingers back into the mousse. "He's incapable of affection."

"Affection? Are you telling me that man can't fuck?"

"Jesus Christ! Of course he can fuck. He fucks better than anyone. That's not the point."

"Yes it is. I'm married, and I know what's important for domestic harmony. You're just addicted to your image as a blighted lone wolf. You won't be the youngest for the rest of your life, Cordelia."

Yes I will, Cordelia silently mouthed.

"Why do you have to make things so complicated?"

"You don't know him."

"Never mind! I will never offer you advice, for the rest of my life. It's not as if that was my role anyway. . . ." Amelia's voice began to quiver.

"Amy . . ."

"You'd listen to this if it were Cynthia talking."

"Stop it." Cordelia sank to the floor with the bowl of chocolate mousse between her knees, the phone balanced on her shoulder.

"I've done all I can. If you want to be lonely for the rest of your life, that's fine. Tom wants to say something. . . . Come here, honey! Come talk to Auntie Deli."

"Auntie Deli—"

"Don't call me that, Tom. Call me Aunt Delia."

"Aunt Delia?"

"Yes, ducky?" There was a lot of heavy breathing before he spoke again.

"Can Harrison come over tomorrow?"

"No, sweetie. He went back to Washington. He lives in the same city as the President. The one we don't like."

"Oh." There was a brief silence, punctuated by more breathing from Tom.

"You want to tell me anything else?"

"When's he coming back?"

"I don't know."

"Why?"

"Because Harrison doesn't tell me all his secrets."

"He told me he'd be back soon."

"Well, good. I love you."

"Bye."

"Does Mommy want to talk to me again?"

"Bye."

She held on to the receiver until the phone began to make terrible noises.

That night she went to see *Annie Hall* at a revival house. Crying into her second box of heavily salted and buttered popcorn, she marveled at the injustice of not knowing Woody Allen well enough to inspire screenplays about her life and flattering close-ups of her being confused and adorable.

Some of her tears were due to what she recognized as the movie's hopeless attitude toward love. If she could rewrite her own affair with Harrison it would have ended with him down on his knees, begging her to stay with him in Dublin. Instead he had stood on his head and then had left to acquire a selfish, unfaithful wife who stole his son and corrupted his best friend. He came to Cordelia a humiliated man, hoping she would provide him with comfort, give him the strength to go off and reclaim his family. So he could leave her again. He asked comfort from someone who was slowly sinking into a sea of despair, who considered the act of opening her eyes some sort of victory.

When she left the theater, an icy wind was blowing down Broadway. Walking downtown, Cordelia contrasted her own cold solitude with the snuggly warmth she observed behind the glass windows of the restaurants. She felt like the Little Match Girl on Christmas Eve. As she passed the newest, most fashionable restaurant in her neighborhood, so chic it had no name, she practiced her most woebegone expression and, to her horror, found herself staring directly into the cold gray eyes of Philip Syrianos.

He was seated at a table next to an extremely thin woman whose hair was cut into such a geometrically perfect square she appeared to be constructed from cardboard cut with a straight-edge blade. The woman's face was averted, but Cordelia noticed she wore a lot of heavy gold jewelry. Her nails were lacquered a reddish purple, and while she spoke to Philip she punctuated each word by tapping his arm with her finger. Philip looked bored. He was staring out at the street, wearing the same expression as a big dog trapped inside the house on a nice day. When he saw Cordelia he grinned, licked his lips, and then slyly tapped his wristwatch, pointing first toward himself, then to Cordelia. The woman continued her monologue, oblivious to his gestures. At first Cordelia thought he was commenting on the lateness of the hour, but then she realized he was telling her that it was only a matter of time before something happened between them. Cordelia's face grew hot despite the freezing air. Philip nodded and licked his lips again. She turned back toward the street, no longer depressed, simply agitated.

She was working on an audition piece from Pinter's script of the movie *The French Lieutenant's Woman*. It was the scene in which Sarah, the miserable governess, tells Charles, the engaged gentleman, why she never stopped waiting for her treacherous lover. She describes her desolation: "But . . . after he had gone . . . my loneliness was so deep, I felt I would drown in it."

Cordelia put down the book and tried to breathe. After her sister's murder she kept waking with the feeling that her lungs were filled with salt water. She had a bitter taste in her mouth, and her breathing was shallow, stopped somewhere in her throat. She would get up, choking, and stagger half asleep to the window, to hang her head over the sill and try to take in the fresh air. She did not see a doctor, as she suspected that she was drowning in her own unshed tears. It would be hard to describe the symptoms. She had enough Valium to float away on a cloud of denial. The pills frightened her. She had begun to take them whenever the level of anxiety made it impossible for her to function. One day she found herself downtown without them, and she began to feel so anxious she thought her entire body was about to shatter. When she reached home that night she swallowed three times the normal dosage and slept for nearly twenty-four hours. It had been lovely to sleep like that. No dreams, no feelings. She put the Valium away.

She could not complete her work on the monologue. Each time she came close to Sarah's state of mind, she found herself down on all fours, pounding her fists into the floor. Mr. Stetzler began to beat on the ceiling with his cane. Finally, she stood up. Cold water made her swollen eyes feel better. She put the script away and cut a large piece of carrot cake to eat while she read an article in *Vogue* about preventive dieting.

In her dream she was dressed in a pinafore and a black velvet hairband. Her hair was very long and straight and blond, exactly like the illustration in her English edition of *Alice in Wonderland*. She was sitting astride a large object that looked vaguely like a toadstool. Her sister Cynthia was dressed as Billie Burke playing Glinda in *The Wizard of Oz*. Swathed in gauzy silk and speaking in the same sort of tinkly tones, Cynthia kept saying "Fiddle-de-dee!" and hitting Cordelia with her fairy wand, quite hard. Finally, Cordelia grew tired of her perch and tried to get down. Peering over the edge, she saw her sister, no longer dressed as Glinda but wrapped like a mummy or a corpse in the same white gauze. She kept trying to unwrap the shroud, but there were too many layers. The material crumbled in her hands. She woke up just before dawn. Her pillow was soaked with tears, and the sheet was torn between her fingers. She had scratched her own arms until they were bleeding. Her sister's body had been cold.

CHAPTER

5

A T SEVEN A.M., SHE UNLOCKED THE CLUB AND TURNED ON the power. The coffee was brewing and she was labeling towels when Philip stepped off the elevator. He was dressed beautifully in a charcoal-colored cashmere coat and muffler. He smelled of lilac water and expensive leather. Cordelia was speaking on the phone to Manny, the beer distributor, when she felt Philip's icy hands on her neck. She screamed and dropped the receiver.

"So don't buy the Kronenbourg if it's too much," Manny said. "You don't gotta yell in my ear!"

Philip smiled, picked up his briefcase and a towel, and went whistling upstairs to the men's locker room.

Dr. Schwartz arrived promptly at seven forty-five and handed Cordelia a warm bagel. "For the woman I adore, one sesame with a schmear."

Dr. Schwartz had given her a gold chain for Christmas, and when she tried to refuse his gift he had slumped over the desk.

"Let me have my few pleasures," he had groaned. "I'm an old man, about to die."

When Cordelia pointed out his being merely sixty and in perfect health, he had stood up and shouted, "Don't be such a goy! Accept in the spirit it was given!"

At nine o'clock, all three telephone lines began to ring. For the next hour she was responsible for scheduling the week's squash courts. The members of the club took their squash games very seriously. They frequently called a minute before the official time and tried to chat with Cordelia until they were allowed to make a reservation. As each call came in she would put that person on hold and check the times they had requested courts against what remained open. For most of the hour the incoming lines flashed red. At the same time she was expected to give people towels and register them for classes. She did not look up from the telephone until after ten. There was an engraved card on the counter. The card said PHILIP SYRIANOS. Written in black ink was *Call me.* The words were underlined three times. She put the card in her wallet and tried to decide upon a convincing outfit to wear at an audition for a miniseries about nineteenth-century coal miners. On her last audition she had managed to peek at the stage manager's notes. Next to her name was written: "Too health club."

She had not auditioned for a long time. Shortly after Cynthia's funeral, an agent who represented a friend of hers put her up for a small part in a Broadway showcase. Cordelia didn't know him well enough to explain that her sister had just been murdered. She thought he might be completely turned off and associate her with depressing things. He was a pretty important agent, and she hoped he might offer to represent her if she managed to do well at the audition. She tried to think of a way she might mention it casually: "Oh, by the way, the part sounds great, but since my sister was raped and stabbed and left to die, I've been a little tense." She couldn't get the words out.

During the audition, which was for an ingenue who did nothing but giggle, she began to see the director's face as if it were behind a fish-eye lens. Under ordinary circumstances she would have stopped, but she felt that the director was impatient and only seeing her out of courtesy. She began again, but when she looked up she saw his face again, the eyes stretching down to meet the nose, the mouth gaping. The distortion of his features terrified her, and she ran out of the theater, screaming. That evening she returned home with the sense that she was being pursued by winged furies, tiny demons that whispered hideous truths into her ears about how dangerous and vicious the world was.

"This is just the beginning," they hissed. "You're going to ruin everything!"

She was scheduled to work a lunchtime shift at a restaurant called Benny's Hideaway the next day. She usually cleared about seventy bucks in tips, which supplemented the low wages at the club. She was dressed and ready to leave at nine, but she could not open the door. Wearing her coat, she sat frozen in a chair next to the phone, unable to pick up the receiver and call in sick. The manager from Benny's left three messages on her machine. That evening she missed her acting class. The next day she took a leave of absence from the club. She told them she was going to Paris. She was fired by the restaurant and removed from the Acting Studio's roster of active students. Her teacher yelled over the answering machine for her to pick up, that she had to come back. The agent called and said he'd spoken to her acting teacher and for God's sake why didn't she tell him what had happened to her before he sent her to an audition for a part that made Betty Boop look like a Rhodes scholar and if she ever needed someone to talk to he'd lost his best friend and it did get easier but it took forever and he was interested in her career, she had a quality that he admired, and he hated talking to machines so when she felt better she should call him.

Finally, she simply unplugged her phone. Each morning she called her mother, so she wouldn't get worried. After talking to her mother about things she wasn't doing, she'd pull out the plug and lie on the couch under Cynthia's baby blanket, which she'd taken from her sister's apartment. She'd cry until her eyes were no longer producing tears, until her cheeks were chapped and the fabric of the couch was soaked. She didn't eat anything, but she sometimes slept, and when it was late enough she went from the couch to bed. When she was afraid of the dark she took sleeping pills, which made her fall into the sort of slumber that feels like a half-conscious death. Underneath the pain was relief that she had given up. But she didn't want anyone to find her. It was a complete humiliation to her that she could not summon up the courage to leave the house.

There were three sisters, Cynthia, Amelia, and Cordelia. Cynthia was the eldest, Cordelia the youngest. They were each separated by three years. Cynthia was murdered by an enraged mugger, who thought she was lying when she told him at knifepoint that she had no money. He had raped her and then stabbed her eighteen times, leaving her in a pool of blood two blocks from her own house. He had told the police when they picked him up in a local bar that he didn't like her attitude, she was too "uppity," and anyway, he said, he wanted to fuck her and he wanted her rings. The cops said he talked about her as if they'd had some sort of relationship, like she'd been his girlfriend, and evidently he had said he enjoyed talking to Cynthia about how hard it was to stay off drugs. It was all written down by one of the cops. One of the cops who had put his coat over her sister's body.

Cynthia had chosen to live in the East Village, where she had opened a neighborhood health clinic after she finished her internship. She had been found dying in a pool of her own blood by two of her downstairs neighbors, who were walking home from a movie and thought they heard a kitten crying. When they found her she had looked up at them and tried to explain that she didn't think she was going to die. "Don't worry, I'm going to be fine," she said.

A month after Cynthia's death, a memorial service was held in a Ukrainian social club on the Lower East Side. The small hall was packed with weeping people, ranging from mink-swathed dowagers to a lady with an invisible dog and twenty plastic shopping bags. A Hell's Angel stood by the back door, dressed from head to toe in black leather, and wiped away tears.

The night Cynthia had been dying on the operating table, some of these people had stood outside her apartment building in an impromptu candlelight vigil. Someone had a guitar, and someone sang old Joni Mitchell songs. It had been on the local news, with the introduction "An angel of mercy is murdered for rings."

Cordelia had come to the service in place of her mother. Dr. Cavanagh could not face all these strangers who loved her daughter.

"Honey, just smile and try not to cry too much. You're much better at that than me."

Cordelia nodded. She was sitting at her mother's dining room table, staring at her dinner. It had been such a long time since she had eaten that she couldn't remember whether she liked what was in front of her. She managed to cut up the meat and hide it under the lettuce. It was like being a child again, concealing the hated lima beans under the remaining mashed potatoes. Her mother was too depressed to notice. Sometimes it seemed as if her mother had forgotten Cordelia was her daughter and viewed her as a dependable friend who lacked any emotional connection to what had happened. Cordelia believed she interpreted her daughter's numbed shock as some sort of acceptance. But Dr. Cavanagh's picture of her daughters had always been distorted. She saw them as she wanted them to be: invulnerable, self-confident, and happy.

After some of the neighbors spoke of Cynthia's goodness and bravery, they turned to Cordelia. The entire room was staring, and she struggled to breathe, afraid she would faint.

A woman began to speak. "We are all so concerned about Cynthia's family. Her sister Cordelia was kind enough to come here tonight. None of us can say anything to help you through this terrible time. We just needed the opportunity to thank someone for giving us the chance to love your sister. We needed to express our sorrow together, as Cynthia would have liked to see her neighbors." The woman's voice broke, and she became silent.

Cordelia stood and looked down at the faces of the people who thought they loved her sister, and what she felt was pure hatred. They didn't know her. None of them had been taught how to read, how to spell, how to put on makeup, by Cynthia. None of them had lain in bed staring up at the ceiling while Cynthia explained why their parents had to get divorced and Daddy was moving away from them. None of them had to think, when people asked how many sisters she had: How do I answer that question? Two, she always said, I have two sisters. None of them had known her. How dare they think they felt anything real?

"She was my oldest sister," Cordelia whispered. "She was always there. I don't know how I'll live without her. She was always there."

Looking into the faces of her sister's neighbors, their expressions kind, she tried to hide her conviction that Cynthia's murder had no meaning outside of finally proving that life was a bad joke. She despised them for what she perceived as an ignorant trust that the death of someone as lovely as Cynthia would somehow cause the living to be more loving. They spoke as if her sister was going to rise like a phoenix from her own ashes and be placed as the lead star in the brightest constellation in God's heaven. Cordelia believed Cynthia was left as dust, that her death completely negated the years she had lived. The emptiness Cordelia embraced was attractive in its simplicity. The hatred that filled her was somehow comforting. The service ended, and she walked quickly outside, nodding and smiling, avoiding their outstretched hands. She was stopped on the street by an elderly woman, whom she recognized as Cynthia's downstairs neighbor. She had come to tea once when Cordelia was visiting. She was a very kind and educated woman who had graduated from Smith. They had all discussed Samuel Beckett while Cynthia baked muffins. Blueberry muffins.

"My dear," she said, her hand heavy on Cordelia's shoulder, "does anyone know?"

"Know what?" She kept her eyes on the sidewalk.

"How much she meant to you in particular. How very close you were. . . . What are you going to do now?"

"I'm fine," Cordelia said quickly, smiling into the tear-filled eyes of her sister's friend. "There's nothing to do but wait."

"Wait?"

"Until it's over. I mean, until . . . well, anyway . . ." She raised her hand to hail a cab.

"It will never end, Cordelia. Forgive her." The cab stopped.

"I can't," she muttered.

"What?" asked the cabbie. She didn't answer. The cabbie turned up his radio. Terrible things were happening in the Middle East.

She stayed in her house for nearly two months, rarely getting up, not working, not eating.

Eventually Amelia grew tired of leaving unanswered messages on her little sister's machine or being told by the operator that the phone was not plugged in. She drove into Manhattan, with Tom buckled into the child's seat, and forced Cordelia to allow her into the apartment. It was nearly noon, but the room was pitch black since there were blankets nailed over the windows. Cordelia had lost nearly thirty pounds. Her hair was thin, and the color of her skin was a pale but definite green. She was wearing an old flannel nightgown over a pair of sweat pants. When Amelia saw her apple-cheeked little sister she screamed, and Tom, in absolute sympathy with his mother's distress, burst into tears. His mother never cried. Cordelia sat on the edge of the sofa, rocking back and forth, holding her ribs as if she might fall apart. Amelia dressed her, trying not to yell at the sight of her sister's emaciated body. She took her home to her house in New Jersey and then called a local doctor, who insisted Cordelia be put into the hospital for tests and observation.

They diagnosed her as being severely depressed, anorexic, and malnourished. The doctor also suggested she was completely out of touch with reality and in a state of shock, which had existed since Cynthia's murder. After several days in the hospital, where she attended a support group for anorexics, group therapy for relatives of dead people, and individual sessions with the staff psychiatrist, she was released with the recommendation that she seek long-term professional help.

Her denial had been difficult to break through. Cordelia had continued to insist that she didn't have suicidal feelings, until the counselor interrupted her and asked: "Did it ever occur to you that deliberately starving oneself is a very slow and painful form of suicide?"

Cordelia opened her mouth, but nothing came out. She interlaced her fingers and saw that her knuckles had become grotesque, as the flesh had shrunk away from the bone. Her father had always loved her hands; he had kissed the dimpled fingers when she was a little girl, telling her they were sweeter than candy. She put her hands in her lap and felt how weak she was. Slowly she began to eat again. With each mouthful she felt Cynthia's soul, the faint light, grow dimmer.

All of it was kept secret from their mother, except for the fact that Cordelia was staying with Amelia for a while. Dr. Cavanagh was pleased her girls were finally becoming friends.

"Cordelia's so tough," she remarked to Amelia on the telephone. "I don't know how I could have survived this without her."

"She's having sort of a hard time," Amelia said, looking out her kitchen window to where Cordelia was sitting in the backyard with Tom. "She's a little too thin."

"Well, it's because of that ridiculous profession she's in. I can't tell her that acting makes people crazy. She always accuses me of sabotaging her career. How thin is she anyway?"

"Oh, it's no big deal. Look, Ma, I'm making lunch. I really gotta go."

"Bye, honey. Are you okay?"

"Fine." Amelia glanced out the window again, to where Tom sat building a sand castle and Cordelia stared vacantly into space. "For God's sake," Amelia muttered, "when do I get my nervous breakdown?"

After two weeks out of the hospital, Cordelia rolled over in bed one Sunday morning and realized she felt almost happy. The sun was pouring into the room she had been given in their nineteenth-century farmhouse, and she could hear Tom and Michael chopping wood.

"I'm going home," she announced at breakfast. "I feel like a human being."

"What's a human bean?" Tom asked, dropping his pancake in his lap.

At first New York was impossibly threatening. Running up the stairs at night, she would feel the presence of a shadowy figure armed with a steel blade behind her. At the door she would fumble for her keys and then drop to her knees, head bowed, resigned to the knife between her shoulder blades. When she was walking on the street, she often believed the person coming toward her was going to kill her. She would cross against the light and run into a store, where she would cower and wait to be attacked. On the subway she felt that anyone who sat beside her had a weapon, and she was constantly running out of trains and then becoming convinced the people standing on the platform were going to push her in front of the approaching train or onto the third rail to be electrocuted. Invariably she ended up back on the street, dark glasses in place, hailing cabs, trying to locate a policeman, having what a doctor called a panic attack, feeling as if she would surely die from the pressure in her chest. She witnessed her own murder in the eyes of every person she encountered. Violence seemed inevitable. Her friends were put off and alarmed by her behavior. She seemed continuously distraught; they felt an inner tremor that made them look away from her out of pity and a horror at how she had changed.

CHAPTER

6

THE ACTING STUDIO WAS ON WASHINGTON SQUARE, IN THE basement of a brownstone. A self-appointed security guard named Clarence was hanging out on the front steps, smoking a joint.

"Hey, Sunshine," he called out, waving a large joint. "Have some bad reefer!"

She had made the mistake once of taking a toke just before she was scheduled to do a short monologue in the class. She could not remember any words after the opening line. She began to laugh and then to cry, falling down on the floor, clutching her sides, unable to breathe. She was handed a glass of water and told to start again from the top. She managed to remember the rest of her lines, but she was stoned as a koala bear chewing eucalyptus leaves. When she finished, she sat staring into space while the class waited patiently, thinking it was part of the piece. Finally, her teacher said, "Is that it?" and she nodded and stumbled off the stage. During the grimmest section of a scene from 'Night, Mother, her giggles returned. Clearly Clarence bought his dope from someone who considered getting stoned a religious experience.

"No, thank you, Clarence," she said, smiling. "I can't act and comprehend the meaning of the universe at the same time."

The smoky basement room was filled with students. A bulletin board contained audition notices, apartment rentals, and several rather mysterious notes, such as: "Daphne, remember—completion is crucial." Periodically the board would be purged, and Cordelia always wondered if anyone ever answered the poignant pleas for mercy.

Her friend Maxine was eating a Dove Bar and reading the *Ross Report*, a monthly publication that listed all the casting agents in town, as well as other sources of rejection for actors in New York. Cordelia had met Maxine at so many auditions where neither of them had been cast that they felt as if their relationship was the only positive result of their going to those cattle calls; since it was clear they'd never compete for the same part, they decided to be loyal friends. Maxine's quest was for a diet that included an unlimited amount of butter and sugar. Her eating habits were, according to Maxine, the result of being raised by macrobiotic parents on a diet of brown rice, seaweed, and onions. None of the kids from school wanted to sleep over at her house. During adolescence she discovered junk food and binged on Doritos, Ring Dings, Cheez Doodles, and cherry liqueur. Her parents' open attitude toward sex precluded any experimentation with boys. Her mother once suggested to her that she might lose weight if she got in closer touch with her sexuality. Maxine simply ate herself into a state of hysterical rebellion against her thin, organic, liberated parents. Her clear white skin belied her unhealthy appetite. She had curly black hair and high color, which caused her to resemble a rather plump version of Disney's Snow White. She was far too lovely to be cast as an ugly fat girl but far too heavy to be considered for most other roles.

"Well, well, if it isn't Little Ms. Nautilus! Come over here and let me try and pinch an inch!" Maxine patted Cordelia's belly, which was indeed quite flat. "Holy hell, Delia! There's nothing here for a real man to sink his teeth into!"

"Hi, Maxine." Cordelia automatically removed the Dove Bar from Maxine's hand but was stopped before she could throw it out.

"Don't! That cost two bucks, and I want it!"

Cordelia shrugged, took a bite, and returned the ice cream. "Why are you eating that? Do you know how many calories there are in those things?"

"Six hundred and something. I don't care. Depression. Sexual frustration. Masturbatory substitution. Impending nuclear annihilation, if you wanna get political. Rejection."

"Who rejected you?"

"Mick Jagger."

"No kidding."

"Swear to God! I ran past him on Riverside Drive. He had on this really crummy-looking sweatshirt, and he was towing two kids. One looked like Bianca, and the other one must have belonged to that Texas twat who's always trying to prove she's smart but just proves that perfect bodies and brains rarely come together."

"Jerry Hall."

"Yeah. The one with the nose. Anyway, I stopped. I jogged backward. I dropped all my loose change on the sidewalk. And Mick just ignored me."

"He's old. He must have bifocals. He didn't see you."

"I wanted to tell him the story of my life: how I lost my virginity listing to 'Ruby Tuesday' and I felt it was him I was fucking and I was just like Ruby Tuesday—no one could pin a name on me—and he just looked right past me. . . . Rock stars don't like fat girls."

"Max! He's almost fifty! He's short!"

"Rock stars like skinny girls. He probably would have asked you to come to Martinique or something to baby-sit his kids."

"Let's go down front."

"Okay. Are you sad about something, Delia?"

"I'm fine."

They found two seats in the second row and watched another student perform a memory exercise that ended in an intense physical experience. He recreated his first homosexual encounter. Maxine filed her nails while Cordelia tried to pay attention, failed, and then began to think about Philip Syrianos and the long muscle at the front of each of his thighs. Their teacher cautioned them against using sexual experiences for the exercise.

"Memories of sexual encounters are rarely accurate," he said. "We normally glorify them to assuage guilt."

The temperature had dropped during their class. Cordelia shivered as they walked down the steps and stood on the pavement.

"So what happened with Harrison, the great white god?"

"Not much." Cordelia shrugged.

"You didn't fuck him, did you?"

"Not really."

"What's that mean? Sort of? Heavy petting?"

"He's destroyed, Maxine. His wife went off with his best friend and his son."

"Like you didn't have any troubles?"

"That's not the point."

"It's exactly the point! You just climbed out of the deepest hole—no, correction, I think you're still in there—"

"Maxine . . ."

"The guy's a blood-sucking leech, Delia. Men don't change."

"I still love him."

"Oh, Cordelia!" They were circling Washington Square Park, brushing past the dealers, who were muttering, "Sens," and the joggers, who were gritting their teeth and panting. Maxine stopped and took her hand from Cordelia's shoulder.

"Well, maybe I don't love him, but when I see him I feel sick and my palms itch and I want to do things for him. Crochet one of those hideous blankets; can jam."

"This is really disgusting! And you don't can jam, you stupid slut! You put it in jars with wax on top. My mother used to do that. It was so neat! All that lovely organic jam in your peanut butter sandwich! Little pieces of wax with your sprouted wheat bread! I want you to go to a Women Who Love Too Much session."

"What's that?"

"It's for women who are addicted to their own pain."

"Fuck you!"

46

"I mean it, Cordelia! I'm sick of this shit! We're going to be getting our Oscars together! You can't sacrifice your brilliant career for some guy's dick! Or any other part of him. There is no place in your current life for that whining ex-husband of that kidnapping bitch! Okay?"

"Okay."

They parted at Eighth Street. Maxine lived in a Brooklyn brownstone with three other actors and two cats. Cordelia had turned down Greenwich Avenue when she heard her name. It was Harrison. Instinctively she fluffed out her hair and bit her lips. When she realized what she was doing, she felt furious. What was Harrison doing in her city? If he wouldn't stay in Africa, where he belonged, he should at least have the decency to remain in Washington, waiting for his wife, and not roam the streets of Manhattan.

"What are you doing here?"

"Visiting friends." Harrison bent over and kissed her nose. Her face was very cold, and the touch of his lips was warm. His hair was standing straight up in an appealing fashion.

"What friends?"

"Old ones. Male ones. I remembered you said your studio was down here, so I took a chance. Let's go and have a drink, shall we?"

Without waiting for an answer, Harrison took her hand and steered Cordelia toward the Lion's Head. The bar was almost empty. The bartender was rinsing glasses and watching a taped baseball game. They ordered hot whiskeys, and the bartender pushed a button that froze the action of the game. Cordelia began to sulk. It seemed unfair somehow that Harrison would not just go away and leave her alone.

"I was thinking about your sister," Harrison said slowly, staring into the bottom of his glass. "When I called your mother in October I couldn't ask her for any details. It had just happened. You never told me how she died."

"You never asked."

"I'm asking now."

"She was stabbed." The sharpness of her voice seemed appropriate to her choice of words. Harrison flinched. "Raped and stabbed and beaten. Left to die in a pool of blood. Murdered."

He put his hand over hers.

"Oh dear God, Cordelia. I'm so terribly sorry." He pressed his lips against her fingers, and she sat staring down at his wonderful hair.

So there it was, her dream that someday Harrison would emerge like a Greek god from a cloud of dust and tell her how sorry he was. She saw their reflections in the bar mirror and was shocked by how beautiful they both were. Her own face seemed unrecognizable, sharp-boned and stern. Now he would take her in his arms and she could cry out her despair, her awesome rage at having to let go of her sister. She had loved him so much in Ireland, waited for him to turn away from his view of the sea, to turn around and tell her, yes, he did love her. He never turned around but simply walked into the cold water, swam far out beyond the breakers, not caring if she followed or stood alone on the sand smiling at the other people so that they wouldn't feel sorry for her, the other people who probably wondered what this godlike man was doing with such an ordinary girl. She remembered standing like that waiting for her father to come home after he had left for California, after she had turned her back on him and refused to join her sisters in a hug. "Go," she had whispered under her breath, but later she had stood on the curb in front of the house until Cynthia had come out and held her hand and told her about how Daddy was going to see the sun rise three hours later every day. She became something made of concrete and stone, a dead weight, a monstrosity.

"Thank you." She could not look into his eyes for fear he would pity her. Pity was the worst thing in the entire world, she thought; pity was as close to death as one could come without actually dying. She felt it from people, felt it wrap around her until it was impossible to breathe.

"He wanted her rings."

"Jesus Christ." Tears were rolling down Harrison's cheeks. The sight of water clouding those perfect blue eyes fascinated her. She couldn't remember ever seeing him cry when they were together.

"You were such good friends. You told me so many stories about her. How wild she was and how she took care of you when your father left . . ."

"I did? People always say that. They always say: 'Not the sister you talked about all the time?' And I'm surprised. I loved her more than anyone. She kept me from giving up. I don't think I realized that until I had to go and see her, when they called and told me to go to the hospital . . . that she was what I defined my family as. I don't think I ever knew how important it was to me to do things for her. I suppose that's why we lose people. . . ." Her voice trailed away. She felt very tired.

"And now?"

"I can't love her anymore. I can't do anything for her. She's dead."

"But how is it?"

"It?"

"I mean, is it better?"

"No. She's just been gone longer. I miss her more. I have more to tell her when she comes home." Her lips twisted. She could not get her breath. Harrison put his hand over hers, but she pulled it away. "Except she won't ever come home. I keep forgetting that part. Did you ever dream your family moved away and didn't tell you where they went? Sometimes I think she's wandering around somewhere in the wrong neighborhood, looking for us."

No one could help her. No one could take away the pain that still connected her to Cynthia. She stood, pulling on her coat.

"Leave me alone, Harrison," she said, putting down some money. "This is much too little, far too late. I don't exist anymore."

A cab was discharging a fare at Sheridan Square, and she ran for it. As they pulled from the curb she saw Harrison, coatless, looking down the street, in the wrong direction, for her. His behavior was baffling. How could he imagine she'd be willing to hand over her grief as if it were a heavy child she had carried on her hip for too long? He should go after his wretched wife, reclaim his baby, and return to Africa, to squat with his childhood black friends in the bush, smoking reefer. He didn't belong in New York City, with his loping stride and his beauty that was almost painful to contemplate.

As the cab threaded its way uptown along Eighth Avenue, Cordelia realized that she didn't feel safe. Her sister's blood had been spilled on these streets, and there was no reason to believe that such an event would not occur again. She glanced into the rearview mirror and saw that the driver was staring at her.

"Everything okay?" he asked, attempting a smile, which Cordelia saw as a leer.

She took out her address book and wrote down his medallion number and name. In her mind a picture formed of him taking her to Harlem, forcing her to the roof of a building, raping her, and then pushing her off. She tried to do her yoga breathing, deep in the stomach, through the nose. It was not helpful.

"This is fine."

"You said Sixty-ninth."

"I've changed my mind." She threw a ten-dollar bill in the front seat and began to open the door.

"Hold it, lady," the cabbie said, pulling over. "Don't try and leave a moving car!"

She was on Central Park South and Broadway. As she walked she tried to visualize herself as someone who didn't deserve to die. It was all she could do to stop herself from walking into traffic. She sang herself home. A song her mother used to sing when they couldn't fall asleep.

This is so exhausting, she thought. Trying not to die is so fucking tiring. When she reached her apartment, she went into the bathroom, turned on the shower, and began to cry.

She fell asleep as soon as the blankets were pulled up, seeking escape. Instead there were hooded creatures in black, armed with thin steel blades, pushing Cynthia and herself through a city street that resembled Dresden after the bombings of World War II. Each turn was more desolate, until it was Cordelia alone, ringed by fiends, her arms raised in supplication as the knives flashed in the streetlights. She was shouting. She awoke to the sound of someone pounding on her door. It was morning. A pale gray light filtered through the blinds. She told her neighbor that she'd had a nightmare, and the woman went away muttering something about "psychotics."

CHAPTER

7

A T EIGHT A.M. PHILIP SYRIANOS STEPPED OFF THE ELEVATOR wearing a leather bomber jacket, jeans, and black lizard cowboy boots with silver toes. Cordelia did not look up from her book, merely putting out a towel, which he ignored.

"What's wrong with you?" he asked, dropping a new copy of *Back Stage* on top of the squash schedule.

"What's this for?"

"*Back Stage?* I thought you were an actress. You're supposed to read the trades. I was thinking about you. You got it already?"

"No. Thanks."

"You look like hell this morning. You were better in my thoughts."

"Thanks again."

"Hey! Sweetheart, what's going on? Your boyfriend go limp or something? I look forward to doing two things when I come to this lousy club—a nasty game of squash and the sight of you smiling behind the towels. *Capisce?* What's with the terminal depression? Let me take you out to dinner. You look hungry."

"No." Philip's voice had been surprisingly gentle. She did not dare look at him, in case she began to cry.

"No? You forget I saw you, kiddo, wandering around the Upper West Side on a cold Sunday night looking like all the other unmarried biological clocks going home to microwave the Lean Cuisine. Who are you to snub my dinner invitations?"

"Who was that horrible-looking woman?"

"Her? The one with the hair? She looks like she's wearing a goddamned pyramid on her head! Nefertiti!"

He had such a disgusted expression on his face that Cordelia laughed.

"There's my girl," he said endearingly. "Now let me take you out to dinner. Have some laughs."

"I don't think so."

"We'll go somewhere really *luxe*. Four stars. Wear something weird. One of your actress dresses. Pia Zadora."

"I don't do Pia Zadora."

"Well, something else, then. Just don't wear one of those little-girl-wearing-daddy's-pants gigs. I hate the look of a broad in a necktie."

"You have a lot of demands."

"I'm worth it, darling." He beamed at her, raising his eyebrows, and she shrugged.

"Well, all right."

Her mother had given her a black sheath cocktail dress. "It's a Galanos," she had said, zipping Cordelia up. "Until you became Twiggy, no one could get into it. It never fit me. I just liked the way it looked hanging in the closet."

Cordelia bought a black lace corset, a garter belt, and seamed sheer black stockings. She didn't know why the props felt necessary, but the costume was extremely effective. At the back of the hall closet she found a black velvet coat lined with red silk, stolen the summer she worked in the wardrobe department of the Shakespeare Festival. An old pair of black velvet pumps and elbow-length gloves completed the outfit.

She made herself up as a sort of vampire rock star, with magenta lips, pink eye shadow, and violet mascara. She sprinkled gold powder across white cheeks and down the plunging front of the dress. She rubbed perfumed oil into her shoulders, her breasts, along her inner thighs and her back, which was bared nearly to the waist. Her hair emerged from braids into a wild, rippling mane, which she brushed until it fell down her back in a cloudlike mass. The overall effect was frightening, but three men tried to pick her up before she managed to flag down a cab. Her range of movement was limited, as the dress clung to her hips and wrapped around her legs like a glove. The heels were high enough to make her sway, and her Achilles tendons ached.

When the elevator doors opened, she walked across thick gray carpeting into a reception area. He had asked her to meet him at his office. There were two leather couches, a chrome-and-leather sling-back chair, and a pile of European Vogues. The view from the window framed the Empire State Building, still red and green from Christmas.

"Walk this way." Cordelia followed the sound of Philip's voice to a corner office, its walls painted a dusty rose. Above his desk hung a glass-covered Helmut Newton fashion layout featuring two gaunt models in black leather and three large dogs. Philip was seated behind a malachite desk, which was balanced on a base of carved wood. He was chopping up a sizable amount of cocaine cut from a larger rock. A phone was clutched between his ear and his shoulder. There was a beautiful Japanese screen in one corner, next to a low couch covered in gray suede. In another corner there was a rowing machine and a rack filled with chrome weights. On the opposite wall she saw the Hoboken skyline. A poster of a naked woman wearing a lot of diamonds was hung on the remaining wall: someone was about to blindfold her. The lighting was low.

When he saw her framed in the doorway, teetering slightly on the too-high heels, Philip's mouth opened and the phone dropped.

"Lemme go, Lou," he said into the dangling receiver. "Something incredible just strolled into my office. Yup. Fucking mouth-watering. Yeah. Yeah. Nah. In your dreams, pal. She'd stop your pacemaker. Classy. Young. I'll call you later." Philip hung up the phone, his eyes never leaving her face. "You ever fucked on malachite?" he asked quietly.

Cordelia frowned. The dress was meant to convey something:

54

her acceptance of being attractive and her sense of drama, not that she was a whore. He seemed to understand her discomfort.

"Hey, it was a joke. This is the first time I ever saw you out of sneakers and sweats. I mean, I had an idea, but this is kinda radical. You sorta take my breath away. I'm not sure I would have recognized you." He smiled. "Where'd you get those shoes, kid? You need a little more practice."

Cordelia leaned slightly against the door, raised her leg, rolled her shoulders.

"Okay. So you want a drink or something?"

"A glass of wine?"

"Sure." Philip touched a button by his desk, and a complete bar was revealed behind a wall panel. Cordelia felt slightly dizzy. The bar reminded her of a scene from an old James Bond movie. The villain offered James a drink just before he was dumped into a pool full of piranhas. She had not eaten that day, for fear the dress wouldn't zip.

"White, red, rosé, or champagne?"

"White."

"You like coke?"

"Uh, yes. Sometimes. I can't afford it, so I try not to do very much. I mean, I don't really do it at all. I mean, I don't buy it. Much. Also, it's really bad for your skin." She was babbling. Her hands were shaking so she wrapped them around her glass and gulped some wine. The glass was lead crystal. She looked up and saw that the ceiling was covered with a dark reflecting glass. She saw her breasts, her legs, the absurd amount of makeup she had on. She blushed and saw that Philip had seen the same reflection.

She stood and walked over to the window, feeling as if she were wrapped in Saran. The dress was like a second skin. The office resembled a set in one of those late-sixties movies about executives who were fooling around with their secretaries. Philip was chopping the cocaine with an ivory-backed razor blade.

"Man, you look like you were born in that dress."

"It's my mother's," Cordelia said very primly. "It's some famous designer's, but I've forgotten his name." She giggled stupidly.

"What was your mother? A movie star or a hooker?"

"She's a doctor."

"Your mother's a doctor?"

"Yes. A pediatrician. Early childhood. She's very good. Children love her." She felt hysterical, as if she wanted to leap out the window and swim to New Jersey.

"Hey, honey, what are you doing way over there, and why are we talking about your mother, the doctor? Come over here and do some of this good stuff."

Cordelia crossed the carpet and bent low over the table, a straw in her nose and Philip's hand caressing her bare back. It moved slowly downward, his hand almost touching her ass as she snorted the line.

"Do another one," he said, his hand pressing down on the small of her back as he inserted a knee between her legs.

She handed the straw back to him, and he ran a finger along her jawline, his eyes sweeping the length of her until she turned away. He finished the remaining lines.

"Save the rest for later," he said, replacing the vial in his pocket. "Have a seat."

Cordelia perched awkwardly on the edge of the leather chair. The skin was as fine and soft as velvet. She wondered how she was going to manage to eat anything. The dress stretched so tightly across her stomach she could see her own ribs. The cocaine began to make her jaw ache, and then she was overwhelmed by the sensation that everything that was happening was predestined. A sort of spiritual déjà vu. She was an actress in a completed film, and the performance was already reviewed. Her lines had been spoken. She leaned back and crossed her legs, the dress sliding up her thighs. Philip beamed at her.

"So how's the acting biz?"

"It's about a word called rejection," Cordelia said, leaning forward so her breasts were offered to him. "I'm too big, too small, too thin, too healthy, not blond, too old, young, white-bread, or ethnic. I am not Procter and Gamble, nor am I American Express."

"Who said?"

"Casting directors. Agents. Clients and acting teachers. You name it."

"So what do those putzes know? What you have is great—it's sincerity."

"Yuppies don't go for that. It's image, gloss, brand-name sneakers—"

"Yuppies? Don't talk about them to me! Those tight-assed little wet-nosed slimes don't buy anything. They hoard their pennies. They wrap the fucking things and turn them in at the bank! It makes being rich something to be ashamed of! It's cheap hoods like me and working stiffs that tip! Don't tell me any of those big Wall Street stockbroker squash players gave you anything for Christmas."

"Dr. Schwartz."

"Well, he's a Jew. Jews go in another category. Anyway, ask any waitress in one of those downtown fern bars. The worst tippers are those obnoxious little turds."

Philip's enthusiasm was infectious. Cordelia began to relax. His referring to himself as a cheap hood was disconcerting but, at the same time, endearing. She picked up an alabaster egg from the surface of his desk. The egg was a deep jade color, perched in a golden basket. Her fingers stroked its smooth sides as she looked around the room. There were no personal touches, no family snapshots.

"Where's the wife and kids?" she inquired, arching an eyebrow and tossing the egg in the air.

"You want that? The basket's solid gold." It was an odd thing to be offered an alabaster egg on a first date.

Cordelia hastily replaced it and stood up. "No, thanks."

"Ready to eat?"

"Sure."

"Great coat."

A white stretch limo was parked in front of the building. As

Cordelia began to walk down the street, Philip caught her arm and gestured toward the car. Cordelia giggled. The license plate said "P.S." A chauffeur emerged from the shadow of the building, hastily dropping a cigarette.

"Sorry, boss," he said, opening the door with a low bow.

Philip shrugged. "If it was up to her," he said, "we'd take the subway."

Cordelia gave both men her most dazzling smile and slid sideways across the leather seat. She felt as if she were in a straitjacket, the dress was so tight. As they drove uptown, the traffic seemed to part to allow the limousine to pass. She saw someone she knew riding his bicycle and the urge to hang out the window and scream "Hey! Look at me!" was very strong. Instead she turned on the television and watched three very thin women wearing spandex lip-sync a song by the Supremes. She picked up the phone and heard a distant hum.

"What sort of acting do you do?"

"Theater. But I'm trying to get commercials. And I love film."

"You got a good look for commercials."

"Sincere?"

"Partly." She frowned.

"What's the face for? You don't like that?"

"It's boring. I like to think I'm sexy."

"Sure you are. It's a nice, clean look. I think clean's sexy. What do you want to look like? Some sort of hooker?"

Cordelia raised one leg in the air until the dress fell back, exposing her thigh in black stockings, the lace garter above. A velvet pump hung from one toe. "You think I'm the young-mommy type? Or more like the crazy next-door neighbor who needs to borrow stuff?"

Philip ran his hand slowly down her leg as if he were estimating its worth. "Why do girls like you think they want to be whores? Whores are just hungry junkies. There's nothing like a smart lady from a good family getting excited. Whores just lay there counting up their money, figuring out how long they have to be on their backs. When a nice girl gets excited, it's like watching a fucking orchid bloom. Something beautiful."

Cordelia smiled. Philip's fingers were tracing a slow path from the tips of her toes to her inner thighs. His hands pressed her hard against the seat. She felt the electricity between their skin, between his hand and her body. The image of Harrison sitting on the edge of her bed crying for his lost child began to fade. Philip had begun to stroke the outside of her breast.

"Girls like you fall in love with the men they fuck." Philip had his tongue in her ear, his hand was down the front of her dress, his fingers were pinching her nipples. "Girls like you fall in love every day."

The restaurant was crowded, but they were ushered past the other patrons to a table in the corner, which was reserved. Cordelia stood straight in her mother's black dress, feeling invulnerable and somehow in charge. The maître d' bowed so deeply she almost curtsied, but she smiled instead, an enigmatic, mysterious smile. He deposited her, like a valuable jewel, on the velvet chair.

Philip ordered caviar and champagne, escargots, lobster, and some sort of pasta with black truffles. The meal cost more than her month's rent. Waiters became increasingly obsequious as their gratuity grew. Cordelia felt like a queen bee, with eager drones ready to satisfy her most mundane whim. Her gestures became languid and dramatic. She thought of Maggie the Cat from *Cat on a Hot Tin Roof*, who handled her body as if it were about to explode. She almost spoke with a southern accent. Philip ordered strawberries and cream and Grand Marnier. He fed the berries to her slowly, while she continued to purr and stretch.

"You seeing anyone?" Philip pushed her hair behind her ear, his hand following the line of her chin until he forced a finger between her lips and she sucked it. He had his other hand up her dress, with his knee forcing her legs apart. They were in a private corner of the restaurant, where no one seemed to observe what was going on underneath the table. Still, she felt herself to be utterly exposed.

"Not really." He had taken his finger out of her mouth.

"Why not? A beautiful girl like you."

"I'm kind of busy. And I'm sort of in a rut."

He took his hand and put it against the ice bucket. Then he put his cold fingers down inside her dress.

"Bullshit. You're a bitch."

"No I'm not."

"Sure you are, Cordelia. A beautiful bitch. Didn't Daddy ever tell you that? I like it. I like all of it. I like your stockings and what's above them and your mother's dress and those tits you keep flashing at me. . . ." Philip sat back, lighting a cigar.

"It's a game."

"I'm very good at games. I'm very good at squash, and I'm very good at figuring out what to do with girls like you." He snapped his fingers for the check.

She excused herself to go to the ladies' room. Faced with herself in a full-length mirror, under the fluorescent glare, she saw beneath the paint and the black dress, a skeleton, a wild-eyed girl with dilated pupils. Tears of self-pity rolled down her cheeks. She saw the marks of his teeth on her neck like a brand. The attendant handed her a tissue, holding out her hand for a tip. Cordelia sank down on the upholstered couch and tried to become calm, to think of what she should do. The bathroom had no back door. She looked at herself again and, hissing, "You pathetic bitch," applied more lipstick, brushed out her hair, and returned to the table. They drank very old brandy. Cordelia felt the seams of her mother's dress biting into her flesh. Although she had eaten, her stomach felt hollow.

In the limo, Philip opened her coat, kissed her face, covering her eyes with kisses, running his tongue across her cheekbones, nibbling along the line of her neck to her breasts, where he pulled down her dress and began to suck her nipples. Each time she opened her eyes she met the cold stare of his chauffeur, his mirror adjusted to see Philip's hand between her legs, her breasts exposed, her back arched against the seat.

He pushed her into her apartment, ripping the dress away from her body, holding her down with one hand while he slammed the door. She was bent over the couch so that her head was almost resting on the floor.

"Are you protected?" he muttered, his face bright red.

From her upside-down position Cordelia noticed how much dust had accumulated around the legs of her chairs. There was a spoon under the couch.

"Yes." She had inserted her diaphragm before leaving that evening.

When he slapped her across the face she thought he must have misunderstood her answer. She struggled to sit up, but he pushed her back, covering the hurt flesh with kisses. He ripped the remaining material of her dress from her back, tore off her stockings and underwear, pushed his entire hand inside her, rubbing until she was ready, dizzy with the blood that was rushing to her head, her face stinging from his blow, almost tempted to laugh at the picture she had of the two of them in such an awkward position. But his hand kept stroking until she was pushing hard against him, arching forward to meet him, and then he was naked, and bending her back even further, he plunged himself into her so quickly she screamed at the pain. He held her so hard she could feel the flesh beneath his fingers bruise.

She clung to him, her nails scratching his spine, her legs wrapped around his waist while he rode her, pulling her closer to him by grabbing handfuls of her hair and then pushing her back so that she was arched like a bow. He lifted her from the couch, holding her so that she remained impaled, and then lowered her to the floor so that she was against the wall, almost sitting. He pulled her to him hard and shoved a pillow beneath her hips so she was raised up high, and then he plunged into her again, harder still, her head hitting the wall with each thrust. He sank his teeth into her breast so that she screamed, and then he turned her around to enter her from behind.

"You fucking whore," he whispered into her ear. "You hot little bitch."

She remained silent.

When she woke up the next morning he was gone. The mattress was on the floor, with the blankets thrown across the room. He had torn up her favorite Calvin Klein sheets to bind her wrists. A silk scarf, used as a blindfold, was balled up under her pillow. They had snorted the rest of the cocaine and fallen asleep just before sunrise. Cordelia found her comforter and lay on the mattress, curled up into a ball. The sound she was making resembled a puppy's whimpering for its mother. Philip's departure made the wreckage of her room even more difficult to contemplate, but when she recalled the events of the previous night she was glad to be alone. Her body was covered with bruises and rug burns. Her head ached and she felt as if she had fallen down a flight of stairs. He had taken her in every position possible and opened her up more than she was willing.

"You're not the kind of woman I usually like," he had told her as they lay in the dark, his hands still touching her while she tried to calm down, tried to tell herself she was safe, the fear still present. "I liked big tits, small brains. You know, Malibu Barbie. No politics, no opinions, no ambition, no bullshit."

Cordelia laughed. Pulling herself up slightly on one elbow, she lit a cigarette.

"No smoking," Philip said gently, putting it out in the glass of wine by her bed.

"Fuck you," Cordelia said.

"Again? You sure?"

"No." She settled back against the pillows, yawning.

Philip pulled her into his arms, gently stroking her head as he talked. "I liked women that wanted to be put down. Humiliated. You know—dress 'em up and take them someplace really public, no underwear. They had to sit with their legs spread, and anyone who wanted to look—"

Cordelia pulled out of his arms and twisted around to face him. "Why are you telling me this?" she asked, her voice shaking. "You can't expect me to like you if you do horrible things to women."

"Honey"—Philip settled her back against his chest—"that's all history. I don't like those kinds of women anymore. That's why I'm telling you this. When I first saw you at the club I didn't get too excited. I mean, struggling actresses just don't do that much for me. But then when I saw you that morning I asked you if you'd ever heard that Yeats poem—"

"You asked me if I knew who Helen of Troy was," Cordelia said, laughing slightly.

"Yeah, well, I was trying to remember the poem where he says this chick's got beauty like a tightened bow. I took English in college. And you looked at me like I was some sort of loser, some kind of quasi-literate pervert."

"No I didn't."

"Yeah, you did. I saw that I wasn't getting anywhere, but then you looked me full in the eye and I saw there was this orange flame around the pupils, and you had these fucking cheekbones like a goddamned American Indian, and I could see you were really clean . . . just sort of pure. And smart. I wanted to talk more, but your attitude really pissed me off, and then I started to watch you."

"You did?"

"Sure. When you were working out. I looked for you. I liked how hard you pushed yourself. You sweat like a man. And I started thinking about how nice it would be to have all that power underneath me, tied down. But then you disappeared."

"Umm." Cordelia yawned and started to roll away, but Philip put his hand under her chin to make her look at him.

"When you came back after your sister died I couldn't believe how much you'd changed. It was like watching this ghost. At first I thought you looked great that skinny, but then I talked to you and I saw what had happened to your eyes." Philip stopped. He kissed Cordelia's forehead.

"What happened to my eyes?"

"They were black. I mean, completely dull, like the lights were gone, like you'd been put out; the flame was missing. You handed me my key and your hand was so thin. Jesus. You know, I felt something. I never really pitied anyone before."

"You pitied me?"

"It wasn't just pity. It was something else. I wanted to make you feel better, but I could tell that nothing could do that. It made me angry. You seemed totally alone, and I was jealous—"

"Jealous?"

63

"Yeah. Like would anyone ever hurt that much for me? And I knew you weren't really seeing me. You remember?"

"No." Cordelia thought for a moment. "I don't remember any particular time."

"Right. But I kept seeing your face. And it was like watching you run. I thought anyone who could suffer that much would have to be some phenomenal fuck."

"God," Cordelia whispered. "I don't believe you. I'm not who you think I am."

Philip pulled her up and placed her against the pillows. He ran his hands down the length of her body.

"And I thought you must be so good to love your sister like that and what I need in my life is a good woman."

He put his fingers inside her. Cordelia sank down lower, her face hiding in the sheets.

"But I'm not convinced you can do it, Delia, 'cause there's something inside you like steel, something hard and fine that might survive anything. But I want you to look at me now." She opened her eyes. Philip was tying her wrists above her head, tight against the headboard.

"What I want is to break you completely," he whispered in her ear as she twisted under his touch, her body beginning to respond again. "I want you to surrender."

She had closed her eyes and thought he was probably just what she needed.

On the kitchen table she found a note. It said: "Buy a new dress." Underneath the sugar bowl there were ten new hundred-dollar bills. She sat down, still mummied in the quilt, and considered her next move. She had an acting class at five and was expected to work at the squash club from one to four. It was a little before eleven. She decided to call in sick and go home to see her mother.

CHAPTER

8

CORDELIA'S MOTHER WAS A WONDERFUL DOCTOR. CHILDREN actually liked to visit her, in an office that was furnished with child-sized brightly painted furniture and all the latest toys. There was a complete library of children's books and some over-fed gerbils, who dedicated their lives to rotating on a squeaky exercise wheel. Dr. Cavanagh felt it was important for all children to feel superior to something, and what was less intimidating than a gerbil? The Cavanagh cellar was filled with boxes containing macaroni-encrusted spray-painted ashtrays and shellacked objects meant to be worn as jewelry. The children presented their pediatrician with offerings on every possible holiday. Brocaded pot holders, gilded pine cones, and painted Easter eggs were standard props in the Cavanagh household. When Cordelia was little, she spent many afternoons sitting in the waiting room reading old *Ladies' Home Journals* while her mother finished work. Because she was the youngest, she didn't have cheerleading practice or an after-school job like her sisters. The magazine articles made her wonder when it would be her turn to make Jell-O molds and wear a white veil. When Cordelia turned thirteen, her mom gave her a box of tampons and told her to feel free to ask any questions. Cordelia asked her how long she had to wait before she could start planning her wedding.

"Marriage is a crock," her mother said bitterly. "Learn a craft."

Cordelia's father was an actor. He never seemed to be the correct age for the current trend. His looks and style were always somewhat behind or ahead of what was considered "hot." He walked out on the family when Cordelia was seven, moved to Hollywood, and, to earn a living between auditions, started an employment agency for other actors between jobs. The agency specialized in supplying short-term talent for highly paid jobs. It was open only to industry professionals who needed a second income. The response was overwhelming, and the company became franchised. Mr. Cavanagh was now wealthy enough to accept poorly paid parts in showcases and small movie roles.

Cordelia's father lived in the Hollywood hills with his girlfriend, Sunflower. Sunflower was an est graduate who had been a follower of someone who had been a follower of Charles Manson. She had hang-glided off every cliff face and dune in southern California. When Cordelia finally visited them she was disgusted by the fact that Sunflower was nearly twenty years younger than her father, but the worst thing about her father's girlfriend, as she told Cynthia over the phone, was that she was so incredibly naive, even by Hollywood standards.

"She does nothing but analyze her own head," Cordelia hissed into the phone, while her father's and Sunflower's Buddhist chanting filled the living room, "and it's as empty as a scooped-out gourd."

Cordelia refused to attend a workshop one of Sunflower's friends was giving on introductory fire-walking and instead picked up a boy who was working the grill at the local Denny's and went to Baja with him to take psychedelic mushrooms. Her father was understandably upset to discover his seventeen-year-old daughter gone and his live-in girlfriend crying over being called a gullible sheep. When Cordelia turned up, sunburned and raving about the conversation she'd had with a school of humpbacked whales, her father accused her of being selfish and mean-spirited.

"Well, at least I don't have a boyfriend old enough to be my father," she screamed at him. "I'm not some sort of pathetic aging has-been who can't stand the fact that he's almost fifty-five." She'd caught the next plane back to New Jersey.

She didn't visit them again. Her father phoned her on major holidays and her birthdays. When he called her at other times, she sat outside her mother's room and wished it were possible to speak to him. Her mother always put down the phone and yelled for her. Then she would tell him there was no answer but she'd let Cordelia know he'd called. Sunflower tried some sort of astrological counseling by letter, but Cordelia threw away her charts without looking at them.

Mr. Cavanagh's initial reaction to his eldest daughter's murder was to disappear. The funeral arrangements were left entirely to his ex-wife.

On the day after Cynthia's autopsy, Cordelia had asked her mother, "Where's Daddy? When is he coming?"

Her mother shrugged and sighed.

"That cowardly scumbag," Cordelia said, laughing. "He can't even show up for his own daughter's death?"

"You don't understand, darling," her mother said slowly. "This is something he can't accept. His heart is broken."

"And yours isn't?"

There was a silence. Tears were rolling down her mother's cheeks.

"Yes. But I have something else. I have my belief that somehow I did everything in my power to protect her, and he feels as if he's failed. I don't know how to explain. . . . Your father and Cynthia were almost like best friends. She understood him the same way she understood you—"

"I am nothing like him!" Cordelia screamed. "He's a cheap liar! He doesn't love us! He didn't love her! He didn't understand anything!"

Her mother held out her arms. "Honey, I'm sorry. He loved her more than he loves himself. He loves all three of you like that. You girls mean everything to him. He doesn't know how to let go."

Cordelia walked out of her room and went downstairs to the

living room. She removed from the wall a picture that was taken of all of them on a vacation in New Mexico before her parents' divorce. The three girls were laughing at something the photographer had said, and her father was smiling down at his giggling daughters. It was a look of complete pride and happiness. She went outside and smashed the glass of the frame until her hands were red with blood, and then she tore the picture into tiny pieces and burned what was left and threw the ashes over the neighbor's fence. It occurred to her then to stop eating.

The funeral was held in the Quaker meetinghouse where all three girls had attended Sunday school. Cordelia had learned the little she knew about scripture there; mostly the children built lost cities in the sand. Her religious training was incomplete and sporadic. She had thought for most of her childhood that the Statue of Liberty was God. Someone played the flute. Someone sang "Chelsea Morning" in a clear soprano. Everyone wept. It was perfectly awful, and when Cordelia cast a desperate eye around the church she was shocked to see her father standing in one of the back pews. He was just taking off his dark glasses, and the sight of his eyes terrified her. They were completely black, red-rimmed and blank. He looked like a blind old man. He saw her and waved feebly, attempting to smile. She could not bear to look at him again.

At the grave site, Amelia crossed the grass to hug him, but Cordelia stood alone, completely rigid, her hands clawing at the air by her sides as if she were a spastic. She refused to speak to him. She held a rose meant to be left on the coffin so tightly the head snapped off and petals scattered across the ground.

Her mother put her arm over Cordelia's shoulders and was shocked to feel the bones protruding through the skin. It had been less than a week since the murder, and her youngest child had begun to disappear; her eyes were strangely bright and empty. She could not read her daughter's thoughts. Cordelia's relationship with Cynthia had given Dr. Cavanagh tremendous relief, as she believed herself to be a failure as a mother. She tried to unclench Cordelia's fingers from the rose stem.

"Baby," she whispered into her daughter's hair. "Let go."

"That's not her," Cordelia said slowly. "I saw her leave before the autopsy."

"It's no one's fault, Cordelia. Try to forgive whoever you think is responsible.

Cordelia shook off her mother's arm. "It's everyone's fault, Mom. You never taught us how to take care of ourselves. I bet she thought that bastard would put down his knife and talk to her if she could just figure out the right approach to the situation. She thought everyone was basically good. You never taught us anything about evil."

Back home, Cordelia had slipped upstairs while the guests were arriving. Changing into sweat pants and sneakers, she escaped out the back door to the road. After seven days without food, her body was feeling oddly strong yet light, filled with energy that might have been supplied by drugs but was, in fact, the high one experiences during the first stage of starvation. In the fourth mile her pace increased and she felt a second wind rush through her body, giving her more power and evening out her breathing. She felt the stretch in her muscle, and her mind was a perfect blank, a clean slate, charcoal gray. The white line down the center of the road carried her forward, and it occurred to her to keep running until she fell and everything was over. She realized that a car was slowly following her. She waved it on, but it didn't pass. She looked over her left shoulder and saw her father's rented Mercedes.

"Oh, Christ!" she said. "Leave me alone!" She ran faster, but the car continued to crawl along until her father pulled up slightly in front of her and leaned over to open the door.

"Get in," he said, his hands tight on the steering wheel, his eyes hidden behind the dark glasses.

She sat as close to the door as possible, as if she'd been picked up by a leering stranger. He pulled into the parking lot of a nearby playground. Cordelia opened the door.

"Mind if I stretch?"

"Of course not."

Her father got out and walked around the front of the car to watch her. She put her leg up on a bench and reached toward the toe.

"That's a bad stretch for your hamstring," her father said. "It overstretches the muscle."

Cordelia ignored him.

"You're too thin."

"No I'm not." She reached toward her toe again, wishing he would leave her alone.

"I'm in the business, Delia, and I'm telling you, you're too thin. You look hungry. That's not the look anyone wants. It makes agents nervous. You couldn't even model."

"I'm not trying to look like one of your bicycle-pump temps, Dad," she said in a nasty tone. "I don't like to look like a born-again earth mother either. I work out, and I've just changed the way my body looks. You can't remember me as anything but fat."

"You were never fat, Cordelia. Don't try to make me feel guilty. You're starving yourself. You don't even have an ass anymore."

She stood up. "Don't you look at my ass! How dare you! You don't even know me! What do you know about my body?"

"What's to know? Pretty soon your hair will start falling out and your gums will recede. You keep it up and you may never have children. When was your last period?"

She turned around to face him, her face distorted by tears, her finger pointing.

"You shut up! Who do you think you are? My father? That's none of your business! It's disgusting of you to ask. You weren't even around when it first started." She saw a mother slowly buckle her toddler into a stroller and wheel the child away from the screaming couple.

"Why did you bother coming here? What right do you have to try and throw your weight around?"

"She was my daughter, Cordelia. You have no idea what you're talking about."

"So what? How much time did you spend with her?"

"Six years before you were born. Seven years after that. And all of her adult life by phone and spirit. She was the miracle baby, the first child you can't stop watching. We took her everywhere we went. We stayed up all night watching her sleep and wrote everything down that she said and told people stupid stories about things that she'd done, until everyone referred to her as the Wonder Baby. We didn't know anything about failure then. It was all perfectly golden. All about love. And then someone, a woman you can't really communicate with but you'll always love, the mother of your children, calls you up and tells you that one of those children, that daughter of the sun, is no longer living, that you'll never see her again. The best thing you ever did has been destroyed by some arbitrary act of hideous greed. She came from my temple like Zeus's daughter." She could see the tears dropping from beneath his dark glasses. Her impulse was to bolt, to run as fast as she could away from the sight of her father raging at the sky. "I talked to her for at least an hour every week. How do you think I found out how you were? I paid for the lease on her clinic. You never call. You don't answer my letters. She liked Sunflower. They were friends—"

"No they weren't."

"Yes, Cordelia. They liked each other very much. Sunflower's absolutely devastated by this. And Cynthia always thought I did the right thing by leaving. You had to stick by your mother—"

"Don't talk to me about my mother! You always try to rewrite history to fit your own fucking idea of what sort of person you are! I hate you! Cynthia thought you were a fraud and a bum and a seducer of women! She hated that bleached-blond Hollywood High surfer-chick bimbo! Leave me alone!"

She stuck her fingers in her ears, squeezed her eyes closed, and hummed "Moon River" until she sensed his departure. The playground was deserted. She was muttering under her breath: "I hate you and I'll never eat until I die and then you'll feel really bad."

She stood on the hill overlooking the woods where she'd played as a child. She was always younger than her sisters. Always smaller and stupider and easier to fool. They often found her worship of them embarrassing, but Cynthia's protection was absolute. Once when she had fallen hard and split her lip open, she had stood in a circle of children, who were transfixed by the sight of the blood pouring from her mouth. She could see her sister breaking through that ring of silent, staring children, kneeling over her and whispering, "Delia, I'm here." She had turned to all the other children and said, "Leave her alone. She's my little sister." They had walked home together, and Cordelia had thought she would fall again soon so as to be rescued by her own angel.

"Cynthia," she screamed. "we have to go home now!" She sat down on a swing, her head between her knees, crying tears that seemed to rip out her insides. It grew dark, and a car pulled up and honked. It was Amelia.

"Daddy's gone back," she said as Cordelia opened the door. "He said to tell you goodbye."

"Thanks for picking me up," Cordelia said. "I didn't feel like running."

"I wanted to leave the house. Mom's kind of drunk, and she's telling horrible baby stories. Were you crying when I drove up?"

Amelia asked the question so abruptly that Cordelia could not think of a way to deny her. She nodded.

"I can't cry," Amelia said in a flat tone, her forehead against the steering wheel. "Michael told me he thinks I'm still in shock, but I don't think so. I know she's dead. But it doesn't seem possible. I think it will be three birthdays from now or something when I realize this is forever. That she'll never come home. Winter. Always cold. I feel frozen, Delia. I feel as cold as I did that night, all the time. Like my insides are made of ice. Michael thinks I'm in shock. Do you think she was frightened? Did he hurt her terribly? Do you think she knew she was dying?"

"I don't know." Cordelia watched the lights go on in someone's kitchen. Everyone but them seemed to belong somewhere.

"I hope she didn't know, Cordelia. She loved everyone so much!" Amelia was hitting her forehead against the steering wheel. Cordelia put her hand in the place where the skin was hitting the plastic. "And why are you so thin?"

Cordelia stared at her hand. It seemed translucent. She believed she could see the veins, with the blood moving through them.

"I'm not." They sat in silence in the car until the stars came out, and then they drove home.

CHAPTER

9

CORDELIA LET HERSELF INTO HER MOTHER'S HOUSE BY THE side door, which was always left open. The living room had recently been painted white. She looked at herself in the hall mirror and was happy to see that the bite marks left on her neck by Philip were not visible above the collar of her sweater. Snow dusted the outside deck, and squirrels and small birds were perched on the railing, nibbling nuts and seeds and staring boldly at her through the picture window. She slid the door open and took a deep breath of the cold, clean air. The pain behind her eyes diminished considerably. Her mom was scheduled to be at the hospital until dinnertime. When Cordelia had called her she acted surprised that she could just take off for the afternoon.

"How nice to have such a fun job," she had said sarcastically. Dr. Cavanagh did not want Cordelia to be an actress.

The house hummed with the comforting sound of expensive machinery catering to all possible human needs. The most discouraging aspect of Cordelia's life was a budget that failed to allow for any form of luxury and was upset completely by any unexpected expense. In fact, she was operating on a deficit; her money nearly always ran out before her next paycheck was due, and for several days of the month she walked hundreds of blocks and subsisted on canned soup. Her refusal to accept help from her mother somehow made her choice of career less unfortunate.

The thought of the previous night's dinner brought back her headache. It seemed acceptable somehow that Philip would give her money. She was so hopeful and poor. Acting money often arrived disguised as a windfall, which she blew by treating her starved senses to Zabar's deli or expensive sneakers. A friend of hers had attempted to work out her budget, but when he informed her that she was not capable of surviving on her current income, she ignored his advice and simply trusted in the kindness of strangers for occasional charity.

Her mom loved gadgets. She owned air conditioners, two microwave ovens, humidifiers, a CD player, a Dolby stereo system with speakers in every room, and three televisions complete with cable and VCR. While Cordelia did her laundry, coffee brewed in a machine that roasted and ground its own beans. The kitchen VCR showed Raquel Welch performing impossible yoga poses while she talked about achieving inner tranquillity by eliminating salt. Cordelia flipped through the mail, putting aside the latest issue of *Gourmet* to read with her lunch. Underneath the magazine she found a note written on a doctor's stationery: "Sarah, mastectomy is scheduled for Saturday as discussed. Call to confirm."

Cordelia's stomach contracted. On her mother's wall calendar she saw a red star drawn on next Saturday's square, with "9 A.M." written in black ink.

"Mommy! Why didn't you tell us?" It was a sobbing accusation.

"Tell you what, Delia? You sound hysterical."

"The operation! About the cancer!"

"Oh, that . . ."

"What the hell do you mean, 'Oh, that'? What's wrong with you? What's going to happen to us? What's happening to our family? You're going to die!"

"Cordelia! Stop this at once! Calm down. Watch a tape, and I'll come home for lunch. We'll talk. People don't die from this sort of operation. I just got the biopsy result back last week."

"Why didn't you tell me you found a lump? When did you see the doctor? Don't lie to me!"

"It all just happened, sweetie. All at once." Her mother's voice sounded tired.

"How can they cut off your breast? Mom?"

"Yes, honey bunny?"

"Are they cutting off your breast?"

There was a short silence, followed by a sigh.

"I think so, darling. It's safer."

When Dr. Cavanagh arrived home she found Cordelia in front of the VCR, watching the deathbed scene from *Terms of Endearment:* Debra Winger, the spunky daughter, is dying of cancer, and her mother, Shirley MacLaine, has finally broken down and admitted she can't imagine life without her child. Cordelia's face was so swollen with tears she could barely see. She was sitting on the floor sobbing when her mother rushed through the door.

"You morbid little duck," she said, turning off the machine. "You look like you were attacked by bees! And you aren't allowed to watch this miserable movie."

She gathered Cordelia into her arms, making clucking noises in the back of her throat and stroking the tangled hair out of her daughter's eyes.

"Don't you worry about your tough old mom," she whispered.

"You're going to leave me just like she did," Cordelia wailed.

"No, baby. Cynthia didn't leave any of us, Cordelia. She was murdered. Stop trying to bury me before I'm ready to go. You'll be appalled by my longevity, and your children won't be able to stand their senile, ancient granny! Now go and wash your face with cold water and come back, and we'll have éclairs and cappuccino for lunch. Did you see the new machine? Refined sugar and caffeine—just what the doctor ordered!"

Cordelia splashed water on her eyes and returned to watch her mother arrange straw mats on the table. Dr. Cavanagh had picked a few winter roses on her way in, and she put them in crystal bud vases next to a plate filled with pastry. One of Cordelia's favorite activities as a little girl had been to watch her mother prepare for a dinner party. She had a wonderful sense of harmony, without seeming contrived in her choice of decorations. She could set a table with linen and get away with using brightly colored paper plates. Her clothes were always individual yet elegant. Still, whenever Cordelia told her she looked beautiful, her face never failed to register surprise. She'd stare into the mirror, trying to see what her daughter described.

"You think I'm beautiful because I'm your mother," she'd say finally, turning away to finish her cooking.

When their father had left she had fallen apart, taking to her bed for weeks of weeping. Cordelia stood in the doorway of her room, willing her to turn around and hold her arms out, but she lay on her side staring at the far wall, the room dim, the shades closed to the light. Cynthia had taken care of her two younger sisters. She was extremely angry at their mother.

"I think Daddy's a bastard," Amelia burst out one night, shoving her food around her plate, her eyes filling with tears.

Dinnertime was an ordeal insisted upon by Cynthia, the three little girls alone around the large table, eating badly prepared food under the sharp eye of the eldest.

"Shut up, stupid," Cynthia had snapped. "You don't understand. If I was him, I'd have left her too."

On the night of Cynthia's murder, the police had asked Dr. Cavanagh to come to the morgue for a final positive identification of the body of her eldest daughter. There were papers to sign before they'd let the family claim the body.

"I can't bear this," she had muttered to Cordelia as they sat in the brightly lit waiting room. "This is the worst nightmare, the only thing you never allow yourself to imagine. I mean, how could I? I thought she'd bury me. Oh my God, my darling daughter! Why did they do this to her?"

Cordelia's hands were marked by red ovals left by her mother's nails digging into her flesh. As they waited to be summoned, Cordelia felt she was standing at the edge of a pit filled with unbelievable horrors. She presented God with everything she held dear, every dream and past triumph, in exchange for sparing her mother such grief and allowing her sister to come back to life.

"I'll be a prostitute," she whispered into her fists. "I'll die of AIDS. I'll never have children. I'll be a nun. I'll stop acting and clean houses. I'll be fat and ugly and unloved for the rest of my life."

But Cynthia was already dead from multiple trauma, and her mother brushed her lips again and again across the pale skin of her daughter's face. She gently pushed the thick chestnut hair back from her brow and for a moment rested her cheek against that of her dead child.

"Yes," she said to the medical examiner. "This is my daughter."

Cordelia stared down at the still face of her sister, and for a moment she felt her heart stop completely, a flutter and a pain in her chest unlike anything she had ever experienced. She thought, with relief, that she too must die.

She looked at her face reflected in the fluorescent light of her mother's bathroom and spoke aloud. "I hate you. You have no talent. You are exactly like your father."

Her mother looked up from putting out the coffee cups, to catch the stricken expression on Cordelia's face.

"Now stop this," she said gently. "Come and sit down." She patted the chair next to her. "I'm sorry I didn't tell you guys."

"Why should you have? It's not as if I'm of any help! All I ever worry about is my scummy life and my lousy ambitions. Everything as it affects me. Everything is about me. You're getting operated on, and I'm afraid you won't take care of me. That's all I think about: What's going to happen to Cordelia? When Cynthia was dying, you know what was going through my mind? How could she do this to me? Who's going to be my best friend? Who's going to deliver my babies? She was the one who lost everything, she was the one who'd been cheated, and I felt like the victim."

"That's because you loved her so much. We love people selfishly, Delia. You probably loved Cynthia too much. Anyway, stop being so melodramatic and have an éclair."

Cordelia broke off a large piece of pastry and stuffed it into her mouth, which made her mother smile.

"How'd you get your belly that flat, piglet? I've never seen you this skinny."

"There's a machine at work called the abdomen compressor."

"Where does the fat go? You think I could do that?"

"Sure."

"Met any millionaires?"

"Huh?"

"One of my nurses, Doris, told me *Cosmo* recommended squash clubs as the best places to meet rich men."

"I guess it is, but most squash players are pretty neurotic about playing squash. I mean, they come there to play mostly." She ate the rest of the éclair.

"Are you dating?"

"Dating doesn't exist, Mom. I sort of have this one guy—"

"What's that mean? To 'sort of have'?"

"He took me out to dinner. It cost a fortune. I wore that Galanos thing you gave me."

"Well, dinner's a date. Is he nice? What's his name?"

"Philip. He's very rich."

Cordelia thought about the money on the table and her torn sheets. The way Philip had hit her. A shiver went down her back.

"If he isn't nice, get rid of him. Money won't make up for not being loved properly. Try to do what Amelia did. Fall in love with a lawyer." Had her mother ever been loved properly? There was a nice man in her life, a sculptor named Ed.

"How's Ed feel about the operation?"

"Sad for me, but he says he'll just concentrate on the other one. Symmetry was never that important to him."

"That's good. You want me to stay until Saturday?"

"No, honey. Go back to New York to not get cast in a few more major motion pictures. The sooner you realize you're casting your pearls before swine . . . which reminds me, that slasher movie you did is out in video. It's called *Scream Until You Die*

78

or something like that—one of my patients' older brothers saw it. He recognized you from that production of *Glass Menagerie* you did a few years ago. I told him those weren't your boobs, and he looked very disappointed."

"Mother! Why are you so negative about my work?"

"Not at all, darling. If I really wanted to discourage you, I'd beg you to stay."

"I almost got cast in this coal-mining miniseries, but the director said I was too healthy-looking."

"You mean not anorexic? What a disgusting industry."

"The producer said they'd reconsider me if I lost fifteen pounds."

"You will do no such thing, Cordelia!" Her mother's fist came crashing down on the table. "Do you think I was blind to what you were doing to yourself?"

Cordelia stared at her plate. The last éclair was oozing custard. "I wasn't doing anything—"

"You were starving to death, and I was not able to stop you. I have never been able to protect you from anything. I am a lousy mother."

Cordelia stood and crossed to where her mother sat, her hands cradling her head. She put her arms around her.

"I'm sorry, baby," Dr. Cavanagh whispered. "Everything's going to be fine."

On the train back to Manhattan, Cordelia realized she would not see her mother again before she went under the knife. That's how she thought of the operation, a black figure performing human sacrifice on her innocent mom. She might die under the anesthesia. Cordelia had found her mother's will in the living room breakfront while she searched for a stamp. The house had been left to her. She wished she could stay, but there was nothing to do or say. Her mother was a doctor and viewed the procedure as a normal part of life. She had once broken the neck of an injured pigeon, picking up the bird in front of her horrified daughters and throwing its limp body on top of the compost heap.

"Don't be sentimental, girls," she had said briskly. "A slow and painful death is a terrible thing."

Cordelia had sneaked back after dinner with a cotton-lined shoe box and buried the bird with suitable morbidity and tears.

Just before it entered Penn Station, the train went into the tunnel and the lights flickered off. For a moment Cordelia was blind, the only sound the thumping of her heart. She said a silent prayer: Please, don't kill my mother.

CHAPTER

10

THE ANSWERING MACHINE WAS FULL. THE FIRST MESSAGE was from her service. Someone named Brad asked her to call him back. Philip's voice was deep and slightly hoarse.

"Last night was fantastic," he said. "Let's do it again really soon."

Maxine's words were more poignant. "Call me, Cory," she said. "I ate an entire Sara Lee chocolate-chip cheesecake last night, and I have an audition for a fat part tomorrow, which will probably be over by the time you hear this, and I'll be even more depressed and considering a serious binge. So call me."

Amelia sounded grumpy. "Mom called me about the operation. She might have told us about the lump or the biopsy, but what can you fucking expect from fucking super fucking woman. Fuck it. Also, Tom wants Harrison. He told Michael he was a better horsie than he was, and Michael's very upset. What, honey? Oh, he says to tell you to tell Harrison that he can borrow his sword and also that he's got the new Nintendo game. That's this video shit. What? No, Tom. He thinks you made him leave. I've got to go. What, honey? No, no, Harrison's not on the phone. I'm talking to Auntie Deli's machine. He's more obsessed with Harrison than with Kermit. Look, don't worry about Mommy. God can't do anything else right now to fuck us over.

We'll be all right. Don't worry." Her sister sighed. "I love you, Delia."

There was a second message from Philip. "Still not home? I can't stop thinking about your body. Let's make the mattress fly again. Call me."

The final voice belonged to Harrison.

"Hello, Cordelia's machine. I've decided to stay in the city for a while. I think I've got a sublet on Avenue A. The number's 202–3460. We need to talk."

Cordelia turned off the machine and considered what she'd do if her mother died. She stared into the mirror, fascinated by the tears she could summon at the mere thought of herself as a motherless child. Of course she could sell the house, but Amelia would hate her. She could pay to go to graduate school. She allowed her eyes to fill with unshed tears and admired the way her face looked suffused with false emotion. The phone rang.

"You're home." It was Harrison.

"Yes."

"What were you doing?"

"Watching myself cry in the bathroom mirror."

"God, I love to do that! Shall I come over and help?"

"No." There was a short silence.

"Why'd you run off like that?"

"I didn't want to discuss my sister."

"You could have just said that."

"I didn't know it. I just needed to get away from you."

"Why?"

"Who knows? Because people adore you. My nephew prefers you to his own father. Strangers on the street want to touch you. I feel like a leper in the company of Jesus Christ. Everyone seems to bask in your beauty except me. I feel shut out. The world sees Cary Grant, while I'm stuck with the Underground Man. Harrison, my mom has cancer." She whispered the last part.

"Oh, no. Cordelia . . ."

"She's having a mastectomy."

"I'm so sorry."

"She's acting like it's perfectly normal. She didn't even tell us.

I found a memo from her doctor. My mother has beautiful breasts."

"Did you just go home?"

"Yes. I read her will. She's left me the house. Because I'm such a failure. I'll never make any money, and I'll never have a nice husband like Amelia. I'll never have my own babies—"

"What are you talking about?"

"My life! It's horrible. I slept with this man—this man from work. He left me a thousand dollars underneath the sugar. I mean, underneath my sugar bowl. A thousand dollars." Harrison didn't say anything. "It was to pay for my dress. I mean, the dress he ripped off my back. That's what the money was for. He ripped my dress off. Shit. Except it's way too much money. But he's very, very rich, so it doesn't seem like anything to him. He'd give me more if I wanted it. But I don't want it."

"Should I come over?"

"Why? Do you want a short-term loan?" She giggled a little.

"No, Delia. You sound a little shaken."

"Oh, I'm fine. Well, I'm not exactly fine, but that's what I always say. I said that to the medical examiner after we went to see her body. Cynthia's body. They had her laid out on one of those shelves. Like a television show. But she was really dead. Everyone in there was really dead. He was talking to me about shock. I shook his hand, and I said, 'Thanks for all your help. I'm fine.' Then I punched the wall. He told me shock sometimes lasts for years. People do all these weird things. Get terrible haircuts. He said it was like a drug. Or it could kill you. Your heart just stops working."

"Cordelia . . ."

"I need to be by myself."

"You're all right?"

"Sure. Good night, Harrison."

"Good night, darling."

She hung up the phone. It was snowing a little. Snowflakes glittered like diamonds as they danced across the street lights. Reflexively she thought that her sister would never see this again, the city perfect underneath a blanket of snow. Sometimes it was when she tasted something delicious or laughed. *Cynthia will never do this*, she would think, and the taste would become bitter, the comedy flat. She put the kettle on, picked up *The Portrait of a Lady*, and fell asleep dreaming she was an unhappy heiress traveling across Europe in a coach.

The next morning, a box containing a dozen long-stemmed white roses was left on her desk. Lacking a vase, she borrowed the coffeepot, which caused a minor altercation among the early exercisers.

"The receptionist gets flowers, and we don't get our coffee?" Lucy Van Castle, wearing a Donna Karan bodysuit and dozens of gold bracelets, stood in the middle of the front lobby, trying to incite the other members in a rebellion against Cordelia.

"What's the matter with you, Van Castle?" snapped Dr. Schwartz. "Didn't anyone ever send you roses?"

The janitor found an empty orange juice bottle, and the problem was solved. The card was simply signed "PS."

When she returned the call from her service, she was given an audition time for a commercial that featured a new yogurt being marketed as the best snack to eat after working out. The spots featured "real people," jock actors and actresses exercising and then eating yogurt. The concept of yogurt as a refreshing thing to consume after a workout was somewhat implausible, but the ad campaign was well done and the company was spending a lot of money on a television and print campaign. Her audition was scheduled for the next afternoon.

She had a friend at Macy's who was a makeup artist and had offered to give her a free facial and makeup session anytime Cordelia felt like visiting the store. When her shift ended, she took the elevator to the lobby. Harrison was dozing on the front steps. He looked slightly hung over but, as always, handsome.

"You finished work?" he asked her, slowly straightening up to his full height. He leaned forward to tuck her scarf more securely into her jacket and to pull up her zipper.

"Yes, but I'm on my way to Macy's to get my face done."

"What's wrong with your face?" Harrison was squinting at her worriedly, as if she were contemplating cosmetic surgery. "What do you mean by 'done'?"

"Nothing's wrong. I'm getting a facial and some makeup ideas. I have an important audition tomorrow."

"Can we talk? I really need to work some things out with you."

Cordelia had started walking briskly down the street toward Herald Square. The air was very cold and dry. Harrison's nose was pink, and his shoulders were hunched into a lightweight tweed jacket. His appearance infuriated her. What was he doing in this brutal winter? He belonged barefoot on a sandy beach or in the gentle mists of Ireland. New York was too unforgiving; its sharp edges and frenzied pace could not accommodate someone like Harrison.

She wished she could turn to him, explain why it was impossible for her to go back, to allow herself to think of that girl who had expected life to be filled with epiphanies, who put herself center stage, the lights gradually coming up to reveal her, Cordelia, perfectly posed, her lines all memorized. Having learned how badly things turned out, she had no desire to begin. She saw her sister's death as a logical fate for someone who had once fully embraced life. In Ireland she had decided she would simply love Harrison without anticipating a return. She convinced herself it was enough just to be near him.

During the Easter break in Trinity, they had decided to go away to the west of Ireland, to Connemara, where a friend of Harrison's owned a small stone cottage stuck out on a spit of land, across the fields from the sea. Ponies ran wild in the long grass, and the air smelled of lavender, which grew up the sides of the hills. The cottage had no electricity or running water. They pumped it from a small pond behind the house, on which lived two white swans. Each morning Cordelia snuggled under the down comforter watching Harrison, his back bare, priming the pump. The swans stretched their long necks, gently crisscrossing the surface of the lake, always touching, seemingly madly in love.

When the water began to flow into the tank, she would jump

out of bed to light the gas stove for their morning tea. Harrison would straighten and stretch toward the sun and then turn to smile at her. She would wave at him and turn away, unable to stand the perfect blankness of his eyes. She wondered if it was the effect of the sun hitting the window that made him look that way. The simplicity of their activities supplied a sad tranquillity. They rarely got completely dressed, and neither of them had a watch. They ate what they wanted, without considering mealtimes. Mostly they ate brown bread baked by Cordelia, tomatoes, cheese, and apples. Sometimes Harrison made a frittata from eggs and potatoes; on several occasions they broiled freshly caught mackerel with lemon and butter. At sunset they did their yoga stretches. Instead of meditating, she stared at Harrison, trying to breathe, trying to imprint his face somewhere in her brain.

In the evening they sat by the fire reading their books, until she would fling hers down and he would open his arms and she would sit on his lap and listen to stories about Africa. Sometimes it was as if someone had died and his death had brought great peace. She'd take aimless, endless walks along the shore and stare moodily across the waves, wishing she might come upon Harrison's body and finally be able to mourn his loss properly. She imagined building a great funeral pyre and watching the smoke blow across the bog.

One morning during their second week she woke up sick, dizzy with fever. She did the grocery shopping anyway, but on the way home her perspective narrowed until she felt she was in a dark tunnel. When her vision failed completely, she fell off the heavy, tired bicycle. Her last thought was for the eggs that were balanced on top of the rest of their supplies.

She woke up in bed, a fire in the fireplace. Her throat burned, and her body ached. She was alone. She thought perhaps she was dying and now Harrison would feel terrible for not loving her. She cried at the tragedy of her short life. It was unfair that no one would ever know what a fine actress she was and how nice she would have been to her children.

She fell asleep and dreamed her mother was stroking her forehead and telling her how sorry she was. She awoke again, and there were stars in the blue-black sky. The swans were entwined, their beaks resting on each other's backsides. She wept at the idea of a world so cruel that it was easier for birds to find true love than humans. Harrison was asleep in the chair by the fire, a book fallen at his feet. The sound of her crying woke him up. He stood over her, and Cordelia saw that his eyes were full of tears. She played the dying Melanie from *Gone With the Wind*.

"Don't cry," she croaked. "It doesn't matter anymore."

Harrison sat down on the side of the bed, his shoulders shaking.

"I'm the one who's sick," she whined. "Come to bed and tell me a story."

Her fever broke in the middle of the night. The sheets and mattress were soaked with her sweat. Harrison's arms trembled as he pulled her nightgown off and gathered her into his arms. His naked body felt as cool as snow. She believed that nothing would ever hurt again.

"I love you, Harrison," she whispered into the quiet. "I can't help it; and I think you love me too."

"Flower gatherer," he whispered into her hair. "My brave love who smells of roses."

She was very weak. Too weak to hold up her head. "Love me, Harrison," she murmured into his neck. "Make love to me."

He held her like a piece of crystal, delicate and incredibly fine.

"Love me," she whispered. "I want to feel you."

Pushing off the covers, he loomed above her, kissing her from her forehead to the tips of her toes, returning to lick and suck her breasts until he buried his head between her thighs, and she felt herself letting go, falling backward until the expectation of some sort of landing, the inevitable pain, brought her back and she tried to push him away, but Harrison would not obey her feeble attempts. Turning her over, he mounted her from behind and, holding her hands down, rode her until, arching her back, she saw through the window the coming of dawn and the two birds, throats exposed, mirroring their movements, and at that moment she stopped questioning his motives and surrendered completely, and it no longer mattered if love was possible at all.

That was then and this is now, Cordelia thought, setting her jaw more firmly against the cold wind. *We have both changed. I am on my way to Macy's to discover my cheekbones.*

"There's really nothing to work out, Harrison. What do you want from me?"

"I don't know."

"Well, figure it out!" He stopped at the tone she used, then he shook his head and turned in the opposite direction, heading east fast. His posture was more stooped, the hunch of his shoulders more pronounced. For a moment she almost ran after him to tell him that it didn't matter what he wanted, she would accept anything. She wanted to ask him if he remembered their swans. But the impulse passed. It was time, she thought, to stop running after someone who never looked back.

CHAPTER

11

MACY'S WAS A ZOO. WOMEN IN WHITE DRESSES, WITH PRINcess Di haircuts, patrolled the aisles, spraying innocent customers with the latest designer fragrance. The makeup counters were mobbed, but Cordelia spotted her friend Melinda, dressed as a southern belle, by the Estée Lauder counter.

"Hey, Cordelia," she said, smiling and taking off a large straw hat. "You gonna finally let me do your face?"

Cordelia sat on a stool, surrounded by Japanese businessmen, who snapped away on Nikons while Melinda applied various lotions from an assortment of unmarked jars.

"Any auditions coming up?" Melinda asked, dusting her cheekbones with iridescent powder.

"Yes. Tomorrow, in fact."

"What's it for? Career gal? Young mommy?"

"Young mommy who jogs and eats yogurt."

"Ooh, Delia! That's perfect for you! You're so healthy!"

Melinda was someone Cordelia's mother would probably refer to as a "dim bulb." She was very pretty and had been Miss Akron, Ohio, during her freshman year in college. She wasn't a very good actress, but she had a large heart.

"Take a look, honey."

Melinda held up a mirror, and Cordelia gasped. The businessmen looked ready to pounce. Her cheekbones were razor edged and slashed with scarlet. Her eyes were painted to the brows with violet and pink shadow, and her lips were bright fuchsia.

"Thanks, Melinda," she said. "It looks great."

She crossed Herald Square, dodging bicycle messengers who appeared from nowhere, leaping off their machines to suggest sex. On the subway she was accosted by two men and by a child who seemed no older than ten. She slapped his hand, and he stuck out his tongue.

She attended the audition in her normal daytime makeup. It lasted for a little more than nine minutes. Her line was simple enough: "Oh! Thanks, honey!" The intrepid young-mommy jogger has just run five miles, and she's all wet and tired, when daddy and adorable child arrive with mommy's yogurt. It was filmed on a high school track in Brooklyn. The kids stood outside camera range, saying encouraging things like: "Boy, mama, you sure is ugly!" Cordelia's competition consisted of two women whom she recognized from national television spots.

After she said, "Oh! Thanks, honey!" twelve times, she was photographed, introduced to the client, and thanked. She was back on the street by lunchtime, feeling that her chances of getting the commercial were almost nonexistent.

There was a message from Philip on her machine.

"It's Phil. I've got a winterized place on Montauk. I'd like to take you there and continue to explore your inner resources—or just fuck you stupid. Call me at the office." She ate yogurt for dinner, trying to cast a spell on fate. Then she finished a jar of extra-chunky peanut butter and a bunch of celery. She stood in front of the mirror and tried to look perky. but she appeared seasick. Her mother was right. Acting was the career choice of insecure parasites. It would be a noble gesture to give up the profession before her mother's operation. Instead she called her father. The phone was answered by his "mate," Sunflower. Cordelia barely resisted hanging up.

"Hello?" Sunflower answered in her breathy Malibu whisper.

"Hey, Sunflower. Is my dad there?"

"Cory?"

"Yes. Cordelia."

"How are you, sweetie?"

"Fine."

"No, I mean really. How are you? Are you eating?"

"I'm fine. I had an important audition today. Is my father there?"

"An audition! You'll get it. Your chart was really goal-oriented today."

"You did my chart?"

"Not the whole thing. I do it for your daddy, honey. He asks every day, 'What's it going to be like for my girls?' Except the day that Cindy was murdered. I couldn't find anything, and there was this terrible storm brewing off the coast. All day I could feel that something was wrong with the planets, that something incredibly terrible was going to happen and I was powerless. Oh, God, Cordelia—"

"Sunflower! Is my father there? Please put him on the phone."

Cordelia was stunned at the idea that her father asked his lover to examine the positions of his daughters' stars instead of picking up the phone to call them.

"He's taking Turkish lessons, honey. You want him to call you later?"

"No." She refused to ask why. "Just tell him I called."

"Sure. Can I say you love him or anything?" The woman was hopeless.

"Fine. Yeah. Tell him anything you want."

Cordelia was, of course, named for Lear's faithful daughter. Her father's departure from his marriage coincided with the time she needed him most and, being the youngest, was still completely entranced by everything he said or did. She was in second grade, and suddenly she couldn't read or write. The teacher told their mother she stopped being a good sport and wouldn't share her things. She wet her bed and was sent to the principal for biting a classmate. She wouldn't let her mother tell her anything about how Daddy would call every night and how she was going to get to fly to California. She hated them both, and she thought that if she prayed hard enough, God would give her back her daddy. She kicked her mother in the shins, had a temper tantrum in the A & P, and finally tried to set fire to her teddy bear in the hopes that the sacrifice of her own child would bring back her parent. She was sent to a child psychiatrist, who was impressed by her ability to mimic movie stars, her intelligence, and her despair about the future.

"Your daughter's a fighter," he told her mother, "but she feels things too much."

When her mother entered the worst stage of the depression she experienced after her husband's desertion, Cordelia was convinced their mother was going to die, the family would be destroyed and the children split up and sent to live in foster homes. Her Catholic grandmother had once explained to her the meaning of martyr-dom. "A martyr," her grandmother had whispered while they stood in front of a nearly life-size painting of Saint Sebastian with blood pouring from the arrow wounds of his body, "is someone who dies in a state of grace rather than betray his faith. A martyr has the divine privilege of sacrificing his life for a principle."

Cordelia decided to sleep in the yard until her father came back. On her second night of sneaking outside, she was caught by Cynthia.

"Where are you going?" Cynthia asked, her face heavy and soft with sleep.

"I'm sleeping outside," Cordelia answered, clutching her stuffed rabbit. "I'm a martyr."

They made cinnamon toast, and Cordelia explained about her fear that their mother would die and they would be put into foster homes. Cynthia pulled her onto her lap and, stroking her back, said:

"I'd never let anyone separate us, stupid. We're sisters. Mom's not even sick. She's just tired. Martyrs are dumb."

Her sister had lied, Cordelia thought. She didn't have any power to stop terrible things from happening, and her death on the streets was as hopeless as Saint Sebastian's passive bleeding.

Philip picked her up in an emerald-green 1965 Porsche with leather seats and a rosewood instrument panel. They listened to

Mozart on the CD player, driving fast on the Long Island Expressway. She fell asleep and dreamed she was a child riding in the back seat of her parents' old Volvo, returning from the World's Fair in Flushing, Queens. She was squished warmly between her two sisters, lulled by the rhythm of her parents' talking in the front seat. When the car stopped, she woke up suddenly and saw they were halted at a red light on a country road. She rolled down the window and sniffed the soft salty air.

"Bad dream?" Philip touched her knee softly.

"No."

"We're almost there," he said. "The housekeeper should have left some dinner for us."

Montauk was cold. The sound of the waves crashing against the shore was soothing. Her mother had asked her not to come to the hospital. Philip had promised to hire a private plane to fly her home if necessary.

They turned into an unmarked driveway flanked by stone phoenixes. The paved road through the woods was nearly a mile long. In a grove of trees, she saw a converted barn with a peaked roof and many skylights. The dining room table was set with a roast chicken, French bread, a plate of cheese, and an open bottle of red wine. The crystal and the linen were very fine. Fires burned in the fireplaces. The furniture was chrome and leather and glass, as in his office. Philip touched a switch, and an unseen stereo system played Keith Jarrett.

"Have some chicken." Philip handed her a drumstick and went into the study to use the phone while Cordelia explored, opening doors until she discovered a room under the stairs converted into a closet and filled with women's clothing. As she quickly closed the door she felt Philip's arms around her.

"My ex-wife and I share this place," he said, nuzzling her neck. "She has a lot of clothes."

The only source of light in the room came from the fire. It cast long shadows sculpting the lines of Philip's face into a finer mask than the original. He lay with his head in Cordelia's lap. Both of them were silent. He stared up at her while she gently stroked his temples and stared into the flames. She was imagining a clearing

93

in another continent where wild animals circled a ring of light. A tall man, naked to the waist, arranged their bed, a nest of grass covered with a blanket.

"Jesus," Philip groaned. "You are so fucking beautiful, Cordelia."

With a slight start she looked down and saw that Philip's eyes were soft, the lids heavy. He pulled her down hard to meet his lips. His hands were strong on her neck. Her hair fell down around them like a shining scarf. She shut her eyes and thought: *It's easy to forget who it is you love.* He continued kissing her, pulling her down on top of him, turning her over on the floor so he could caress her breasts. He removed her shirt and jeans, put his fingers inside her while he remained clothed and would not allow her to touch him. Each time she struggled to sit up he pushed her back, hard. She began to gasp, to arch up to meet his fingers. He kept one hand inside her, bringing a breast to his mouth to suck and bite. He took a pillow and, raising her up, shoved it beneath her hips so she was spread open, offered to him. Each time she was about to come he slowed down to leave her hanging, removing his tongue or his fingers, whispering in her ear that she was going to beg for him and he was going to hurt her. When she tried to reach for him again he slapped her hard enough to knock her sideways, and then, quickly removing his own clothes, he took her. Plunging down hard, pinning her shoulders to the floor, he could see her heart knocking against her ribs while she writhed beneath him.

"Why is your heart beating like that?" he asked her. "What are you afraid of?"

When she moved too much he put his hands around her throat with enough pressure to keep her immobile. At one point she struggled and he pressed down so hard she gasped.

"Don't move," he whispered. "Don't move and it won't hurt so much."

She became perfectly still, and he was excited by this impenetrable calm and beat down into her so hard he was barely conscious of her breathing. Her tears did not affect him. With his hands pulling her hair, she felt his teeth sink deeply into the side of her neck, and the pain seemed to merge into all of it. The silence in the room was terrible. She bit her lip and closed her eyes, and he said in a soft voice: "This is how I want you. honey. This is how I always want you."

After he rolled off her, she lay curled on the rug, her knees drawn into her chest, her nails digging into her palms. She thought about Ireland, how they all had so many plans. How ignorant they had been. She was barely aware of him picking her up and carrying her into the bedroom. Lying in his arms, she slept as if drugged. Just before morning she dreamed she was driving, but she was a very little girl and did not know how to control the car. She was running over people who stood on the sidewalk. She did not know how to stop.

CHAPTER

12

THE FOLLOWING EVENING SHE SPOKE TO HER MOTHER, WHO sounded weak but was able to joke. "The way I see it," she said, "I lost five pounds of fat without a diet."

After she hung up the phone Cordelia burst into tears.

Philip had brought her breakfast in bed late that morning. Her body was bruised and stiff, and her bad dreams had tired her out. There were teeth and hand marks around her throat. The tray was silver, covered by a lace cloth. A deep dish of strawberries was next to a bowl of crème fraîche and a small pot of coffee with a side pitcher of hot milk. There was cinnamon toast and a small crystal vase containing a single white rose. Around the base of the vase snaked a single strand of pearls. She held them up to the light and saw that they were genuine and perfect. The necklace rested on her collarbone, looking strangely out of place on her naked body, while she stood in the bathroom counting the marks he had made. His fingers had left their prints inside her arms and along her spine. It was difficult to breathe. She sat down on the lowered toilet seat and put her head between her knees. She said a brief prayer for her mother. The medicine cabinet contained Valium. She took a pill and swallowed it, the pearls catching the light with the movement of her throat. When he had put down the tray, he kissed her and she flinched. He had seemed not to notice. She thought it would be better not to thank him for the pearls. She put the necklace in her cosmetic bag.

In the afternoon they drove to the beach. Cordelia wanted to swim. Philip didn't argue with her, despite its being late winter. He went back to the car to fetch a blanket and then stood at the edge of the breaking tide, waiting for her. The water was cold enough to numb her body instantly. She caught her breath and swam out, long powerful strokes, away from the shore. The salt water carried her, and she felt a surge of energy in her legs and arms. She thought she could hear her sister calling to her. She wondered if she had become a mermaid. She dove into a wave and opened her eyes, but it was as black as night and as cold as snow. He wrapped her up like a baby and put her down in the weak winter sun while he took a walk. His silent understanding and respect for her feelings astonished her. She sat and cried, her entire body tingling with the shock of her swim, while Philip threw pebbles into the surf.

"Feel better?" He was standing above her, looking down, holding her clothes. She nodded.

"You looked like something from a Florentine painting," he said. "Venus on the half shell, the fisherman's wet dream, the answer to mortal man's prayers."

"Hardly," she replied, pulling on her jeans and a sweater.

"That's what I think," he said, lifting her to her feet.

"What?"

"That you're the answer to my prayers, if I said them, if I knew what to ask for." He pushed the salty hair out of her eyes. "A key to redemption . . . Beauty at the beginning of the world . . ."

"God doesn't want someone who wishes him great harm in his kingdom," she said slowly. "Besides, I'm just a would-be actress having a minor nervous breakdown who likes swimming in cold water."

Laughing slightly, she turned toward the car.

Philip caught her arm. "Cordelia, the most important thing is that you're mine, right?"

"No," she answered, avoiding his stare. "I'm not anything. I'm a vampire. I have no reflection. I don't exist for anyone, so I can't be yours.

Philip held both her wrists in one hand and pulled up her sweater to touch her breasts. "But if you did, you would be, right?" He bent his head down and gently kissed each breast.

Far down the beach, a dog leapt to catch a stick. She stood caught in Philip's grip, and yet she felt that of the two of them, he was the weaker. She laughed and kissed his scalp.

"Yes, m'lord. If I were alive, you might own me. Perhaps I might love you."

Philip didn't smile. He let go of her wrists and put his hand gently against her cheek.

"You are alive, darling. Sometime soon you're going to have to accept the fact that you lived and she died."

"Why? Maybe she just went somewhere else. Maybe she'll come back, and we'll all have given up too soon. Maybe it's some sort of test of our faith." Her voice rose. "Maybe it's just some sort of horrible joke!"

"She's never coming back, Delia."

"Maybe . . ."

When they returned to the house, Cordelia took a shower while Philip made phone calls. He argued with the overseas operator about his connection to Geneva. Then she could hear him shouting at someone in Switzerland.

"I'm telling you, Carl, I'm gonna have that cocksucker's legs broken!"

When he slammed down the phone she called her mother. He stood in the doorway holding a bottle of Chivas, watching her make the bed.

"You don't have to do that. The maid will come."

"I wanted to. Sometimes I like to clean."

"How's your mother?"

"They cut off all of her breast. She told me a joke about losing weight."

"Come here, honey." Philip sat down on a chair and held out his arms. She sat in his lap, sighing with relief at the feeling of his arms encircling her. He smelled of Scotch and lavender soap. He gently stroked her back. Before her father went away, he used to hold her like that.

"What's that outfit you just auditioned for?"

"Yogo-Lite."

"They're owned by Fine Foods, right?"

"I think so."

"Go pick out a movie for us to watch. Nothing foreign. I'm going to make a couple more calls."

Philip knew a lot of very important people in advertising and show business, and he'd offered to call them for Cordelia. Her father's failure had taught her that ego was not a useful trait for an actor. How good you were had nothing to do with getting work. Her father had always insisted that talent alone opened doors, and now he owned a franchised employment agency. Cordelia was determined to succeed where he failed, and she already knew that ninety percent of getting a part was the right connections. Even if her father never loved her he would be forced to recognize her success when she appeared on the David Letterman show, telling David her personal philosophy, and on Johnny Carson, modestly explaining why she was such a hot property.

She fell asleep in front of the fire, and when she woke up he was carrying her to bed.

"Make love to me," she whispered into his neck.

He put her down on the bed, and then, taking off his belt, he bound her wrists together and then to the brass headboard. Her arms were stretched tightly above her head. He slowly undressed her and then covered her eyes with his shirt, her mouth with a scarf. She felt her heart beating so hard she could barely breathe. He tied each ankle with a cord and then to the brass baseboard, so that she was spreadeagled, completely open. She felt something inserted into her, something cold and hard.

The silence in the room was broken only by Philip's muttering. "Whore! You deserve to be frightened." He touched her until she was screaming, the fabric in her mouth making it difficult to swallow. He moved the thing in and out until she was begging for him, but it went on too long. Whenever she felt herself let go he would slow down and then, after a minute, begin again, until finally she was just crying, screaming for him to stop hurting her, to take off the blindfold, to stop. When he entered her she was almost unconscious. He removed the scarf and kissed her, but he left the blindfold on. Her hands were numb, and the muscles of her legs ached. It seemed to take a very long time. Afterward he untied her wrists, massaging them gently until the blood returned. She had grown used to the dark, so it was a shock to see that they were in the bedroom still. He kissed her very tenderly, rubbing her ankles where the rope had cut into her skin. He tucked her into bed and then went into the living room. She could hear music, a Brahms lullaby, and the sound of bottles.

On the drive back to Manhattan late Sunday afternoon, she stared out the window and tried to think about something other than the feeling she had in her chest. "I.N.R.I.," her sister had said in response to Cordelia's question as to why those letters appeared on their grandmother's crucifix. "I.N.R.I. means Iron Nails Ran In." Cordelia could not stop thinking about that phrase. She could not stop seeing Jesus with his punctured hands and feet, but then the features melted and became feminine and familiar.

Philip drove with one hand on her thigh, looking at her as often as possible.

At breakfast he had started: "About last night . . ."

"I don't want to talk about it," she had said sharply. "It didn't happen."

He had sighed and returned to the *Times* crossword puzzle. She could see that he was relieved and that she had passed another test.

Her answering service called to tell her she was expected on the set of the Yogo-Lite commercial Tuesday morning. It was difficult to believe anyone would pay her to sell something to the American public. She wandered into the bathroom and gave the mirror several of her most dazzling smiles. She held up a bottle of ammonia, gracefully, the fingers curved and relaxed and not hiding the label, as she'd been taught in her commercial class.

"You want to know what really makes me happy?" she asked, showing all her teeth. "Knowing my family has had their cup of ammonia this morning!" She shook down her hair and growled. The effect was not overwhelming. She put a cork in her mouth and practiced rounding all her vowels. She had gotten her first real job, and she didn't have anyone to tell.

She wanted to call her mom, but since the shooting would delay her trip home, she decided it would not be tactful. And Amelia was always awful about any success she had. Despite her child, her house, and her husband, Amelia acted as if there were some sort of conspiracy that kept her from the joy of being a rarely employed actress. When Cordelia had been cast in the horror movie, Amelia suggested that the director had made a mistake.

Cordelia started to dial the first three digits of Cynthia's number, but then she stopped, her fingers frozen, her entire body shaking. It was hard to remember the lack of something you had once taken for granted. It had been months since she'd made that mistake, run home with her throat full of news to tell her sister— a wonderful audition, the chance to play a major role in an off-Broadway show. When the computer told her the phone had been disconnected, she had screamed obscenities at that mechanical voice.

A week after the funeral, she had been packing up boxes in Cynthia's apartment with Cynthia's boyfriend, Robert. It was another ordeal their mother could not face. The operation was performed largely in silence, until one of them sat down with something significant and began to wail. The other one would simply stop and wait for the crisis to pass. The doorbell had rung. When Cordelia answered, there was a friendly-looking couple standing on the steps, holding a bottle of wine.

"Hello," the man said. "We brought some wine."

Cordelia took the bottle and smiled. She didn't know what the couple wanted. She thought they might be from some sort of cult.

Then the woman spoke. "Are we too early?" she asked. "Cindy told us to come around seven."

Cordelia had been folding one of her sister's shirts. She had to resist throwing it over her head and running away. By then Robert had joined her, and he was opening and closing his mouth like a guppy.

"Hey, Bobby," the man said. "Where's our girl?"

Cordelia couldn't understand how these people had failed to read about the murder in the paper. There had been extensive coverage. They looked rather tan; perhaps they had been away on vacation.

"My sister is dead," she said flatly, willing these people to understand. "She was stabbed, murdered by a mugger." For a moment there was an absolute silence, the calm, restful period that comes before terrible news is received. Cordelia felt herself fall into that peaceful gap and tried to remain there.

The woman swayed, her hand holding her belly; she clutched at her companion. "Oh my God!" she shrieked, holding her hands out toward Cordelia. "She was going to deliver our baby!"

Cordelia stepped closer to Robert. She was tired of this scene. She did not want to be touched by this stranger. The woman was not visibly pregnant, and anyway, what did it matter? She would find another midwife. The man seemed to understand.

"We loved her very much," he said quietly, his eyes filling with tears. "I can't imagine what your family must feel." He turned to Robert. "We'll go now."

The two men embraced, while Cordelia avoided catching the eye of the weeping woman. They all shook hands in a strangely formal manner, and then the couple limped off to hail a cab.

Cordelia realized as she was walking back into the apartment that she was still holding the bottle of wine. Robert looked at the label. "Good wine," he said. Suddenly they both began to giggle. Robert got a corkscrew and opened the bottle.

"Did you see their faces?" Cordelia gasped, rolling on the bed. "I wonder if they went to Burger King."

"Probably not." Robert chuckled. "He's the food critic for *Details*."

"We didn't handle it well. Cynthia would have given on-the-spot grief counseling."

"God, Cordelia, your sister loved a tragedy. She knew exactly what to say to people, how to defuse psychos and calm down angry mobs. Each time we planned a romantic dinner à deux, we seemed to end up in a situation where she was talking to a sniper through a megaphone."

"Umm. I remember that crack addict who held the people hostage in Mamma Leone's—"

"Twenty day trippers from Paramus, Delia! A matinee crowd who kept asking the poor bugger for more mozzarella. Nobody listened to his demands."

"What did Cindy do?"

"Well, he had a crush on her from the clinic. He asked to see either her or Cher, and Cher wasn't into it. So Cindy came and stood outside and talked to him."

"What did she say?"

"She agreed to marry him. And to have his baby. I'm not sure of the order. We had a table at Le Bernardin, and she's getting engaged to a serial killer!"

"I hate her for this, Robert." Cordelia put down her glass and looked around the nearly empty room. Her sister's life seemed very meager. She had lived surrounded by more friends than objects.

"She didn't want to leave us, Cordelia. She didn't want to die."

"So why didn't she have any money? Or why didn't she run away?" Cordelia tried to continue packing, but her hands were shaking too hard. "Did she think she was some kind of angel that didn't bleed?"

Robert put his hands on her shoulders and turned her around to face him. "Sweetheart," he said, pulling her into his arms. "your sister loved you very much. She thought you were a wonderful actress. And a good person."

"I can't remember the last thing I said to her," Cordelia sobbed. "All I want to do is remember what it was!"

When she'd finished reading the theater section of the Sunday paper, Cordelia decided she'd call her father and tell him the news about the commercial. It was about two in California, so she thought he'd probably be home.

"Hello?"

"Dad?"

"Amelia?"

"No. It's me. Cordelia."

"Hey! Hi, sweetheart. Sunflower told me you called. I tried calling back, but there was no answer. Everything okay?" It was a stupid thing to say to a person with an answering machine.

"I got a commercial."

"What, honey?"

"A commercial. A real one—it's national."

"You're an extra?"

"No. I'm a young mommy. It's that Yogo-Lite campaign. I jog and then I eat yogurt."

"Never seen it."

"You must have, Daddy. It's on all the time. They have this voice-over, the guy who does the Heartland wheat bread ads—he always sounds like he's about to start crying over bran."

"No, but that's terrific. Aren't you a little young to be playing a mommy? Well, maybe not. I keep forgetting how old I am." The self-pity in his voice was obvious.

"Aren't you happy for me?"

"Sure. I just hoped you'd focus on the theater a little more. You should be doing *The Seagull* or something. Anyway, it's a scummy industry. How's your mother?"

She felt as if there were something dry stuck in her throat. She tried to swallow, but her neck muscles wouldn't relax. Her father knew nothing about the operation, she realized.

"She just had a mastectomy."

There was a sharp intake of breath, a gulp, and then Cordelia heard the thick sound of tears in his voice.

"When?"

"Saturday."

"What hospital is she in?

"Jersey General."

"I'll call you back, Delia. I gotta talk to her. Are you and Amy all right?"

She considered telling him the truth; telling him that since the murder she was terrified of living and eager to die. She might describe her weekend with Philip. Explain how easily she had discovered someone like that. He would not stay on the phone long enough to listen. In the background she could hear Sunflower singing an old Joni Mitchell song in a slightly flat soprano.

As Cordelia replaced the receiver, she heard a clicking noise that indicated an incoming call. It was Maxine.

"Cordelia?" Maxine's voice was barely a whisper.

"Max?"

"Yeah."

"What's the matter?"

"Can I come over?"

"Sure."

"No men!"

"I'm alone. What's wrong?"

"Everything. I'll be there in half hour."

Maxine arrived with a Food Emporium bag containing a six-pack of Diet Coke, rice crackers, a pint of Tofutti, and a jar of supercrunchy peanut butter, which Cordelia kept closing but Maxine refused to yield.

"Take your bony mitts off my peanut butter," she growled. "Why didn't you call me?"

"I went to Montauk."

"Montauk?" Maxine crossed her eyes. "Why would anyone go to Montauk in the middle of the fucking dead winter?"

"It was nice. I went swimming."

"In February? What was nice, exactly? Did you go with that South African giant? Tell me you didn't go swimming!"

"I went swimming. In the ocean. I didn't go with Harrison."

"Don't tell me you went alone! Were you spiritual? I could have come! We could have fasted. I've gained six pounds in three days!" Maxine's hands went toward the peanut butter, but Cordelia snatched the jar away.

"So stop this! My mother had her operation."

"Is she okay?"

"Yeah . . . I don't know. She isn't dead. Her breast is gone. I'll see her on Wednesday."

"So what's with Montauk?"

"I just went there. With that man . . ."

"What man, you stupid slut?"

"The squash man. The rich one that ripped my dress off."

"The creep? He tore up your Calvin Klein sheets."

"It's a beautiful house, Max. A reconverted barn in the woods. He was very nice to me."

" 'Nice' again. You describe swimming in arctic ice water as nice. What's with this 'nice' shit? I bet that's what Sylvia Plath told everyone before she stuck her head in the oven. She probably kept telling her best friend how nice her husband was. So what's with this compulsive fabric-ripper?"

"He gave me a string of real pearls."

"You're kidding."

"Nope." Cordelia went into the bedroom and returned holding the necklace. It glowed in the palm of her hand as if it somehow contained life.

"Holy shit," Maxine said, holding the pearls up to the light. "These are very expensive baubles. My uncle Seymour is an appraiser. He taught me how to judge these things." Maxine put the pearls in Cordelia's lap. "So what does he expect from you?"

"He's sort of weird." Cordelia had opened the peanut butter and put her finger into it. Now she stared at her coated finger as if it were all a mistake.

"Define weird."

"Umm . . . he hits me. I mean, it's part of our fucking, but it's kind of . . . weird. Very erotic. He's strong." Cordelia stared at her bare toes and Maxine's red boots. She had great taste in shoes. "Hot boots."

"Cordelia . . ." Maxine had put down the carton of Tofutti. Her face was very pale. "He hits you?"

"Not all the time. I mean, it's very spontaneous. And he's affectionate. Especially afterward."

"Afterward?"

"After he hits me."

Maxine was shaking her head slowly. She leaned forward and grasped Cordelia's wrist. There were several bruises on her inner arm.

"Oh, Christ," she murmured. "He's hurting you. Why are you doing this? Can't you forgive yourself? Can't you forgive her?"

"He's very good to me, Maxine."

"Cordelia! You need therapy. Doesn't your mother care if you go on being this traumatized waif? Hasn't she asked you any questions?"

"About what?"

"How you feel."

"She's busy. She's a doctor. And she's got cancer."

"Before she got cancer. Months ago, when you were in so much trouble."

"My mother doesn't notice things like that, Max. Hey, I got a commercial!"

Maxine's Diet Coke went up her nose. "You got a commercial?"

"Yeah. One of the Yogo-Lite spots. I'm a young mommy jogger. Philip knew the president of the company or something."

"So if he gets you a movie can he break a few bones?"

"Maxine . . ."

"Don't try to wheedle me out of this, Delia! I'm very worried about you. You're like a bimbo lost sheep these days. Your judgment stinks. I wish I could lock you up in a tower with a drawbridge until you get your mind back."

"Spinning straw into gold?"

"Fuck it. Who am I to talk? I think food loves me. My parents think I have a ying-yang imbalance. I can't believe you got a national spot! I'm really proud of you."

"What happened this weekend? Why are you eating like this?"

"I don't know. I had a canceled Saturday-night date, and I stayed home making s'mores, those gross graham cracker things, over the electric burner. The whole place stinks of burnt marshmallows. I'm sick of going to O.A. Those people are all so weird . . . and fat. Or fat people waiting to happen. It's boring. When's the shoot?"

"Tomorrow. I have to be on the set at seven."

"Shit. I'd better go home and let you sleep. Elevate your feet and put cucumber slices on your eyes. Try to sleep without a pillow so you don't wrinkle your face."

"I called my father."

"And?"

"He said he wished I were doing Chekhov."

"He's a jealous son of a bitch! He's got a stinking chain of employment agencies and a moronic girlfriend."

"I dropped the news about Mom on him."

"Good. He deserves to feel rotten sitting out there in la-la land with that air-bubble starfish, sending out bimbos to screw up someone's Xerox machine! Why doesn't he pay attention to his daughters? You really need therapy, Delia. Is he coming to see her?"

"No. I thought my audition was terrible."

"You always think that, and you get hired. I think I'm perfect, and I get nothing."

"Max, why are you eating like this?"

"It's just depressing being an actress, fat, and single all at the same time in New York. If I was in Reading, Pennsylvania, right now, I'd probably be thin. Or I'd be married to a steamfitter who didn't care, and we'd go to K mart on Sundays and buy stuff for the mobile home. I could cook with Crisco! Ben & Jerry and Sara Lee help me forget."

"Go back on your diet."

"Yeah. Now put on your answering machine, drink some hot milk and honey, give yourself an orgasm, and go to sleep." Maxine hugged Cordelia, picked up her jar of peanut butter, and left.

CHAPTER

13

"READY ON THE SET! READY, CORDELIA?" THE DIRECTOR WAS wearing pink corduroy overalls, which caused him to resemble a large, demanding toddler.

"Yes."

"Okay. Roll 'em." The gaffer snapped the block, and Cordelia gazed adoringly up at her handsome husband and down at her cute son. Her cute son chose that moment to roll his eyes back in his head far enough for her to see nothing but the whites. She said her line with the intensity of a person attempting to avoid a fit of hysterical giggling. This was the fifth take, and she had heard a shoot was considered bad if there were more than three takes.

She was surprised by the calm, relaxed attitude of the crew. The director seemed strangely protective of her feelings.

"Cut and print! Well done, Cordelia."

As she was leaving the studio, an extremely well dressed man in his early forties moved quickly forward to open the door.

"Ms. Cavanagh?" He extended a perfectly manicured hand.

"Yes?"

"I'm the president of Greene Industries. George Franz."

Cordelia shook his hand. "Very nice to meet you, Mr. Franz."

"You did a good job today. We're extremely pleased."

"Thank you."

"I hope it was a pleasant experience."

"Oh, yes. I was really grateful that everyone was so kind. This is my first commercial."

"It won't be your last. My best to Phil." The last was thrown over his shoulder as he walked toward the director.

The studio was in Secaucus, New Jersey, and provided a van to bring her back to Manhattan. Gulls circled over the garbage scows that were burning along the sides of the turnpike. The sky was low and close; steely gray. Greene Industries owned Fine Foods, which owned Yogo-Lite. It was strange that the president of a major corporation would visit the set of a commercial to meet an unknown actress with one line. She wondered how Philip really made his money. Would her performance have been acceptable without the connection? Her father's voice in her head described the basic truths of the world: "Talent is meaningless. Nepotism is all-powerful. Contemporary theater is shit."

Philip had a squash court booked for six. When she looked up from the script she was reading, he was leaning on the desk.

"How'd it go, kid?"

"Great. Mr. Franz must owe you a big favor," she replied in a teasing tone. "I was treated like visiting royalty."

Philip frowned. "You complaining?"

"Of course not. They were very kind to me."

"So shut up. And get me a towel."

Philip was competing in the final round of the Chivas Tournament, one of the most important amateur squash events held in New York. His opponent was ranked beneath him, and Philip was expected to beat him easily, winning the trophy for his division. During the third game there was a radical change in his opponent's strategy. Instead of using agility and skill, he used his age to tire and outrun his older challenger. He returned Philip's shots with all the strength and endurance of a twenty-two-year-old man. He dominated the best position on the court, sending Philip from corner to corner until his aim became sloppy and the match was lost.

She heard the sound of a racket being smashed against the wall, and then the door opened and the two men left the court. Philip was holding his broken racket. He was panting and very red.

"I'll appeal this to the Squash Association!" he hissed at his embarrassed opponent. "You called bullshit lets! I'll have you thrown out of this fucking club!" He walked up to the desk and threw down the racket.

"Get rid of this fucking piece of shit," he roared at her. "Be at the elevators in five minutes!" It was almost time for her to leave anyway. The next shift was covered by a quiet guy named Tod, who was studying cello at Juilliard.

"You shouldn't go out with that thug, Delia," Tod drawled in his southern accent. "He's supposed to be in the Mafia."

"Syrianos is a Greek name."

"The new Mafia is filled with Greeks. How do you think they got all the diners in New York? Anyway, he hates women. He thinks they should all be forced to get pregnant and stay home. He said women don't know how to reason and that all these women in business are crazy because they've waited too long to have children. I heard him in the sauna—"

"I thought I told you to be ready!" Philip muttered at her through clenched teeth. Cordelia's hands shook as she picked up her books.

"Bye, Delia," Tod said, raising an eyebrow. "Call later?"

"Bye, Tod." She was led away, feeling it was time for her punishment for a crime she didn't commit. When they reached the street she began to walk very quickly, almost running.

Philip caught up with her. "Where are you going?" He reached for her hand, but she jumped so fast he missed her.

"Home."

"We'll get a cab."

"I don't want you to come. You're too angry. I'm afraid of you."

"What did you say?" Philip was so close she could feel his breath on her neck.

Cordelia kept moving, pretending to stroll although she was close to a jog. She thought they must look slightly ridiculous, the well-dressed man following on the heels of a young woman dressed in rather scruffy workout gear, a young woman with an inexplicably frightened expression on her face. For a moment she feared a bullet in her back. The idea came from nowhere. Was it possible to stop someone and say: "Excuse me, this man is scaring me. Help!" She did not turn around. She dashed across Sixth Avenue, and when he saw he missed the light he made a gesture of dismissal and hailed a cab. She found a token in her pocket and went down into the subway.

"This train is *mmph*." The conductor repeated the same message for the seventh time. No one could understand what he was saying, but no one wanted to admit to confusion. The doors on the Broadway local had opened and shut a dozen times. People stared straight ahead or pretended to sleep. The train sputtered and sighed. A man sitting next to Cordelia began to swear and mutter under his breath.

"Shit," he said softly. "I hate this fucking train! I hate this fucking Transit Authority! I hate the fucking mayor of New York and the governor and the President and the President of Russia! I hate this fucking city, country, world, and universe! I hate the moon, the sun, and all the stars!" It was difficult to resist applauding this sentiment, but the man looked quite deranged.

By the time she got home it was after seven. A phone message from Amelia said she would see her at home the next day. There was nothing from Harrison, and she wondered for a moment if he'd finally gone off to locate his prodigal wife. She heated some frozen soup left from before Christmas, when she'd bought a few capons and made enough soup to last months. She took a bowlful to bed, with a stack of butter-drenched toasted pita. Her toes were against a heating pad, and she was surrounded by magazines and books. It was much nicer not to have a man around, acting fierce and competitive over stupid, inconsequential matters. That night she dreamed Philip was forcing her to drink from a body of water filled with strange-looking insects.

"Hi, honey!" Dr. Cavanagh was sitting and grinding coffee, a receiver glued to her left ear. She gestured to her youngest daughter to come hug her.

Cordelia held her mother gingerly, fearing contact with something that was no longer there. The two bunches of tulips bought from a Korean grocer seemed silly in the face of her mother's apparent health and the abundance of early roses that were in the garden. The only time she could remember her mother staying in bed was during the period just after their father left. None of them had been sickly children. Their mother believed you were either deathly ill or perfectly healthy. No one was put to bed with a cold or cramps.

"Doris, tell Mrs. Robinson I'll see Jason tomorrow morning. At nine. Yes. Yes, I'm coming back tomorrow. Doris! You would never dare talk to a boy doctor like that!" Dr. Cavanagh hung up the phone.

"Delia! My little star! My yogurt-guzzling Academy Award winner!"

"Who told you?"

"Daddy. You shouldn't have dropped the news on him like that. The poor dope wanted to fly here immediately to hold my hand."

"He's a fraud."

"Sometimes. But he loves you very much. He loves all of you."

"You mean both of us." She muttered this under her breath, searching for a vase for the flowers.

Her mother flinched. "We still love Cynthia."

"I'm sorry, Mom."

"Well, I know you're angry at me for having cancer."

"I am not!" She stamped her foot in a gesture worthy of a toddler.

"Of course you are. I have a degree in psychology, baby. Your father's not having a very good time—"

"I told him about the commercial, and he was mean! He started making noises about the 'legitimate theater' and how I should be doing Chekhov."

"That's because *he* should be doing Chekhov. His girlfriend's absolutely worthless. She wants him to retire so they can live on a commune dedicated to hang gliding."

"That's disgusting!" Cordelia vehemence was rather surprising.

Her mother raised an eyebrow. "Disgusting?"

"All of it. He's pretending to be someone he isn't. Like an actor. Or young. Or a father."

"You want to see the scar?"

"No!" She spoke without thinking.

A shadow crossed her mother's face, darkening her eyes and deepening the fine lines near her mouth.

"I didn't mean that, Mommy. I do want to see it."

Her mother unbuttoned her shirt. Where there had once been a perfectly shaped, pretty breast was a scar. The stitches were still visible. It was not so bad, really. More like a man's chest than anything else. Still, Cordelia began to cry, thinking about how much had been lost. Her mother said something about being an asymmetrical work of art, and the tears became giggles.

Amelia returned from the playground with a hungry Tom. The minute her nephew saw Cordelia, he ran up to her, put his hands on her knees and said: "Where's Harrison?"

"Who's Harrison?" her mother asked.

"A friend of mine who's married," Cordelia said quickly, before Amelia could open her mouth.

"His wife left him, Mom. He's incredibly handsome and charming and smart. Remember? He was Cory's boyfriend in Ireland."

"Why don't *you* go out with him," Cordelia snapped, glaring at her sister.

"Because I'm a married mother," Amelia replied, drawing herself up to look taller. "I don't have an empty life. Besides, it's you he loves."

It was still difficult to believe Amelia was Tom's mother. In her faded jeans and sweatshirt, she looked like a high school baby-sitter.

"No he doesn't. He loves his wife."

"He said he did. And he said his wife was an unfaithful b-i-t-c-h." Tom giggled. Cordelia's face felt hot.

"Amelia . . ." Dr. Cavanagh rested her hand on Cordelia's shoulder.

"I heard him say that, Grandma," Tom shouted, eager as always to defend his mother. "I heard him tell Mommy that!"

"Shut up!" Cordelia snapped.

"How dare you tell my son to shut up!"

"You meddlesome bitch!" Cordelia stalked out of the house, slamming the door and scaring the birds that were clustered around the feeder. When one of them began timidly to hop back, she stamped her foot and it flew into the branches of the maple tree, screeching at her cruelty.

"Delia." Her mother stood in the doorway, her mink coat thrown across her shoulders.

"What?"

"Come back in."

"I don't want to." Her mother sighed. Her sigh seemed to weigh a hundred pounds. "Amelia's such a bitch."

"So are you."

"Thanks a lot!"

"Amelia has too much to worry about. She misses Cindy so much, and Michael's always working, and she has to stay cheerful for Tom."

"So what? I don't have anyone to defend me. I don't have a little boy who thinks I'm wonderful. I don't have anyone to be cheerful for. I don't have anyone to take care of me."

"I think you're wonderful."

"You said I was a bitch."

"My wonderful bitch daughter."

Inside the fur, her mother's body was warm. Cordelia put her head against her left breast and wished there was a way to return to a time when they were all perfect and unscarred.

CHAPTER

14

O N FRIDAY NIGHT CORDELIA WAS IN BED WHEN HER BUZZER
sounded. She spoke into the intercom and heard a voice
say: "Open the fucking door." It was Philip. She pressed the
button to release the lock and then found herself pacing the
room, wringing her hands, wishing he were not on his way up.

"Where have you been?" It was the first thing he said to her,
unbuttoning his cashmere coat, his face flushed by the cold.
Cordelia was wearing a pair of boy's flannel pajamas bought at
the K mart near her mother's house. The pajamas were too short
and stopped above her ankles. They had a repeating pattern of
little rocket ships.

"Is that what you sleep in?" Philip gave her one of his bewil-
dered looks. "You look like Beaver Cleaver."

Cordelia began to feel better. She went and got one of Harrison's ancient sweaters, a stretched-out jersey that nearly reached
her knees. She sat down on the couch and smiled.

Philip pulled out a vial of cocaine, a gold razor blade, and a
small mirror. "Got any vino rouge, babe?"

There was a bottle of Beaujolais in the cupboard. She went
into the kitchen.

"You should make me a key, honey. I hate being locked out."

She saw herself reflected in the kitchen window, looking like a strangely mature child in funny clothes. "No," she mouthed to her reflection. "I am not giving him a key." She put the bottle of wine and a glass in front of Philip.

"Come on, Delia. I can't drink alone."

She got another glass, but she didn't want any cocaine.

"Sorry about the other day."

"What happened?"

"I lost the fucking match."

"It's just a game."

"Yeah, well, I don't lose at anything. And I don't lose to little kike bastards like that punk."

"Philip . . ."

"What? Jews are too fucking competitive. They compete over everything, including which race got the worst deal. I mean, who denies the Holocaust was a terrible shame, but do we have to spend the rest of our lives apologizing? I mean, what about the Irish? You guys had the potato famine. What about the niggers? What about the Japs? *We* put *them* in concentration camps. You like that Weinstein jerk? You wanna fuck him? Is that what it is? You want to fuck him and find out if what they say about Jews is true? He'd never marry you, sweetheart. You aren't good enough to take home to mom, but he'd probably love to get his hands on your shiksa ass. Is that what it is?"

"No."

"Here." He had snorted two lines, and she could tell from the way he was speaking that he had done more earlier. He pushed the mirror toward her.

If she didn't do the coke, he would do it all. The drug cut through her sleepiness. She felt her heart skip a beat. She took a sip of wine.

"You look sort of cute in those pj's. Sort of like a sleepy little boy."

"Do you have any kids?"

"Kids? What makes you think that?"

"Before you were divorced."

"Nah. No kids. Hey, it's a terrible thing that happened to your sister."

"Yes." Cordelia snorted the other line, drank some more wine, and leaned back. Her pulse began to beat in the area behind her eyes. She didn't want to talk about Cynthia.

Philip continued. "The case hasn't come to trial yet, right? I heard the fuck got himself the best criminal-defense lawyer in the city."

"I try not to read about it. It's useless. She's dead. It just makes me crazy. I guess we'll go to the trial, but I'm afraid." Cordelia's head felt filled with air.

"The bastard's a butcher. He butchered your sister."

"Philip . . ." Her skull felt as if it were about to explode. She held up her hand to stop him.

"I know the guys that run the jail he'll go to. I'm gonna have that prick rubbed out."

Cordelia shook her head. It was like being on some sort of crime show. Somehow her pajamas were appropriate.

"I know what it feels like. My little brother stepped on a land mine in 'Nam. Two weeks before his tour was over. Boom."

"Oh, no," Cordelia said. "I'm so sorry."

"He was twenty-one. Steven. He was sent home in pieces, in a garbage bag. My mother never got over it."

Her mind filled with the images she remembered from watching the Vietnam War on the CBS News with Walter Cronkite. It was strange, sitting at home in America, watching young men with blackened faces and frightened eyes, children really, wading through rice fields, their rifles held above their heads, dodging copter blades, crying over their dying buddies. She saw her own mother standing on the porch, her right breast missing, her daughter murdered. Families destroyed by a single act of brutality, the country permanently damaged. A generation defined by death.

Philip pulled off her sweater, unbuttoned her pajama top, and pushed her back against the cushions. "I miss my brother," he murmured, his teeth teasing her nipples while his hand moved between her legs, beneath the pajama bottoms, his fingers inside her. His other hand was across her mouth.

When she started to tell him she had no birth control, he

tightened his grip across her face and bit her nipple. He had her pinned against the couch, kneeling above her, holding her so she could not move. He pulled down his pants and entered her without waiting, while she tried to keep him from penetration and struggled to breathe. When he was deep inside her he took his hand from her mouth and kissed her; she could feel his teeth against the inside of her lips. His hands dug deeply into the flesh of her buttocks. He pulled her against him so hard she was almost upright and then plunged down so powerfully she screamed. She began to arch up to meet him thrust for thrust, the knowledge that her body was ready to produce a child part of the terror she felt. But this was preferable to the numbness, and when she came she sank her teeth into his shoulder and scraped her nails along his back until he moaned.

Afterward she lay next to him in bed, sleepless, trying to still her imagination, trying to blacken the screen on which she observed her mother down on her knees in the hospital, the lowering of her sister's coffin into the waiting grave, Harrison crying into his hands over the loss of his son. Philip slept heavily, one of his hands holding her thigh in a grip that, even in sleep, promised unyielding pressure. She wanted to call her mother, to ask her for advice, but she was too ashamed to admit to what she'd done.

That Wednesday brought false spring. The sun burned down so brightly she left her apartment without a coat, a sweater wrapped around her waist. Central Park was full of people who resembled confused moles; their pale snouts pointed toward the light. A group of businessmen had shucked their jackets, loosened their ties, and joined an impromptu baseball game. As Cordelia cut across the Sheep Meadow she heard someone shout: "Ho!" It was Harrison. His hair was cut very short, and he was wearing oddly feminine red-framed sunglasses. They looked far better on him than they should have. He was eating a bagel, clutching a Styrofoam cup in the other hand. He waved the cup beneath Cordelia's nose.

"Come and drink my coffee, little girl," he said, smiling. "Come and have your medicine!" He knew how she adored coffee.

"Hello, Harrison." Cordelia squinted up at him, wondering who had cut his hair.

"Off to work?"

"Eventually. I got a commercial. I just did a major promo for Fine Foods."

"So the new boyfriend's got decent connections, I take it?"

"What new boyfriend?"

"The dress ripper. The wealthy sleazeball you've been bestowing your priceless favors on."

"He's not a sleazeball. And yes, he has great connections."

"That's a real fucking relief, Delia. I'd hate to think you'd let your emotions dictate who you fuck."

"What's especially nice about this is that I do! And he also happens to know a lot of important people. So I don't have to continue the charity fucks!" Each of them glared at the other, and Cordelia spilled most of Harrison's coffee, since her hand was shaking. Tears filled her eyes, and she saw Harrison trying to swallow his own. They looked at each other again and drew deep breaths. He reached out to touch her cheek.

"I'm just jealous," he said quietly. "I just don't understand why we can't be together."

"Because I still love you, and it never works," she sobbed. "I don't want to."

"Cordelia, darling—" Her hand stopped him.

"This is a disgusting conversation," she said sharply. "I haven't had any breakfast, and the weather's making me crazy. How are you?"

"Good. I'm making movies."

"What do you mean?"

"Well, I'm just a gofer. That's why I'm hanging around here. They're shooting a scene at Tavern on the Green. It's Lumet's new film. Wanna meet Dustin Hoffman?"

"No," Cordelia snapped. "Movie stars are tedious." She took a swallow of his coffee to try and keep from screaming. "Well, isn't this just groovy." She saw that what she'd taken for a Walk-

120

man hanging from his belt was actually a walkie-talkie. The coffee had sugar in it, which she hated. It made her furious to think that Harrison would simply arrive in New York and immediately start infiltrating her chosen profession. It was just like Ireland, when he began to take over her friends. People liked to see him succeed. Pretty soon, she thought, he'd be spotted and pulled from the sidelines to be a movie star. He'd take Jessica Lange away from Sam Shepard, and Sam would still want her and not Cordelia.

"How'd you get the job?"

"Oh, I met some people at a restaurant. I was looking for a waiter position, and there were these movie people hanging around the bar. I mentioned to the woman in charge of production the work I'd done in London, and she called me."

"Are you sure she's hired you for your ability to fetch sandwiches?" she asked cattily. She gave him back his coffee. "I've got to go."

Dodging his outstretched hand, she blew him a hasty kiss and headed quickly across the field, walking so stiffly erect that she failed to see a fly ball, which came over the fence and nearly hit her on the head. It landed an inch in front of her foot. She attempted to throw the ball back to the pitcher, but her aim was terrible and it went wild, landing next to a bag man, who promptly put it in his pocket and took off. Harrison, glimpsed from the corner of her eye, was laughing his head off. She gave him the finger and then walked until she was out of sight, sinking down in the grass behind a large tree to sulk properly.

Harrison had once told her that he hated being perfect.

"You aren't perfect," she had snapped, enraged at his smug vanity. "You aren't even close to it!"

"Yes," he'd agreed, dumping the old grounds out of her teapot, "but people believe that I am."

"That doesn't make it a fact. People believe anything you tell them! They used to think women shouldn't work because of their periods."

"I believe that," he said, smiling at her. "I believe women's moods are dictated by the moon."

"Oh, shut up," Cordelia said wearily. "You don't even amuse me anymore." She was so tired of discussing Harrison's qualities. "Just fall in love with me!" she wanted to scream at him. "Fall in love or leave me alone!"

They had come back from their vacation in Connemara, and Dublin was dirty, damp, and depressing. Cordelia had a paper due on *Ulysses*, and she couldn't think of anything interesting to say. She didn't want to write a paper. She wanted to go home, return to America, escape from her perfect lover.

"You aren't amused because you know I'm right," Harrison said, pouring tea in her mug. The sunlight streaming into the room from behind a cloud illuminated his face with golden shadows, and she had to turn away to keep from crying. "I am whatever anyone perceives me as. I am everyone's idea of me."

"You are fucked," Cordelia screamed, putting down her mug, her rage choking her. "I want to go back to America! I want to go home to people who love me!"

"But, Delia," Harrison said quietly, "I love you. I just don't know how."

"You don't know what the word means," Cordelia said, putting on her coat. "You say things to keep people away from you. You say that to drive me away. I try to stay away, and then you come and get me."

"But you want me to do that," Harrison murmured, unbuttoning her coat, running his hands up and down the sides of her body. "You want me to come and get you."

"I want to go home," she whispered into his shoulder, all the tension leaving her body as they melted together.

"No, Delia," he whispered, pushing her down on the rug. "Don't leave me."

The breeze that blew across the park had an edge. Cordelia pulled on her sweater and stood up. Harrison had disappeared. The businessmen had gone to work. She picked up her bag and headed toward Fifth Avenue.

CHAPTER

15

"HERE'S OUR LITTLE YOGURT-EATING STAR!" DR. SCHWARTZ was stretching in the center of the reception area when Cordelia got off the elevator. He began to applaud loudly.

Philip was warming up on the glass court with the club's squash pro. As Cordelia crossed toward the desk, he winked at her and was promptly hit by the ball.

"Hey, Cory! Why aren't you getting your legs waxed or your toes polished?" Dr. Schwartz leaned across the desk to pat her cheek. His gray hair curled around his kind, strong-featured face. He was a very kind man. When he heard about her sister's murder he had given her books about coping with death. Nearly his entire family was exterminated in the Nazi death camps.

"You must go on," he had told her firmly. "It will never make any sense, the question 'Why?' will be on your lips until the day you draw your last breath, but you have an obligation to the dead to appreciate and enjoy your life. You must try and find the will to be happy!" He had discovered her sitting like a stone in the reception area, trying to do her desk duties but instead staring into space, shredding paper into little piles. He had insisted on taking her to a local coffee shop for lunch, and when she didn't eat her food he had gently asked the waitress to remove their plates and taken her hands in his own.

"I don't really know you, Cordelia," he had said, "but you try very hard to make other people happy. It's a beautiful way to live life. Was your sister like you?"

"She was better than me. Braver and smarter. She knew exactly what she wanted to do with her life."

"So"—Dr. Schwartz shrugged—"you aren't quite as sorted out. But that doesn't mean anything. You still deserve to live."

Cordelia tried to smile, but her lips kept trembling.

"I'm sorry," she had finally said. "You've missed your squash game."

"Young lady," Dr. Schwartz replied with mock severity, "you overestimate my devotion to that stupid sport."

At first she resented his advice. Her sister had behaved like some sort of Rambo–Florence Nightingale, bicycling into bad neighborhoods with her backpack full of pamphlets explaining how to protect oneself from AIDS. Cynthia dispensed condoms and loving advice to the young women in her neighborhood and taught baby care to unwed teenage mothers. She refused to recognize the danger of the new addicts, the crack users, high and violent in a state of advanced paranoia. They knew where she lived, and they knew she came from a wealthy family.

"It's important that people in the community trust me, Cordelia," she had said in response to her sister's fears about her safety. "People watch out for one another around here. They look out for their own."

No one had been looking when that man had grabbed her, raped her, and stabbed her. The murder took place in a blind alley. Not one of her neighbors rushed out of their double-locked apartments, shouting for the police or screaming for help. Her sister had died in the silence of the streets, in a city filled with people afraid that an act of bravery would only result in their own destruction. Her sister had been wrong.

Cordelia often lay awake wondering if Cynthia had known what was happening, if she was in pain or felt her life slipping away as the blood left her body. She wanted to know if anyone had put a coat under her head or held her hand or told her something kind so that she'd hold on longer. It didn't seem possible to ask the policemen who brought her to the hospital such a question. She was convinced that if she had been there, her sister would not have been able to die. She believed she would have faced that creature from the Bergman movies, the black-robed, sickle-bearing creep, and told him to fuck off and leave them alone. She would have promised Cynthia too much, held her too strongly, to allow her to escape.

Cordelia was furious at the stupidity that brought about the murder. Her sister had no right to think most people would treat her with kindness. She wished Cynthia had been a completely unaware person with no social concerns, whose only joy was found in shopping at Bloomingdale's. Anything was better than death. Anything was better than the void that swallowed the brightness, consumed life with so little effort. Sometimes she was tempted to walk into the stores where her sister had shopped and show the person behind the counter Cynthia's picture and ask, "Do you remember this woman? She was murdered. Do you miss her? Did you notice she never came back?"

Cordelia's resentment toward the living was enormous. She was constantly amazed by the mediocrity of most people, people who she believed did not deserve to live. As for her sister, she wanted to slap her face. To slap her for her blind ignorance and then to kiss her, to hold Cynthia's warm body against her own and feel the heart beating strongly. To forget the touch of those cold fingers she could scarcely bear to feel.

She could still reach forward into space and trace the strong lines of her sister's face. She knew exactly where Cynthia's shoulders would be, the curve of her waist, could feel the weight of her hair. The physical memory of her was so vivid that there were times when Cordelia, riding on the subway, would hallucinate, see her sister standing across from her, hanging on the strap, smiling. She would stop herself from saying, "Where did you go?" and wonder if that was how amputees felt about their missing parts.

One night she awoke to discover Cynthia sitting cross-legged on the end of the bed, staring at her through interlaced fingers. The moon cast sufficient light for Cordelia to ascertain that her sister's body was not covered with bleeding wounds. In fact, she was wearing one of Cordelia's sweaters. She really didn't know what to say to this apparition, so she turned on the television and the two sisters watched *Leave It to Beaver* reruns on cable. It was very cozy. Cordelia cautiously gave Cynthia part of her quilt. She couldn't look at her ghostly companion directly, but seeing her calm profile in the television's light was wonderful, and she didn't care whether they talked. At dawn Cynthia faded without a whisper. Cordelia began to whimper and kick the wall. She called Amelia, who was exceedingly snappish at receiving a phone call before six.

"Go back to sleep," she said. "You dreamed her."

"No I didn't, Amy! She was here. In one of my sweaters!"

"Oh, Cordelia." Her sister sighed softly. "You can't get everything you think you deserve." She hung up the phone, and Cordelia put on her running clothes and ran until the sun rose.

Dr. Schwartz went off to have a massage, while Cordelia counted the missing Heinekens in the refrigerator and then went into the manager's office to get a replacement six-pack. When she came out, Philip was sweating on her *Daily News*.

"Hey, good-looking," he said. "Did the Marriott people call?"

"Uh huh." Cordelia could see Joshua Benson leaning forward to listen to their conversation, his face hidden behind the latest issue of *Manhattan, inc.*

"And?"

"They want me to read."

"You got it, baby!"

"I didn't test yet."

"Believe me, honey lips, there's no test. They owe me. Give us a kiss."

She felt herself shrink from him. Holding the beer against her chest, she tried to steady her voice.

"I really think they might want to meet me. I want to audition."

"So audition."

"Like a normal person."

"You won't get the gig."

"How dare you?"

"How dare I? Hey, grow up, farm girl! You don't even have an agent yet. You wanted help, I'm giving it to you. You could show a little more gratitude."

"Really? What would you like? How about I give you a blow job right here?"

"That would be a start."

Joshua had lowered the magazine, and his mouth was hanging open. Cordelia glared at him.

"Will that get me on a soap?"

"For a lousy blow job?"

"I don't give lousy head!"

"You said it, babe! I love it when we talk like this. Put the fucking beer away, and let me take a shower." Philip disappeared upstairs, while Cordelia refrigerated the beer, turning her back on Joshua.

She wondered how long one could call oneself an artist and still boast about one's skill at certain sexual practices.

Philip did not like stir-fried broccoli. When he'd suggested they go out to an expensive French restaurant, she countered with an offer of a home-cooked meal. While she chopped mushrooms and prepared the broccoli, he sat at her kitchen table, reading the *Wall Street Journal*. She set the plate of food down in front of him and he scowled, pushing the vegetables to the side of the pasta.

"How can you eat like this?" he asked grumpily. "It's like goddamned college hippie food!"

"I'm still poor. I'm poorer than I was in college."

"So we go out! I pay."

"What's wrong with a home-cooked meal? I get uncomfortable with you paying all the time."

"I want home cooking and heartburn, I visit my mother. You have other talents. What's with the money anyway? We got an arrangement, right?"

"Sure." She didn't know what he was talking about. She suspected it was the domestic nature of the situation that made him uneasy.

"Didn't your ex-wife ever cook you dinner?" she teased. "Didn't she ever take off her Lee Press-on Nails and whip you up some gnocchi? Doesn't this remind you of the bliss of married life?"

Philip didn't even smile. He speared the largest piece of broccoli and grimly stuffed it into his mouth.

Later, as they lay in bed, Cordelia thought that this was not a man to get sick with. He would not change the sheets, nor would he be willing to go to an all-night deli to buy lime sherbet. He would sooner hire a private nurse and go to work. Her feelings were not as important to him as how she looked. If she got fat, he would stop seeing her. If she didn't dress properly and make an attempt to be amusing, he would simply find another young woman to keep him company.

She pulled herself up on one elbow to watch him sleep. His face looked softer in the dim light, and with his mouth relaxed she could almost see what he must have been like before he had so much power. She wanted him to want her for different reasons. She knew it was important that he stop hurting her. She believed she could change him into someone who might love her properly, and his money would protect her from the world. Money kept people safe. He would take care of her. She would feel less exposed, and that was all she wanted. Protection and a shield from the violence that had crushed her sister. In return she would stay beautiful. And allow him his pleasure.

As she stared down at him he stirred. Putting his arm around her in sleep, he pulled her into his embrace, holding her tight against his chest, kissing her brow, and murmuring "Sweetness" into her ear. She snuggled into the space between his shoulder and his upper arm, and the regular sound of his heartbeat lulled her to sleep.

Her father was coming to New York. The message on her machine said he had business to attend to, but Cordelia suspected he was going to visit her mother. He asked her to reserve the next evening—the evening of her interview with the Marriott Hotel people.

It was a spokesperson role, a young businesswoman who needed the right place to stay during her frequent out-of-town trips. The image she was meant to convey was that of an intelligent eighties female who was somehow naturally sexy. Cordelia modeled herself on several of the executive women she had encountered as she handed out towels in the health club; she added a certain amount of inappropriate charm. None of these women were sexy. Tense and demanding but seldom warm. Occasionally sardonic. Never sexy.

The interview lasted six minutes. The casting director was a chubby young woman with green-tinted contact lenses that turned her eyes an unnatural shade of emerald green, causing her to resemble a plump Persian pussycat. He name was Dervla, and she chain-smoked.

"You need to project class, Cordelia," she said, slouching back in her chair, blowing smoke rings. "But we have to like this chick. I mean, she can't have a stick up her ass. She'd be friendly to the maid who put the truffles on her pillow. She wouldn't eat those truffles, mind you. Not our workout-princess account-executive mommy—"

"She's a mommy?"

Dervla shrugged. "Too much?"

Cordelia nodded.

"Well, we'll cut the mommy part. Anyway, she's sort of frigid, but she's nice. You know what I mean?"

"I think so."

"So say something in character. Do a little improv. Act."

Cordelia walked around the room, slipped off her jacket and hung it over a chair. She undid the bow on her shirt and sat down, kicking off her pumps to slowly rub her arch.

"You know what I really like about the service at this hotel?" She leaned back slightly, slowly unbuttoning the cuffs of her silk blouse, rolling her shoulders. "At the end of a day like today, which contained four meetings and three disasters,"—she wet her lips slightly and shook out her hair—"I can come back to this room, order room service, watch a minute of television, and go to sleep knowing I'm being taken care of."

There was an endless moment of silence, and then Dervla applauded.

"Great, Cordelia. Except I think she's gonna screw the bell-boy!"

They tried it again without the lip licking, and Dervla was very pleased.

"You strike this perfect balance between ball buster and a piece of ass. I'll call you with all the details. Okay, babe?"

She was meeting her father at her favorite nice-but-cheap Greek restaurant. When she arrived she saw him sitting alone at a back table, an almost empty bottle of retsina at his elbow. He was going over a ledger, bifocals perched on the end of his nose. She had not seen him since Cynthia's funeral, and before that their visits were few and far between. He had grown old without her, and she felt shocked and utterly alone, staring at a man who had willingly left her when she was seven years old.

"Sweetheart." Quickly he removed his glasses and ran a hand through his hair.

With his high-cheekboned face, blue eyes, and golden California tan, he was the handsomest father she had ever seen. He was dressed in a nubby tweed jacket, the color of heather, and a dusty-rose shirt. Sunflower's colors. When he kissed her she wondered if the other diners thought he was her lover. She felt herself blushing.

"Let me look at you." Her father held her at arm's length, admiring her wool suit and white silk shirt.

She was acutely aware of how high his standards of female beauty were, and she felt herself to be woefully inadequate. Cynthia used to insist their father wanted to sleep with them and that his fatherly scrutiny was an excuse to stare at their breasts.

"What's this executive getup, sweetie? Have you finally come to your senses and taken up banking?"

"No. I had an audition for a commercial."

"Another one?"

"Yup. For Marriott." Cordelia's father let out a low whistle.

She had sat down, and he still hadn't asked how she was. In fact, his face looked tense, and he appeared rather annoyed by her news. He finished off the retsina into her glass and raised his own for a toast.

"Here's to great success where the old geezer failed."

For a moment she hesitated, but then she drank.

"Thanks, Dad. Has all that good karma turned you into an old geezer?"

"Nah, it's inevitable, honey. Age and disappointment. Someday, believe it or not, you'll be old too. So you got an agent?"

"Not yet."

"How'd you get the jobs?"

"A friend of mine has a lot of connections."

"Someone should be reading your contracts, sweetie. Is this friend legit?"

Cordelia shrugged. She selected a breadstick from the basket and broke it against her water glass. The discussion might have been appropriate between two business acquaintances, but it was not how she wanted to talk to her father. The waiter brought another bottle of wine. She bit into a roll to stop herself from crying.

"I saw your mom."

"How's she feeling?"

"Fine. I don't know. She said she was feeling fine, but what else is she going to tell me? Don't you call her every day?"

"Yes. No. Amelia does."

"Still the loner, Delia? Cordelia 'I vant to be alone' Cavanagh." Her father's voice had a sharp edge.

She stared at the tablecloth. "I call her a lot!"

"I know. It's hard. How you must miss your sister." His voice was very soft and low.

A sob escaped from her chest, and tears fell on her dinner plate.

"Don't you?" She asked the question too loudly, shrilly. Slamming down her water glass, she reached into her purse for a cigarette.

"Don't smoke."

"I need to." She could not find a match. After a moment her father leaned forward with a silver lighter that had the MGM logo engraved on it.

"Of course I miss her. I think about her every day. She was my first child, Delia. The apple of my eye."

"So who am I? The thorn in your side?"

"No! You're the apple of my eye also. But we're so alike, Delia, that it frightens me to look at you."

"How can I be like you? I don't even know you. You disappeared when I was seven."

"She threw me out. That's why I named you Cordelia, baby—"

"Don't quote anything! I hate that fucking play! I'm the serpent's tooth, aren't I? Well, I am ungrateful, but you wanted to leave."

"I've discussed this with you before, Delia. She didn't want an unemployed actor for a husband—"

"I miss you!" Cordelia had torn her roll apart, creating a pile of bread crumbs.

Her father put his hand over hers. She could not look up. What she really meant to say was that she missed feeling as if the world were a safe place. She wanted to tell him she believed she had made an alliance with the devil, a contract the devil had no intention of keeping.

"So why didn't you stay longer in California?" The moment was over. Her father finished his glass of retsina and ordered another round. He had always been a heavy drinker, but Sunflower watched him like a hawk, so he waited for his trips back east to really hit the bottle.

"I felt I was intruding."

"My own daughter? Sunflower adores you girls. She and Amelia are like that." He crossed his fingers to indicate the closeness of their relationship.

Cordelia felt such a sharp stab of jealousy she could barely speak.

"They are?"

"Sure. Amy's bringing the bambino out in a few weeks. I gotta dust off my grandpop act, and Sunflower has to iron those flowered aprons. It's a rather confusing thing to have a granny who's the same age as your mother."

Cordelia smiled weakly. How dare her sister bring Tom out to California to visit that airhead. She was a traitor.

"So you got a new boyfriend? What's this I hear about a South African basketball player?"

"He's not a basketball player, and he's not my boyfriend. I knew him at Trinity. He dropped by while he was in New York."

"Amelia says he's incredible and in love with you."

"Amelia's an asshole."

"Don't be so unpleasant, Cordelia."

"Let's order. I'll have the pompano."

Her father gave the waiter their orders.

"You in love with this guy?"

"Daddy . . ."

"Don't 'daddy' me! When you deny something with a lot of passion, it's usually because it's true. What's wrong with love, Delia?"

"Nothing. But I'm not in love with anyone, especially not an ex-boyfriend in the middle of a nasty divorce and a custody battle. I sort of have a boyfriend. His name is Philip Syrianos."

"A last name! I'm impressed. I remember when they never had last names. One of you girls would be rhapsodizing over Bill or Ben or Vern, and I'd say, Vern what? and you'd get all defensive and tell me it was utterly unimportant. So what does Mr. Syrianos do?"

"He's a precious-metals broker."

"What's that mean?"

"I don't know. He buys gold, I think. He has a very posh office."

"Rich."

"Extremely."

"He got you that first commercial?"

"He got me the interview. He knows people."

"Why's he doing this?"

133

"He likes me. He knows how hard the business is."

"Single?"

"Daddy! Divorced."

"You see his papers? Greeks like to tell people what they think they want to hear."

"Come on. . . ."

"Watch out, Delia. You're a beautiful girl. A girl any man would lie to in order to keep her around. Men aren't like women. They don't care about what happens. They just want what they want, and they take it. It's a terrible world. I don't want anything hurting my precious child." His eyes were full of tears.

She could not look at him. She wanted to tell him to stop worrying because she couldn't get hurt because she didn't love Philip. She wouldn't suffer because she had no intention of loving anyone again for the rest of her life. People she loved left her. Her sister had believed in love and had been murdered for not having enough cash to pay off a mugger.

"Nobody's going to hurt me, Daddy," she murmured. "I'm pretty tough."

She left her father at the entrance to Central Park on Fifty-ninth Street. He had wanted to stretch his legs with the walk uptown. They had not talked, but he held her hand, and it was nice to walk next to him and feel that despite all the disappointment they both felt, he was still her father.

CHAPTER

16

AS SHE WALKED UP BROADWAY SHE PASSED THE SALOON AND heard someone knocking on the glass. Harrison was sitting at a table with a group of people, apparently a film crew—most of them seemed to be wearing light meters. She paused, and Harrison came out to the sidewalk.

"Hey, Cordelia."

"Hey yourself." He was wearing a bulky gray sweater and black jeans. Through the window she noticed a pretty blond woman watching them with some anxiety.

"I'm really glad to see you," she said, putting her mitten against Harrison's cheek.

"Me too."

"You want to come over for a cup of tea?"

"Sure. Just let me say goodbye to my friends."

She watched him shaking hands, saw the girl's crestfallen expression, and silently mouthed, "He belongs to me."

They walked most of the way in silence. Harrison put his arm around her shoulders and she sagged against him, realizing how very tired she was. She saw with a shock of recognition that the ancient suede jacket he was wearing was the same one he'd owned in Dublin; it still smelled of French cigarettes and almond soap. She had walked beside him then, believing she was in pain and that nothing could hurt so much as unrequited love. It had all seemed so critical before her sister's murder.

"Harrison?"

"Yes."

"I'm very confused."

"I know."

"I don't know what it is . . . how to describe it. I don't seem to want anything."

"It's okay."

"I'm terrified all the time. I think I want to die, but I'm so afraid."

"I know."

"How can you know? How can you understand this?" They had reached her apartment. She pulled free from his arm to face him.

"Every morning I walk to the playground by my house, and I sit and I watch the children. I keep thinking I'll find Sam there, that maybe I just haven't got my facts straight and he's standing someplace holding his Smurfs lunchbox, waiting for his dad to pick him up, waiting for me to get there. Sometimes I see a little boy that looks so much like him I start to go after him, and he looks at me and I see that I'm nobody, a stranger, a possible bad guy. And it freezes me. . . . I can't tell you how much I miss my boy."

"Where is she?"

"Greece."

"What will you do?"

"Nothing."

"Harrison . . ."

"I know! But that's me, Cordelia. That's how I handle pain. It's always been like that. It's part of growing up in a country that allowed such inhumanity: after a while you accept the unthinkable. You don't agonize over right or wrong. You sacrifice what you love for numbness. I know you'd walk into the very gates of hell to get Cynthia back. I see you trying. . . . Somehow it's as if you can force her back to life just by suffering. I've given him up. That's what I did with you."

"What?"

"Nothing. I allowed you to love me, and when it was time for me to respond, I didn't. The moment passed. I used to feel you waiting there, in the darkness, waiting for me to do something. I wanted to take you in my arms, to wake you up in the middle of the night and tell you to stay. I used to watch you sleeping, and I knew I couldn't do it. You walked away, and I just stood there grinning like some sort of jester, the court fool."

"Why didn't you tell me?"

"I couldn't."

"But you never loved me."

"Of course I did."

"No you didn't! Harrison . . . you didn't!" She remembered a scene she'd made in one of Dublin's finest restaurants because she'd decided public humiliation was the only way to hurt him. When her sobs became too loud, he had gently led her from the dining room, smiling slightly at the other patrons, who must have been wondering what this nice man was doing with the hysterical American. When they reached the street he had let go of her arm and she'd slapped him. As her hand struck his face, she saw the look in his eyes, one of terrible suffering. She had not understood.

"It doesn't matter now," she said.

"You don't believe me."

"Not really."

They walked up the stairs, and Cordelia put on the kettle. She brewed the tea, but then she took away his cup and bent over to gently kiss his lips. Harrison let out a small moan. He reached forward and pulled her into his arms, burying his face in the space between her breasts, kissing her neck and her ears until her whole body was tingling. She ran her lips from the bridge of his nose to his chin and down his chest, unbuttoning each button, kissing the exposed flesh. He pushed her skirt above her hips, tore at her panty hose, held her thighs in his hands and kissed her belly, kissed the insides of her thighs, biting gently so that she moaned and arched backward.

When they were both naked, he held her tightly so that her

137

head just reached his chest. Their bodies were so close together she could feel his heart beating. He picked her up and carried her into the bedroom, letting her go into the bathroom for her diaphragm, insisting that he put it in, sucking on her breast as he parted the lips of her vagina and, with the utmost delicacy, put it in. She could not feel that anything that was happening between them was other than part of the dance they had started in the kitchen. He opened her up like a flower, burying his face in her flesh, biting and sucking until she was screaming for him, and still he held her slightly away and was above her like some sort of incredible ghost. Finally, her legs on his shoulders, he entered her, so hard she felt she was splitting, and yet she welcomed all of him, wrapping herself around him as if he were a tree and she some sort of clinging animal. She remembered how he had felt, and yet now they were two different people, and it was not the same. He kept saying, "I love you," until she was repeating the same words, a senseless sort of mantra that lasted until she simply lost consciousness and fell into a present that was just another part of the dream.

When she awoke, Harrison's head was on her shoulder, which was so stiff she could barely move. Their legs were twined together, and he held a piece of her hair between his fingers. She slipped from his grasp, replacing her body with a pillow.

The winter light was pearly gray. Sometime between midnight and morning it had snowed. The sidewalks were lightly dusted, and children outside were trying to build a snowman but mostly just flinging the powdery snow at each other. She brewed a pot of coffee and sat down at the table. The morning of her sister's funeral, a large seagull had incongruously landed on Cordelia's windowsill. Perhaps it was the lack of sleep and food, but Cordelia had felt that the bird was looking at her with some degree of recognition, and she sat by the open window telling the bird various things she might have told her sister. As she sat waiting for the coffee to finish dripping, she hoped that something might happen to indicate her sister's presence. The only sound was that of the children shouting in the street and her own teeth grinding together. She felt utterly alone.

Harrison stood behind her, his naked body pressed against her back. He held her head in his hands; he could easily press upon the vein in her neck, she thought, until the blood stopped flowing. She could feel his heart beating above her head. Her skull pressed into his belly, and his penis rested in the curve of her nape.

"Come back to bed," he crooned into her ear, gently nibbling on the lobe.

"It snowed last night."

"Come back to sleep with me," Harrison pleaded, licking her cheek, removing her empty coffee cup from her tightly clenched fingers.

"I can't sleep anymore."

"Come back to me," Harrison said, pulling her to her feet and turning her around, unbelting the robe to press his naked body against hers. "Stop leaving me, Cordelia."

"I never left you."

"Yes you did. You went back to stupid New Jersey. To Bruce Springsteen and your long-haired boyfriends."

"We were finished. The year was over. You never loved me."

"I knew you'd go."

"That's not the way—"

"I loved you, Cordelia. As well as I could."

"No you didn't. You're remembering someone else."

There were things that happened in her family that she thought had been a mistake in casting, as if they had sent the wrong scene to the set and everyone's behavior was out of character. She had always been the elusive child, neither the dutiful married daughter nor the one who modeled herself after their powerful mother. She was the one people asked about with the expectation of being told something interesting. Amelia was good at being married, Cynthia was an achiever. And Cordelia just kept moving. It was harder to leave someone who was rarely home. Now she had to be present. Her mother needed her. Her family wouldn't allow her to go away.

"I left Dublin before you did," she whispered into his shoulder. "It was only a matter of time."

When she saw that Cynthia must die, Cordelia planned to escape. After she visited the morgue with her mother, she had reserved a one-way ticket on a flight to Shannon. It seemed the only place to go. But that evening she walked into her mother's bedroom without knocking and found her down on her knees, sobbing into the carpet. The bloodstained shirt they had cut from Cynthia's body was clenched in one hand, and she kept repeating the same words over and over again like some sort of incantation: "My daughter! My precious, beautiful child! Oh, God, I hate you! I hate you, God! My baby. . . ."

She had grabbed hold of Cordelia like someone drowning and said: "Don't ever leave me, Delia. I can't stand to lose another daughter."

And Cordelia couldn't tell her she was flying back to Ireland. She stayed in New York, stopped eating, and tried not to kill herself. At times she dreamed of being there, of telling her friends about all of it, feeling their sympathy and their need to see her heal. Her mother's grief pressed down on her with such pressure she wanted to scream. She would wake up in her apartment and cry to find herself alone in New York.

She turned her back on him in bed, but he turned her over as if she were some sort of fish stranded on dry land. While he spoke he gently rubbed her stomach until she felt herself relaxing.

"My uncle owns a farm in Mozambique. No one wants to take care of it. He's offered me a post as his agent. I get a percentage of the crop's profits. We can go there. You can rest and write a play or something. It's such lovely country, Cory! Wild animals in the backyard, waterfalls . . . and it's safe. It's not like here. No one's waiting in the shadows to cut your throat."

"What about the terrorists?"

"It's all protected land."

"What about Sam?"

"My wife won't give him up."

"You have to fight for custody, Harrison."

"That would be terrible for him. Worse than not having a

father. I don't want him to see us ripping things to shreds. We can have a baby." She pushed his hand away and sat up. "Don't tell me you don't want a child, Cordelia."

She got out of bed, still silent, and began to dress.

"You're very confused," he said, watching her search fruitlessly for clean underwear. "I don't think you have the faintest idea what you want."

"I can tell you this, you conceited ass! I don't want to go off to fucking Mozambique with you and have your replacement baby! What am I—some sort of consolation prize? I won't make up for the mistake you made marrying that miserable bitch! If you weren't such a typical idiot male, you'd have seen she was a witch and not fallen on your bloody knees. Now she's stolen your son, and you want to pick another prize? Forget it!"

"That's not what I'm asking you! You make one lousy commercial—"

"Almost two!"

"Whatever."

"Do you have any idea what the odds are against an actor getting work in this city? My career is very important to me."

"What career?"

"My acting."

"Acting? Show me some acting! You're making stupid ads for yuppie imbeciles."

"So what? I'm paying the rent. I take class. I'm going to auditions. It's exposure."

"Exposure to what? Sleazebags that leave bruises all over your body? Who give you money for it?"

"No! To . . . people."

"What people?"

"Agents. Casting directors."

"Why don't you go to RADA or Yale, then? You shouldn't be doing this crap. You should be doing Chekhov!"

"What is this obsession with fucking Chekhov? Am I some sort of reincarnation of Nina? Or is he the only mediocre genius who comes to mind when people are making disparaging remarks about my career? That's who my father keeps throwing in my face. Chekhov!"

"It's better than screwing that ignorant thug for bit parts! And you've got all these marks on your body. Why is he beating you, Cordelia?" He said the last very quietly.

She had dressed and was trying to lace up her boots.

"He's not doing anything. I work out a lot and I'm thinner and I have anemia and it's none of your goddamned business." She threw his clothes on the bed and stalked into the kitchen.

After a moment he came out, dressed and holding his coat.

"I can't fight with you like this," he said. "I feel as if we are destroying ourselves." He let himself out of the apartment.

She ran to the landing. She could hear his footsteps on the stairs.

"You never gave me anything without my asking," she shouted. "I don't want your baby now. I don't want anything from you."

CHAPTER

17

AFTER HARRISON LEFT, SHE HAD TO LEAVE HER APARTMENT. She decided to spend the early afternoon in the Museum of Modern Art. She had an acting class at three, and one of her exercises was set in a gallery. The museum was quite empty. The sculpture garden was white with snow, and she wandered around the third floor, looking at sculptures that appeared to be constructed out of pieces of the insides of machines. The edges were rusted and rough. They looked dangerous.

She wandered into another room and stared at a blank white canvas with a tiny patch of blue on the lower corner. Turning to leave, she saw a man bending over a stroller in the corner, tenderly tucking a blanket around a sleeping child. It was Seth Goldberg, her first lover in college, her first real boyfriend, the man who taught her how to enjoy sex, the first person she'd ever loved.

She froze, trying to locate someplace to hide, but the room was empty. Seth straightened up and looked directly at her. At first his smile was polite and his eyes were perfectly blank, but then he blinked and swallowed. Turning to the woman standing next to him, a small woman with a mass of dark curly hair, he whispered something and then walked toward Cordelia. She gave him a tiny wave. Like Jackie Kennedy, she thought; I just waved at Seth like a president's wife.

"Cordelia," he said. "My God, it's been so long!"

She almost pretended to be someone else, but Seth didn't look confused. She smiled weakly and gave his wife one of her presidential-spouse salutations.

"Hi, Seth," she said, her voice higher by many octaves. "How are you?"

"Wonderful. You look splendid, Cordelia. Grown up. I guess it's almost ten years. But you're very thin."

"Oh, I'm trying to act. The camera makes you look fat." She giggled and tried to breathe.

"That's terrific. You were such a great actress. How are you?"

"Fine."

This was not how she had imagined it would be. Making horrible strained small talk in a major art gallery in front of Seth's family. She had always thought they would meet someplace where it would be possible to rip each other's clothes off and make mad, tragic love until they parted again. All in total silence.

"You live in the city?"

"Yes. On the Upper West Side. It's really great."

"Married?"

"Oh, no."

He had already glanced down at her left hand. His wife walked into another room, pushing the stroller.

"So you're actually making a living as an actress?"

"Just started to. I got a commercial. Yogurt." Inexplicably, her eyes filled with tears.

Seth would not stop looking at her. "That's wonderful, Delia. Would you like to meet my wife?"

"No, Seth."

"Ahh, why not?" His eyes twinkled at her the way they used to on those mornings when he brought her coffee and bagels in bed.

She remembered a pile of newspapers, hours of making sleepy, perfect love, and felt more tears rising in her throat. She swallowed. "Do you live in New York?"

"No. Ruth and I were just visiting her sister."

"That's nice."

"I have a daughter." Seth glanced around the room. "The sleeping lump in the stroller."

"What's her name?"

"Sarah. Ruth thinks it's after her grandmother, but it's really Dylan's Sara. Sad-eyed lady of the lowlands. Remember what a schmuck I was? The reincarnation of Bobby D!"

Yes, she thought. She remembered him singing the complete side of *Blood on the Tracks* to her the night before he left for Colorado. All of it, off key, and that stupid harmonica. While she cried and drank vodka. She knew their love would never survive that separation. Once you let something go, it never comes back. Her reason for refusing to even entertain the possibility of going with him was fear. She assumed Seth would grow tired of her eventually. If she alienated her family—who had no choice but to love her—and then he dumped her, she would be completely alone. When she'd called her father to tell him she wanted to leave school, he had called her "an ungrateful brat" and implied he had no faith in her persevering as an actress. When she told him she loved Seth, he snorted and said love didn't exist.

"Don't you love me?" she had sobbed, watching Seth in the living room, playing with their cat.

"I'm your father," he screamed. "What choice do I have?"

Her determination to win an Academy Award was doubled. It would give her the opportunity to tell the entire world what a shit her father was.

"You'd make such a wonderful mother, Cordelia. You should get married. Give one of the guys a chance." On those words, he reached out to touch her cheek.

She shrank from his fingers, but then, without thinking, she kissed his palm. My sister was murdered, she wanted to scream. I'm having some sort of nervous breakdown.

"How's your family?" Seth asked. "Everybody okay?"

"Sure."

"You're still the most beautiful woman, Cordelia. I'd almost forgotten." He touched her shoulder lightly and disappeared in the direction of the sound of a baby's laughter.

She sat down on a bench and stared at her feet. He was such a nice man. She wanted to run after him and explain why she'd slept with those people after he left. She'd been terrified of being alone again.

"I loved you first," she whispered to her boots. "I loved you always."

But then it was easy to say that, since he was now lost to her for good. The first time they dropped acid, she had hallucinated herself trapped inside the web of a net, with Seth standing outside, a mad butterfly hunter in a pith helmet, beaming at his captive. Sometimes his loving concern weighed as heavy as a wool blanket on a hot and humid day. The pedestal he'd stuck her on was lonely. She had to keep flinging herself to the ground, bruising her joints and shattering his illusions. Eventually they would have destroyed each other. His wife looked very happy. What would she have done with all that well-meant concern?

When she walked into the studio, Cordelia noticed immediately that Maxine had got fatter. She denied it.

"No," she said in answer to Maxine's question, "you do not look like Totie Fields."

They sat in the back of the studio and whispered during a scene from *Extremities*. The woman has turned the tables on her rapist and has him trapped in her fireplace. She's torturing him with insect spray. The two actors were saying their lines so quickly it was difficult to understand them.

"I saw Farrah Fawcett do this," Maxine whispered to Cordelia. "She spent the entire show in a white T-shirt that reached her waist and white bikini underpants. Every time you looked at any guy in the audience, they had this dumb sort of I'd-fuck-her-too expression. It was really a drama about how much of Farrah's tits we were going to see. The woman is plastic. No one's body could be that . . . unflawed."

"Shh." They watched the scene until the actor lost his voice from shouting.

"I'm tired of rape and bondage," Maxine said too loudly from the back of the room. "Let's go get a drink."

They went to the Lion's Head, and Cordelia ordered a martini. Maxine asked for an apricot sour and a double order of potato skins.

"So what's going on? You get the Marriott gig?"

"I don't know yet. Harrison spent the night last night."

"You mean spent-the-night-we-fucked, or spent-the-night-we-slept-and-wished-we-could?"

"We fucked."

"Jesus Christ, Cordelia! I thought you were playing hunt-the-thimble with Zorba the Greek."

"I am."

"Well, that's not fair! This is the eighties, and it's Manhattan! There is point-five man for every two women! Not two for one! You're screwing up all the statistics. You've had more sex in the past week than I've had in a year!" Maaxine's voice carried to the back of the bar, where two men stood and applauded.

"No I haven't."

"Fuck you, Cordelia! I can't be best friends with you. You're thin and you're getting laid and you're getting major career break-throughs. Bartender! Give us more of everything! I'm living in an MGM musical, and I've been cast as a virginal Ado Annie!"

"I saw Seth today in MOMA."

"Seth?"

"You know, my first love—the Jewish guy from college."

"Him? The one you do all your memory exercises about? The one your father hated? The one who gave you your first orgasm—"

"Shh!"

"The one who wanted to marry you, but you fucked his best friend—"

"Shut up, Maxine! This whole bar doesn't have. to know my entire history. When did I tell you all that?"

"The night you got your new blender and we found that copy of *Mr. Boston's Guide to Tropical Drinks*."

"That was a horrible night."

"It was not! Those strawberry-guava piña coladas were fabulous."

"You made a forty-five-minute long-distance call to Japan."

"So what? You tried to get the number of your old boyfriend whose name you couldn't spell in a town he didn't live in so you could tell him he was an asshole."

"It was a horrible night. Those drinks made me throw up."

"I got through to Keith Richards' roadie."

"He was speaking Japanese!"

"Well, that's who he said he was. I think. Forget this—what happened with Seth? Did you hear harp music? Did you fall into each other's arms? Is he bald? MOMA . . . It's a fucking Woody Allen movie! I meet old boyfriends in all-night delis, with my arms loaded with junk food, wearing bunny-head slippers. Smiler's at three A.M. on a Saturday night!"

"He was with his wife. And a child. We said hello. It was really sad."

"Did you tell him about your sister?"

"Oh, no. I couldn't do that. It was already so sad." Cordelia put a potato skin in her mouth, and then she started to giggle. "I don't know. . . . I kissed the palm of his hand, and he didn't even react. I'm not sure what's happening to me. Everything's a bit fucked."

"Drink. Celebrate. I got the part in *Romeo and Juliet*."

"Max! That's so good! The Soho Rep one?"

"Yup. But I'm playing the nurse, which is a terrible part for me. Fat and forty. I'll just have to accept this until I go back to O.A."

"What happened?"

"You didn't call me, Cordelia."

"I'm so sorry, Maxie."

"I need to know you're there for me."

"I'm always here. Let's have another round! To celebrate."

"So what does the confused god Harrison want besides eternal youth?"

"A baby."

"So let him go find his son."

"He's given up. He wants me to have one."

"Oh, God! Why are men so fucking stupid? You've got this sadistic Greek carving his initials on your ass and this ex-boyfriend wandering around major art museums with his wife and a shell-shocked South African looking for an empty womb. . . . Like you have nothing better to do than go around replacing abducted children. Was the sex good?"

"It's hard to describe. It's as if we never stopped loving each other."

"Love? How did that come into it? Oh, Cordelia! You are such a mess! You've had this terrible trauma, and you don't know what day it is."

Cordelia thought for a moment. Her mind was perfectly blank. "That's true," she agreed, draining her third martini. "I have no idea what the date is."

They picked up two investment bankers and convinced them to take them to the China Club, which was near Cordelia's apartment. In the club, Cordelia drank two Stolichnayas on the rocks and had a few lines of coke. The drinks made her tired, and the drugs made her tense. They had a pretty dull time except for one hysterical trip to the ladies', where they discovered that neither of them knew which banker was named Doug and which was Brad. They solved their dilemma by calling one Boug and the other Drad. The men were not amused, and they finally left for the South Street Seaport in search of more upwardly mobile, well-behaved young women. Maxine almost picked up someone who looked like David Bowie, but he told her he'd tested positive for AIDS. So she gave him the name of an excellent acupuncturist who treated AIDS patients without charging very much. They ended their evening in Bagel Nosh, where Maxine had two cinnamon raisin bagels with cream cheese and a hot chocolate.

"I'm a foodaholic," she announced midway through her second bagel. "I need help."

"What do you say at O.A.? 'Hi, I'm Maxine, and I'm a pig'?"

"No. You say you have an eating disorder, you skinny bitch!"

"Am I a bitch? I'm not a bitch. Harrison says I am. God. I hate

149

coke! It makes you feel as if something really terrible is happening just out of range of your peripheral vision."

"No, you aren't a bitch. You're just a mess."

"Should I have Harrison's baby and move to Mozambique? Do you really think I've had a terrible life?"

"No, you can't go to Mozambique and you can't have anyone's baby, and yes, you've had a terrible life. Why are you so demanding? Maybe that's why I eat. You suck the marrow from my bones."

"Max! Oh, Max. I'm so sorry!" Tears stood in her eyes, spilled down her cheeks. She was quite drunk.

"Stop it! What are you, crazy? Goddamn it, Cordelia! Lighten up! You don't know how to have fun. Everything's so fucking heavy!"

"I'm so afraid. I keep thinking something horrible's going to happen."

"That's because of your sister. It did happen, and you had to accept that you could do absolutely nothing to save her. You had to pretend to be strong for your mother. And you came close to dying yourself. When I think of the state you were in when Amelia found you—the curtains nailed across the windows and you like some sort of concentration camp victim."

Cordelia shuddered. Maxine leaned across the table and tenderly stroked her cheek.

"Sweetheart, it's over now. You just need to take care of yourself."

Maxine spent the night. When the phone rang at four A.M. she picked up the receiver, said "Hello?" and then put it against Cordelia's ear, and went back to sleep.

"Ummph?" mumbled Cordelia, wondering why her pillow was talking.

"Cordelia?" It was Harrison's voice. "Wake up."

"What?"

"It's Harrison."

"Oh. It's very late. What's wrong?"

"My wife called."

"Who is this?"

"Harrison. Wake up, Cordelia. My wife called." She sat up, but the throb in her temples persuaded her to slump back down.

"Harrison. Oh, Harrison, is someone dead?"

"No! Oh, I forgot. I'm sorry, Delia. It's just . . . she called. She put Sam on the phone."

"Oh, honey . . ."

"He said, 'Hi, Dada. When you coming home?' "

"Oh, Harrison . . . What a bitch."

"I needed to hear your voice."

"It's all right. I just get frightened when the phone rings in the middle of the night."

"Who picked it up?"

"Maxine."

"Oh." Harrison swallowed. "Delia . . ."

"Yes."

"You're right about my never giving you anything. I just wanted to so much that sometimes I think I must have."

"It's okay." She felt herself slip back to sleep. "I have to hang up, Harrison. I'm so tired."

"Christ! I forgot what time it is."

"Everything's going to be all right."

"God, Cordelia, I'm so sorry about your sister."

"I know. Sam's safe, and you'll see him soon."

"Why did she have to die?"

"I don't know, Harrison. Life's pretty bad sometimes."

"Delia . . ."

"I gotta go."

"Good night, my darling."

"Night."

In her dreams they were playing musical chairs. His wife was able to make the music stop by just snapping her fingers. Cordelia watched her so closely she kept stumbling over the edges of the furniture. Harrison moved like a man asleep. And Cynthia . . . she was a bright light in front of her, laughing, flinging back her hair, and raising her legs like a dancer. Cordelia kept trying to catch up to her, but she would not turn around. At the end there was a single chair in an empty room, the smothered sound of crying.

The first thing she recalled when she awoke was how much she had hated to play that game as a child. There were too many losers. Maxine slept heavily, curled up like a little girl. Cordelia stood at her bedroom window, watching someone search through the garbage as rain fell on the Manhattan streets.

CHAPTER

18

HER HEAD FELT LIKE AN OVERBLOSSOMED PEONY ON A TOO slender stem. She held an ice-cold bottle of Michelob against her temple, and for a moment the pain subsided.

"A little early for a brewsky, isn't it, babe?" Philip stood in front of the desk, his body gleaming with sweat. He had been running on the treadmill.

"Hi." Cordelia moved the bottle slowly across her forehead.

"How'd the Marriott interview go?"

"I'm not sure. She really seemed to like me."

"Did she say when they'd call?"

"No."

"They want you. They'll call. So how's my little kiwi fruit?"

"Hung over."

"Oh, yeah? Where you been hiding the last couple of days?"

"My dad came to town. And I went out with Maxine last night. We had all this vodka—"

"That's the fat chick in your acting class, right?"

"She's more than that—"

"God, I hate fat women!" He shivered dramatically and leaning over the desk kissed Cordelia, patting her stomach with his hand. "Hard as a rock. Jesus, I'd like to rip your panties off."

Cordelia pressed the ice-cold beer she was holding against his bare chest.

"Okay! What's up this weekend?"

"I'm going home."

"Home?"

"To see my mom. You know, she just had the operation."

"Oh, yeah, sure. She feeling okay?"

Cordelia nodded.

"Good. Well, see if you can get a couple days off from this dump next week. We'll go to the Bahamas, Eleuthera. I got some property to check out over there. You can hang out and get some sun. *Capisce?*"

"Maybe."

"Maybe? No maybe, baby! I miss your sweet body. You been a hard girl to get hold of."

Her mother's house smelled of freshly baked bread. Rows of pies were lined up across the counter, lattice-topped fruit tarts, golden brown and glistening with oozing juice. Next to the pies were a platter heaped with brownies and date-nut bars, a plate of sugar cookies, and several loaves of what looked like Irish soda bread. Amelia was sitting at the kitchen counter, looking grimly depressed. At Cordelia's entrance she looked up, her eyes wet with unshed tears.

"Look at this," she hissed. "She's been baking again. I knew this would hit her sooner or later."

Their mother's worst baking binge had occurred just after Mr. Cavanagh had left for California. She had baked, slept, wept, and called in sick at her office until Cynthia had threatened to call the Child Welfare Board to have their custody switched to their father. Frightened of losing her daughters, Dr. Cavanagh had gone to see a counselor, who encouraged her to stop cooking, go back to work, and get rid of all the traces of her ex-husband.

"Where is she?"

"Upstairs. She did this between four A.M. and this morning.

When I arrived she was sitting here covered with flour, crying. Dad didn't help, raving about her perfect breasts."

"Is that what he did?"

"Of course. It was an ideal dramatic opportunity. He beat his chest and raved about their now lost forever perfection. He is such a fucking egoist, Delia! Why are actors so emotionally cheap?"

"I don't know. What did she say to you this morning?"

"Oh, things about Cynthia. Stories about clever and charming stuff she used to do. Because of having to take care of the funeral details, she didn't get to say any of this. She had to identify the body—"

"I saw her too."

"No you didn't."

"I was with Mom. In the morgue."

"You didn't see her."

"I held her hand."

"Shut up, Cordelia!"

"I touched her hand and her face, and she was as cold as ice. I pulled the hair out of her eyes. I was there first. Before you. I was the first one, and I saw what they were trying to do to save her life. Mummy fell down on the floor."

"We have to make her understand that nothing else is going to happen to us. She thinks you're doing something with someone who might be in the Mafia. Is your new boyfriend a gangster?"

"No."

"Daddy said he had strange connections. She's afraid you're going to get hurt. You live in such a ridiculous fashion. You never answer your phone! You have to tell her you'll stop acting if there's no work."

"I've told her that already. Why are you being such a freak? Anyway, I just got a big commercial."

"A commercial? A real one?"

"Yup." Cordelia bit into a brownie. It was very rich and sweet. Something crunched, and she pulled out a piece of eggshell. "It's for yogurt. Where's Tom?"

"With his Grandma Lewis. I told Michael I needed a day off.

It's pretty difficult being a full-time mommy and working. Of course, it's not glamorous work." Amelia worked at home as a free-lance copy editor. Her voice had a definite edge. Amelia's resentment over Cordelia's career had always seemed illogical. She had a family of her own, had given birth to a perfect child and had a supportive and attractive husband. Yet she seemed to think her little sister's irregular and disappointing existence was mysteriously wonderful.

When their eldest sister was alive they had rarely seen each other. Cynthia had been their link, she completed the circle, and neither younger sister ever imagined being forced to deal directly with the other. When Cordelia understood that Cynthia was dying, she thought that Amelia would be sorry it wasn't she, the younger one, that was gone. She was of so little use.

Amelia had always managed. She had a detachment and a self-control that the rest of them lacked. When their father moved west, she was able to be nice to him while still remaining loyal to their mother. Her balance was a sharp contrast to Cordelia's histrionic anger, which caused her to be terrible to both their parents: furious and cold to their father, scornful to their mother. When Cordelia had almost starved herself to death, Amelia had simply said, "No more," and taken her home.

On that drive back to New Jersey, Cordelia had sat huddled up, ashamed at the trouble she was causing. She had looked at Amelia's profile, the hard set of her lips, and whispered, "I'm sorry."

Amelia hadn't taken her eyes from the road. "She can't take care of you anymore," she said. "You'll have to let me and then do it yourself."

But she wouldn't grieve, and Cordelia almost hated her for that. It seemed so important to talk about their past and how this loss of their history affected them both.

"She helped deliver your son," Cordelia wanted to scream at her. "How can you bear it?"

But Amelia didn't tell anyone those secrets. She was a good mother, wife, and daughter. Easy to love but distant and, Cordelia believed, angry to the very bone at a world that defied logic.

Angry at a world that had failed to protect one of the few people she had chosen to trust.

"What is this?" Amelia had bitten into one of their mother's brownies and was picking something out of her teeth.

"Eggshell. Just eat around it. How's Michael?"

"Fine. He'd like to see you. I told him you were very busy, and he said, 'Ah, yes. Cordelia and her lovers.' "

"I don't have any lovers."

"What about the Mafia guy?"

"He isn't in the Mafia. He's a precious-metals broker."

"What's that mean?"

"I'm not sure. But he has a lovely office in midtown. Mafia guys run dry-cleaning stores in Queens. He tried to give me an alabaster egg on a solid-gold stand on our first date."

"Oh, Cordelia!" Amelia wailed, staring into her coffee cup as if she'd noticed a dead insect floating on the top.

"What's wrong?"

"Your life. How can you go on like this? Who is this man?"

"I just told you."

"Will he marry you?"

"I hope not. I don't want to get married. And he'd be a horrible husband. He's a tyrant, and he snorts cocaine and bullies waiters."

"Who's going to take care of you?" Amelia had tears coursing down her cheeks.

Cordelia felt as if she had wandered into a really idiotic soap opera. "No one! I take care of myself. What is wrong with you?"

"We worry about you."

"Well, stop it!" Cordelia lit a cigarette and began to read one of her mother's cookbooks, *Microwave Magic*. "Let's make peanut butter fudge," she suggested to her sobbing sister. "Let's make peanut butter fudge and eat it raw!"

Mrs. Cavanagh slept until five, when Ed, her boyfriend, arrived to take them out for dinner. The two sisters had spent the afternoon eating brownies and playing Parcheesi, fighting over the rules. They felt slightly sick but were hungry for real food. Cordelia went upstairs to wake her mother, but she was up and nearly dressed. She had lost weight since her operation. She turned around and smiled at her youngest daughter. Cordelia noticed how gray her hair had become in the past year but also that her face seemed breathtakingly lovely.

"Hi, darling," she said, hugging Cordelia. "Which earrings should I wear?" The bed was covered with photographs, old black-and-white Polaroids. There were two new, empty photograph albums next to the pile of snapshots.

"Where'd these come from?"

"Your father had them."

"He gave them back?"

"He took them to a Hollywood photo lab and made copies of everything."

"Was it nice to see him?"

"Of course. Except . . . well, it's always strange to see someone you once loved so much . . . couldn't imagine not loving. Now it seems as if it's always been like this." Her mother shrugged. "Know what I mean?"

"Sort of."

"He said you two had a fabulous time together."

Cordelia snorted. "Yeah, we discussed our brilliant careers."

The pictures were mainly of Cynthia and an infant Amelia. Cynthia riding a fat pony, with her two parents looking dashing on their horses. Cynthia and her new Indian friends from the reservation, performing a rain dance in tribal costume. Cynthia grinning from ear to ear, proud in her brand-new all-white Sally Starr cowgirl outfit. Near the bottom of the pile was a picture of eight-year-old Cordelia dressed in the garb of an Arab sheikh, wearing very large sunglasses. Her eldest sister had her arm around her and held up the trophy they had won for the best Halloween costume at a contest held at their local Y. Cynthia had spent days transforming Cordelia into Lawrence of Arabia. The little girls in the photograph dissolved. Cordelia felt as if someone had punched her in the stomach. She started to leave the room.

"Honey?"

"I can't, Mom."

"Are these okay?" Cordelia looked back, to see her mother dangling the shellacked Ritz-cracker earrings she had given her on Mother's Day when she was in kindergarten. She burst into tears.

"I thought they would make you laugh."

"I miss her so much!"

"I know, sweetie pie."

"I hate him!"

"Who?"

"Daddy."

"No you don't."

"He isn't any help. He tells me things about agents. He makes snide remarks about the business and gives me fucking advice! I want to talk about her! I want to talk about what that man did to our family, and I want Daddy to listen to me! I start to tell him how I feel, and he gets so distant." Cordelia was shouting. Her mother put her arms around her and pushed her down on the edge of the bed. "I don't want her to be dead anymore. It's been long enough. We understand how much we loved her. We've all learned something. If this was a movie they'd give her back now. I feel like she's hiding from us."

"It isn't a movie," her mother murmured, patting her back as if she were a baby.

"What are we meant to do now?"

"Just go on, Delia."

"I'm such a fuck-up."

"Who told you that?"

"Amelia."

"Amelia's got a bug up her ass."

"Mother!" Cordelia gave her mother a shocked stare.

"Sorry. I forgot what a little Victorian you are."

"Why are you baking again?"

"Oh, I don't know. It's something to do when I can't sleep. It calms me down. I like knowing something will come out of the oven if I mix it up properly."

"There's eggshells in the brownies."

"I know. I sent home a pound of them with your father to make Sunflower fat and break her perfect white teeth."

"I wish I were dead!" Cordelia wailed, her face buried in her mother's remaining bosom. "I wish I were dead instead of her!"

"Don't be disgusting, Cordelia. Just because you idolized your sister and assumed she had sorted herself out doesn't mean she didn't give us years of misery. I once thought she was a member of that group that kidnapped Patty Hearst, for God's sake. Your sister was far more trouble than you would ever imagine being. It didn't mean we didn't love her, but she said absolutely bone-chilling things to your father. Practically accused him of incest after she was analyzed. And he paid for all of it. And Amelia . . . she's a mess. You might think she's coping, but there's something terribly wrong. Tom and Michael distract her, but she's so angry it's impossible to try and comfort her. Is Ed here?"

"Yes."

"So let's go eat. Is Mexican food okay?"

"I hate Mexican food."

"No you don't. Really, Cordelia, you have so many imaginary likes and dislikes."

She did hate Mexican food, but it didn't matter. They went to a new restaurant in an old shopping center and giggled at the strolling musicians. Ed was very cheerful and attentive to their mother, which made her two daughters very happy. They drank several pitchers of fruity sangria and sang some choruses with the band.

Later that night Cordelia lay awake listening to the muffled sound of her mother crying and a voice softly saying, "Now, now," over and over again.

CHAPTER

19

C ORDELIA?"
"Yes?"

"This is Dervla. We'd like you to be our spokesperson for Marriott."

"Oh. Oh my gosh. Thanks very much."

"Thank *you*. It was a terrific reading. There's lots of paperwork and the shooting schedule to go over. Can you come in next week?"

"Absolutely."

"We'll expect you Wednesday morning. Tenish. Bring your agent if you have one. It's a standard contract."

"Fine."

"See you Wednesday, then."

She called Philip. "I got the Marriott job!"

"What'd I tell you?"

"That I'd get it."

"So I was right."

"It's a very important account."

"You can handle it."

"I hope so."

"No problemo, daffodil! When do you sign everything?"

"Wednesday."

"Perfect. We'll fly to Eleuthera Thursday morning. Get the two-thirty flight from Miami. Okay?"

"I'll miss my acting class. I have a scene up."

"Fuck your class! That's for amateurs. You're in the major leagues now, sweetheart. I'll give you a scene to do."

"Philip?"

"Cordelia?"

"Did I get this job because they liked me and think I'm talented or because you pulled strings?"

"Because I pulled strings. . . . Hello?"

"I'm still here."

"Hey, isn't that the fucking business? Didn't you tell me only two percent of the actors in New York were working? You wanna hang out with those ninety-eight percent losers, be my guest! You want to end up like your old man?"

"I don't know."

"It's called increasing your odds. So we're on for Thursday?"

"I guess so."

"You'll love this place. The sand's pink. Buy a string bikini or something spandex. A spandex string bikini."

"I have a tank suit."

"A fuchsia spandex string bikini I can take off with my teeth."

"Yeah, right."

"I'm serious!"

"Goodbye."

"Good night, Miss Marriott."

"What do you mean, we have to postpone our scene?" Maxine was incredulous.

"I'm going out of town."

"Where?"

"Eleuthera. The Bahamas. It's one of the Out islands."

"An Out island? It sounds like a fucking female reproductive organ! Who's taking you there?"

162

"Philip."

"Oh. Has Montauk become passé? Too accessible?"

"Look, he just got me the Marriott job—"

"You got that?"

"Yes."

"Congratulations. So now you have to suck his dick for four days?"

"Maxine . . ."

"We've been working on this scene for nearly two months. If we cancel now, I don't know when we'll get another time slot. You are being a lousy friend, Cordelia. I'm very disappointed in you."

"I'm sorry."

"Yeah, well, women have to stick together in this business. You can't always be the one everyone helps."

"I know."

"You telling babycakes about this?"

"Who?"

"What's-his-face. The man without a country. Harrison."

"Maybe."

"Can I fuck him, or does he hate fat women too?"

"Maxine . . ."

"Call me when you get back."

"I love you."

"The fuck you do. You're unreliable."

"Bye. Stay on your diet."

"Use sun block. Bitch."

She thought she should call Harrison and tell him she was going away. Then she thought she should simply leave without explaining her whereabouts, so he'd understand she was a creature of impulse. But how would she phrase an answering-machine message to imply a trip to the beach? It would annoy her other friends.

"Hello?" A woman's voice answered Harrison's phone. It was low and slightly nasal. Cordelia couldn't identify the accent. Private school.

"Is he there?" Cordelia used a slightly British tone.

"Who's calling, please?"

"A friend. Who's this?" Now her voice became very English. Clipped and snotty.

"A friend. Hold on."

"Hullo?" Harrison sounded sleepy.

"Who is that bitch?"

"Delia?"

"Who is she?"

"Why are you speaking with an English accent?"

"I'm not. Who is that girl?"

"A friend." Harrison laughed awkwardly.

"She told me that already. You don't have any friends. I never used to answer your phone. It's very sleazy."

"I didn't have a phone in Dublin."

"If you had I wouldn't have answered it," Cordelia snapped.

"Ha! Yes you would have! You'd have picked it up and stopped any female from ever ringing me again."

"Oh, shut up."

"How are you?"

"All right. I'm going away for a few days."

"Home to see mum?"

"No. To the Bahamas." There was a long pause.

"With the lizard?"

"Yes. The lizard's gotten me another national commercial. I'm the spokesperson for Marriott hotels."

"So now you give him head?"

"What is this? Every time I mention this person it's like I give blow jobs for a living! All anyone talks about is my sucking his cock!" Cordelia tried to untangle the phone cord and knocked over a plant. "Fuck!"

"Cordelia . . ."

"First Maxine. Now you! I'm not a whore! I really like this man. He's been very kind to me. He enjoys my company. It's not his fault he's rich."

"Would you like him if he wasn't?"

"How should I know? He is."

"You love me, and I'm not rich."

"I don't love you, Harrison."

"Yes you do. You loved me from the moment you saw me. It was written all over your face. 'I adore that man,' said your eyes. That's why I allowed you to pick me up. You've always loved me. You were born in love with me. I simply had to appear, to unlock your secret passion."

"Are you high?"

"Delia . . ."

"Are you saying all these moronic things in front of that bitch?"

"She's in the bathroom."

"You're snorting cocaine. I can hear it in your voice. So I'm hanging up. And I didn't pick you up, you conceited jerk!"

"So be it. I think you are the most wonderful human being in the entire universe."

"Oh, shut up, Harrison!"

"Have a nice time in Barbados, not giving head."

"It's the Bahamas, and I will if I want to!"

"God, you are a funny woman! I'm sorry I said you loved me."

"Do you love me?"

"Absolutely. Yes, Delia, I do."

"Fuck you."

"Goodbye, my angel."

"Why did you say that?"

"I couldn't help myself. I'm sorry."

"It isn't fair. Who is that woman?"

"Nobody."

"Do you love her?"

"No."

"Do you love me?"

"Yes."

"I don't believe you."

"Stay in New York, Cordelia." Harrison's voice was suddenly serious.

"I can't."

"Don't go away with him. He's dangerous."

"It's not possible. . . . Anyway, you don't understand."

"I do. I see you drifting out to sea, sunshine. I see you going under the water."

"You're high, Harrison."

"I know what you're thinking about."

"Stop it!"

"I came here to save you."

"Goodbye."

"Don't go, Delia."

"Goodbye."

In the bar at the Miami airport she drank three zombies on an empty stomach, washing them down with champagne and caviar. The room began to spin while Philip heaped the caviar on small pieces of toast and put them in her mouth. She was uncomfortably full of Beluga, but she forced down another glass of champagne and found herself drunk enough to forget about Harrison.

The airplane was a single-engine turboprop, and their crossing was very turbulent. Cordelia threw up in the small space between the cockpit and the passengers. The stewardesses kept giving Philip sympathetic pats, as if he were the one who was ill.

CHAPTER

20

"F EEL BETTER?" HE WAS SITTING ON THE PORCH, WEARING pleated white linen pants, an open-necked pale-blue oxford shirt, and espadrilles. The villa was up on a cliff, overlooking a small private beach. On the taxi ride from the airport, Cordelia had barely managed to remain in the cab. She hung out the window like an overheated dog, trying to take in enough oxygen to offset the uneasy feeling she had in her stomach. Little children ran out of their houses and waved at her, while she smiled weakly, sickly, in return. The poverty was jarring. Most of the homes were built of tin and had corrugated roofs. Large families lived in a single room. The children's parents followed them outside but did not wave, standing with their arms folded in front of them, their faces set in grim lines.

When the cab was halfway across a very narrow, unwalled causeway, their driver stopped. "This is the famous glass wall," he said, gesturing toward the water on each side of the road. "Here is where the two oceans meet, the Atlantic and the Caribbean."

On the Atlantic side, the water was rough and gray, and large waves crashed against the concrete embankment. The other surface was as flat and smooth as glass, an impossibly beautiful greenish blue. She hung out of the window and thought it would not be such a difficult thing to jump. Their driver smiled at her in the rearview mirror.

"Feel better, miss?"

"Yes, thanks," she said politely, not looking at Philip, who was reading a pamphlet on water pumps, completely indifferent to her health and the view.

They were staying in a sort of compound that was also a resort. Evidently it had just been built, as a tractor was parked by a newly poured swimming pool, and the roads leading to the other villas were mostly unpaved. They had the largest villa. Made of wood, stone, and glass, it had soaring ceilings, skylights, and picture windows that faced the ocean. The living room was dominated by a large leather couch, which flanked a two-story stone fireplace. The furniture was minimal but very expensive. Oriental rugs were scattered across the polished stone floors. The beds were brass, and there were animal furs thrown over several low-slung chairs. The kitchen appliances were all German, new, and very high-tech.

Weak from throwing up, Cordelia fell asleep on the double bed in the master bedroom. She woke up in the dark with a hangover, completely disoriented. She had no idea where she was or with whom. She felt paralyzed. The room was pitch black, and she was naked, flat on her back. Finally, she wrapped a sheet around her body and tiptoed out to the patio. The air was scented by the purple flowers that seemed to grow everywhere. A house on the far side of the opposite hill had a light on, but otherwise she could see no sign of human life. The sky was pinpointed by thousands of brilliant stars. Philip was sitting in a rocking chair, smoking a cigar.

"Feel better?"

"I'm sorry I got sick."

"As long as you feel better. There's some food in the kitchen."

"No, thanks. I think I'm allergic to caviar."

"Champagne, maybe. What's that dress?"

"It's the sheet from the bed. I didn't see my clothes." She had tied the bed sheet tightly across her breasts and draped it over her hips; her shoulders were bare.

"That's a sheet? Christ! You look good in anything."

"Philip?"

"Yeah, kid?"

"What's going to happen to us?"

"When?"

"After this trip."

"I don't get you."

"After this trip. After we get back. What—" She stopped. The question remained unformed. In fact, the answer didn't really interest her. She balanced lightly on the balls of her feet, weight forward, ready to run. She was free to do anything she wanted. The question was silly.

"We keep having a good time, honey. That's what we do next."

Philip reached out and tugged, and the sheet fell at her feet. He stepped back and stared at her outlined in the doorway, naked, her arms at her sides. The air was cool, and she felt the roughness of the concrete against her bare feet. They were both silent. Philip smoked his cigar, while Cordelia allowed her vision to lose its focus. She saw nothing directly in front of her, just the hills across the way and beyond that a mysterious blinking light.

He circled her, brushing the hair away from her neck, kissing the nape and her shoulders, licking the length of her spine. Taking her indoors, he pushed her down on all fours and held her from behind, his hands cradling her breasts, his cheek against her naked back. The fabric of his shirt rubbed against her bare skin. He raised himself up to remove his clothes, while she stretched forward to allow him to enter her, the thrust unexpectedly hard. With her cheek pressed into the rug, her mind emptied and she felt herself being manipulated like a puppet. She moved as he commanded, allowing him to twist her back and forth. When he turned her around and tried to kiss her, she averted her face.

"Open your eyes," he whispered, but Cordelia did not change the blankness of her expression, the position of the lids. He sank his teeth into the exposed area of her neck, his fingers dug deep into her hips. The noise of the insects in the garden was deafening.

She dreamed of her sister's murder. This time it began like a horror movie, a film that Cordelia was directing. A woman slowly walked down a deserted street. The houses were all dark and shuttered. Shadowy figures appeared from dark alleyways. The woman began to run, but she could not escape the men who were stalking her. The town was designed like a maze. The camera angle was from above, and you could see that all the streets were blocked. She could not escape. Knives glinted in the faint light of a neon sign. The woman was stalked like an animal and cornered, then the circle closed around her. Cordelia heard the woman scream, saw her face, saw Cynthia attempt to struggle, but then she froze, and bowing her head, her hands crossed in front of her, she accepted her death. Cordelia woke up in the bed next to Philip, soaked with sweat and clawing at the air.

By the refrigerator's light she saw a block of cheese and a mango. She ate the mango and a chunk of cheese she broke off. Standing on the porch, she saw that the moon was fuller and brighter than the one that shone over Manhattan. The stars were close enough to touch. The sky was enormous. She wondered if her sister had a star completely to herself or whether she had to share her space. The mango was very sweet. She wondered if her sister could see her standing there naked on this strange island with mango juice running down her chin.

"Cynthia," she whispered, focusing on the brightest and most lively star. "You should come back."

She went inside and found a pad of paper and tried to make some sort of list of things to do when she returned to New York. The only complete sentence was GET HELP. The rest of it made no sense. She could see Philip's body outlined underneath the linen sheet. His arm was flung across the space she had left. Outside, the sun was already beginning to heat up the earth. The sunrise had been very slow and dramatic. She saw there were fresh bruises on her arms. She made coffee.

They spent the morning driving from one empty lot to another, each of them inhabited by a seemingly wild group of farm animals left to graze at will. Philip met with two men at the second lot. One of them was a light-skinned black with an enormous belly; the other was very dark and thin. Both were dressed in beautifully cut Italian linen suits, with pinkie rings and jeweled tie clasps. They had driven up in an enormous black Mercedes-Benz piloted by a man in uniform. They nodded politely to Cordelia when she was introduced by Philip as his "companion," but then all three men ignored her while they strolled around the boundaries of land, stopping occasionally to examine the soil. The men spoke French with Philip, and she could understand enough to tell that the subject was the availability of fresh water.

After visiting several more parcels of land, Cordelia and Philip returned to the villa, changed into their bathing suits, and went down to the beach. There was a restaurant and outside it a pile of snorkel gear, which was meant to be used by the villa's guests. The tropical fish were almost friendly. Schools of tiny tiger-striped creatures brushed softly against her legs as she swam just below the surface of the water.

They lay side by side on chaise longues, their skin glistening with oil in the hot sun. The light reflected off the sand, and Philip's face was not flattered by its direct glare. She thought he looked as old as her father. From her lowered lids she saw her body, the ribs sticking out slightly, the stomach no longer gently curved but almost concave. When had she lost all that weight? Philip leaned over to touch her hipbone, which jutted out sharply.

"Stay thin," he whispered. "Always stay this thin."

She nodded drowsily and wondered how he would react if she suggested he stop aging. His hand rested heavily on her leg, and she shifted to make him remove it. She took off her top and rubbed oil into her breasts, aware that Philip was watching, his eyes hooded like a snake's. The sun seemed to pour over her like warm water. She stretched and began to fall asleep. The heat gradually burned away the cold fear of the previous night.

They ate dinner at the restaurant next to the beach. The room was nearly empty. Several local fishermen were drinking at the bar, and one man was quietly playing a guitar in the corner. There were fishing nets strung across the ceiling; brightly colored ornaments dangled from them. They had dressed for dinner. Cordelia wore a thin-strapped lilac silk dress, which was soft against her sunburned skin. Philip was wearing black jeans and a silk sweater the color of the sea. His skin was already very brown. The food was simple: fish caught that afternoon, roasted potatoes, and salad. For dessert they were presented with a split pineapple filled with fresh fruit and a bowlful of whipped heavy cream. When she'd finished her fruit, Cordelia began to eat the cream by dipping her spoon into her coffee and then back in the bowl. Philip called their waiter over and had the cream removed.

"Bastard," she muttered.

"Oink, oink," he replied.

Just as they ran out of things to talk about, the two men from the building site arrived. Philip was visibly relieved to see them and ordered a round of cognac. As they discussed the benefits of above-ground irrigation, Cordelia wandered out to the veranda to look at the sky. She picked a pink flower and stuck it behind one ear. The air was sweet and tasted faintly of salt. There was the same buzz of insects, but it was less intense. She wondered if Harrison was making love to the woman who had answered his phone. She could imagine him standing above her, naked, bending over to caress her body. She could trace the muscles of his back with her fingers and knew the exact length of his spine.

"Take me back to Africa," she muttered. "Help me."

"Who are you talking to?" Philip emerged from the shadows, holding two snifters of brandy.

"Nobody."

"Do you like it here, Cordelia?"

"Yes. It's beautiful. Thanks for bringing me."

"I'm building a house."

"I suspected that."

"We have water problems."

"Are those men plumbers?"

Philip laughed. "Not exactly. They represent the family that owns every business on the island."

"Why don't they pay their workers? It looks like those people can't feed their children. Can you pay them more? The ones that build your house?"

Philip shrugged. "Mustn't upset the local economy," he said, patting her on the shoulder. "Would you like to live here?"

"I live in New York."

"You could live in both places."

"That would be nice. An island paradise."

"Are you happy here?"

"I don't know." She felt that something strange was going on. Her skin was too tight.

"You've been very distant lately. You have secrets."

"Not really."

"Are you fucking that South African, Cordelia?"

"No."

"But you love him?"

She hesitated. Perhaps that was the truth. She thought of Harrison, and she wondered if Philip would really care if she loved another man.

"No, I don't love him. He's just miserable. And I'm not fucking anyone but you." As she spoke she noticed his clenched fists relaxing. Had she answered differently, he would have hit her.

"No one can take care of you as I shall," he whispered into her ear, pushing her into the shadows by the wall so that he could slip down the straps of her dress and caress her breasts. He pressed against her hard, sucking on her nipple. She could see, from the corner of her eye, the two men arguing. Philip's hands dug into the sides of her hips, the silk wrinkling under his fingers. She saw that Philip's hair was turning gray. She remembered a fairy tale she'd read as a child, "The Snow Queen." She thought it would be nice to live where everything was frozen, cold and clean. Philip dropped to his knees, his face pressed into her stomach, his hands still holding her breasts. She wondered if he'd been taking drugs. He was muttering.

"I'll protect you," he said. "I'll keep you safe."

She patted him on the head and tried to remember why the children had needed the Snow Queen's magic.

When they got back to the villa, Philip began making calls, while Cordelia sat on the porch reading a script. The air was cool, and the stars were so distinct they looked as if they were made of tinfoil hung by giants. Harrison had told her the sky in Africa was impossible to describe, that the night was rarely dark because the moon was so close to that earth.

I live in a city full of fog, Cordelia thought. *Things are concealed by the atmosphere.* But she didn't think she could survive anywhere else. Clarity would probably only underscore the pain. It was easier to miss lost beauty. She went inside, undressed, and got into bed. She could hear Philip in the living room, his voice low but filled with intensity. He was speaking French.

In her dream they were riding gazelles. Cynthia and herself on the backs of these improbably exquisite creatures. The land they crossed was wild. Africa. Lions and zebras and panthers watched as they passed, but they did not attack. They lived together as a family: Cynthia, Harrison, Sam, and Cordelia. It was unclear as to who was in love with whom, but they were very happy and busy, and they made lovely fruit salads, and Sam had two mothers and a father. The last part was terrible. A drought of some sort. Dried bones. A shrouded corpse. Cordelia alone, down on her knees in the dust. Her mouth open in a scream. Everything was covered with dust. The trees were all dead.

She woke with a start and discovered Philip sitting up in bed, smoking and looking at her. The terror of the dream was still with her.

"What do you want?" she cried. "What did I do?"

Philip gently pulled her head into his lap and stroked her hair off her forehead.

"Nothing's wrong, honey. You had some kind of nightmare."

"Everyone died. That's all. Did I make noises?"

"You've been crying, sweetness. I've never seen anything like this, tears coming from beneath closed eyes. It's heartbreaking.

You whimpering in your sleep like a baby trying to wake up or sleep. Like a frustrated baby."

"I'm sorry."

"Don't be sorry. You really get to me, kid. You make me think."

"About what?"

"Crazy stuff. Like getting married again. What it would be like being in bed with you every night." He pushed away the sheets and stroked her naked back.

"I love this body, baby! No woman's body ever gave me so much pleasure. It's too much sometimes."

She felt the gentle pressure of his hand against her skull, felt him growing hard against her cheek. He pushed harder so she would take him in her mouth.

"You really make me melt," he muttered as she began to suck him. His hands were buried in her hair, tugging gently at the roots.

When he began to shake and moan, she pulled up on all fours, still holding him in her mouth, pushing him back so she was the one in charge. After a long time she allowed him to pull out, and she came down on his hardness. She saw that he was utterly helpless, and she felt that she hated him for what he had done to her but that it was not really important. Each time he reached up to pull her closer she pushed his hands away, and she rode him as if he were some sort of machine. Gradually she forgot that he was there at all, and her pleasure was pure and very cold. She touched herself, and when he came she watched his face and thought how easy it was to please him. He fell asleep immediately, while she slipped out of the house and ran down to the beach, to swim back and forth in the silver river the moon had created. She felt the sea's creatures brush against her ankles, and she thought it was probably better that she go back to New York.

CHAPTER

21

THE FIRST PERSON SHE SAW ON HER ARRIVAL AT NEWARK Airport was the yoga instructor from her birthday. He was perched on a large pile of expensive leather luggage, and dressed in a fashionably cut gray wool suit. He seemed oddly out of place. Cordelia thought she might have mixed him up with someone else, but he waved at her.

"I'm going to Brussels for one hundred ninety-nine dollars," he said. "Wanna come?"

"What about your classes?"

"I got a substitute. Life's short, Cordelia—that's your name, right? I remembered because it's my favorite play—except you die. . . . Anyway, life's short and very precious. You look nice and tan, but your eyes are still full of death. You aren't happy?"

"Well, no. Maybe not."

"You should come to Belgium with me. I'll introduce you to some great healers."

"I can't. Thanks for asking."

"Take care, little lamb. Try some affirmations. Tell yourself you deserve to live."

"Bye."

She boarded the bus to Manhattan, feeling very disoriented. Philip was staying in Eleuthera for a few more days to resolve his problems with the water company. After her swim she had gone back to sleep, but she woke up with him already on top of her, about to come inside. She opened her mouth to tell him that she was not ready, and he put his hand over her face and continued to push. She bit his hand, hard. He pulled back to hit her, but she jumped from the bed, pulled down her nightgown and went into the living room. She took a blanket from the linen closet and curled up on the couch to sleep.

Philip appeared in the doorway. "Come back to bed," he said quietly. "I didn't mean to hurt you."

"It's not the first time."

"I'm sorry."

"Why are you so angry?" she asked.

"I was born that way. My mother swore I kicked her so hard she was afraid she was giving birth to a wild animal."

"You can't keep hitting me like this."

"I thought you liked it." His face was hidden in the shadow of the doorway.

"No! You like it. It's just because I can't feel anything. I feel you hurting me, and it seems better than . . . nothing. It's a sign I'm still alive. But it has to stop."

"No problem. I thought it turned you on."

"No!"

"So I'll stop. I want to make you happy."

Philip crossed to the couch and knelt by her feet. He took one of her hands and kissed each knuckle.

"I'm sick of the greedy bitches I've been getting involved with. You're different, Cordelia. So clear. Like an unflawed diamond. I can stare straight into your core, and there's nothing dark there. You show what you feel. Your face is like reading Dr. Seuss. You'd never lie to me, would you?"

Despite the gentleness of his tone she felt fear. Her hand trembled in his hold.

"No."

"Good. I'd know if you were lying, and then I'd really get angry, and I might hurt you for the wrong reasons."

"Philip . . ."

"What?"

"You can't hurt me. It's not fair. After what he did to my sister . . . It's not fair to my family." She had begun to cry.

He sat down next to her and took her in his arms. "Shh, shh, baby. Don't cry. I'm going to take care of you. Always."

He carried her back to bed, and they fell asleep together, wrapped around each other's bodies like kittens.

Her apartment was smaller and shabbier than she remembered. For a moment she almost turned off the light and left again. It would be easy to pretend she had never returned, to take the subway out to the airport and buy a ticket for a flight to Dublin. She'd call her friends from the bus station, or better yet, she would simply arrive at their flat and let them take care of her. She would tell them about Harrison, and they would remind her of how badly the affair had ended. She would describe Cynthia's murder and let them help her feel how deeply she'd been injured. They would put her to bed and feed her homemade bread, and she would sleep very late in a room with a fireplace and the soft light of an Irish afternoon filtering through the curtains. She would borrow a bicycle and go down to the sea, stand by Joyce's tower in Sandycove and try to figure out her next move.

"Cordelia, it's your mother. I forgot you went away this weekend, which is exactly what you should have done except I wasn't sure where you went. Jamaica? Anyway, I just called to tell you how proud I am of you and how much I love you. Aren't you glad you aren't home? Anyway, I'm feeling a little wobbly from this chemo cycle but very well otherwise. Call me when you get back, little bear. Also, change your message. You sound sort of bored."

"Delia, I'm sick and tired of this stupid fucking machine and this stupid game you're playing. It's possible for us to talk to each other. Oh, this is Harrison. Have a nice day."

"Delia, it's Maxine. It's okay about the scene. We got someone's cancellation next week. I'm sorry I was so mean. It's just that I think that guy's a scumbag and I saw the bruises on your shoulders when I stayed over and I'm scared for you. There. I said it. No one should be hurting you like that. Call me."

"Ms. Cavanagh, my name is Sasha Trelawn. We have something in common. Philip. I think we'd better talk. My office number is 822-3489. Please call me after your return from Eleuthera."

Cordelia played the last message twice. How did this woman know where she'd been?

Sasha Trelawn's office was at Seventy-ninth and Park. The sign outside said S. TRELAWN, M.D., PSYCHOTHERAPY. The waiting room was empty, carpeted in thick charcoal gray with vaguely familiar leather furniture. It was the same design as the furniture in Montauk. Cordelia smoked a cigarette and ground the ashes under her heel. She put the butt in the large plant, which appeared to be some sort of cactus. She slipped the new copy of European *Vogue* into her bag. Her anger was unexpected.

"Ms. Cavanagh."

"Call me Cordelia."

Sasha Trelawn was the woman who had been sitting with Philip the night Cordelia walked home alone from the movies. Her haircut was still extremely geometrical, although the pyramid was shorter. Her fingernails were very long, coral colored, and nearly every finger wore a large ring.

"Dr. Trelawn, I guess." Cordelia stood, peeling off her pink mohair mitten to extend her hand. It was not taken but looked at. She felt poorly manicured.

"Sasha. I thought we'd eat lunch in my office. It's private, and we'll have time to talk."

Cordelia nodded mutely. This woman frightened her. She had the look of someone who could focus her concentration elsewhere while the guillotine whistled through the air. She had a body that seemed designed for her clothes but could not be described as beautiful. She was wearing a beige cashmere dress, Maud Frizon pumps, and a heavy gold necklace. Cordelia had pulled on a shrunken sweater that was part of Cynthia's eighth-grade parochial school uniform, an old denim skirt, black wool tights, and high-top sneakers. It had been meant as an act of defiant nonchalance, but now she felt merely pathetic.

The office was large, with windows facing Park Avenue. A small table was set with linen napkins, silver, and large crystal plates. A platter contained a carefully arranged lobster salad. Cordelia settled awkwardly on the couch while Sasha sat in a chair facing her. Nervously, Cordelia reached out to take a piece of lobster meat, but she quickly withdrew her hands and began to play with her fingers. Sasha was watching her with great interest.

She knows I'm crazy, Cordelia thought, trying to relax. *Perhaps she'll have me committed, and I'll die in Payne Whitney.*

"This is incredible," she said finally, longing to break the silence, sitting back and really breathing for the first time since she'd entered the room.

"My office?"

"Uh, well, no. I mean the food and everything."

"Doesn't Philip feed you?"

"What?"

"From what I hear, he thinks *you're* incredible. . . . Usually he's very hospitable."

"I guess you know him."

"Have some salad, Cordelia." Sasha filled a plate with salad and broke off a huge chunk of bread.

Cordelia put the plate on her lap. "Thank you."

"What do you mean by 'know'?" Sasha was delicately holding a piece of celery. Her rings reflected the light.

"Well, do you—I mean, are you his other lover or something?"

"Do we fuck? Sometimes. That's not the point. I don't really mind his being unfaithful. It's the other stuff."

"Other stuff?"

"His taking you to Montauk. Eleuthera. The amount of money he's spending. The jobs he's getting you through my friends."

"*Your* friends?"

"Philip doesn't have any. He's not a very nice person."

"Oh." Cordelia found herself eating the lobster salad with a great deal of pleasure. Suddenly she was starving.

"Are you his girlfriend?"

"No." Sasha paused and lit a cigarette. "I'm Philip's wife. We've been married for fifteen years, and we have two children."

"No you don't." She said it stupidly, heavily, like a child who refuses to believe something she knows to be true. "Philip's divorced, and he doesn't have any children."

"He lied." She waved her hand toward a silver-framed photograph on her desk, but Cordelia didn't look. "There we are. A perfectly balanced family. The nights he's not with you on the Upper West Side, he's in Stamford with Annie and Matthew."

"Annie and Matthew?"

"His children. Nine and three. We aren't divorced. Philip's a Catholic. He doesn't believe in divorce. Anyway, we love each other, I think. In a way."

Cordelia put a piece of lobster in her mouth. It was a reflex. She put down her fork and noticed the extraordinary beadwork on Sasha's pump.

"So you knew nothing about me?" Sasha was so slender it was possible to count her bones.

Cordelia sucked in her stomach. "No. He said he was divorced. No children."

Sasha nodded. "Incredible. He denies them while he has fantasies about being the ideal father." She sighed.

Cordelia couldn't think of anything to say. She ate a Greek olive and winced at its saltiness.

"You don't strike me as the sort of person who'd sleep with someone else's husband. I know about your sister. Philip told me something about you. He actually felt this extraordinary amount of compassion for your family. I think we gave money to that foundation they set up in your sister's memory. He grieved for you. It seemed so . . . incredibly nonsexual. But I saw you that night we were eating dinner, and then I knew it had to be something else. He was sort of vibrating next to me, and you looked much too pretty to be quite so pathetic. I'm sorry this happened."

There was really nothing more to say. They shook hands. Cordelia observed how sharply Sasha's nails were filed and wondered how she avoided hurting the children. Annie probably thought her father didn't like her very much since he was so rarely home. Children are victims of adult evil, she thought.

On Park Avenue she raised her hand and was soon headed home in a taxi. She considered going up to his office and hurling something through the plate-glass window, but she might kill someone on the sidewalk, and windows could be easily replaced.

She stopped the cab too late and found herself standing in front of Juilliard, an icy wind blowing in her face. She had wanted to apply to the theater school there but had been too afraid to audition; her father had told her that she didn't stand a chance without connections and that he considered it a waste of money. For nearly a year she labored over a scene from *The Merchant of Venice*, which she couldn't bring herself to perform. After a woman from her acting class with very little talent was accepted into the program, Cordelia had called Cynthia, choking with anger and jealousy.

Her sister had sighed. "When will you give up, Delia? He doesn't want you to have the kind of life you deserve. He wants you to have the kind of life he can accept, one that doesn't threaten him."

"Doesn't he want us to be happy?"

There was a pause. "No, honey. Not really. But it doesn't mean he doesn't love you. He's just an asshole. He left before you found that out. He left while you still thought he could turn bananas into bunny rabbits."

"What should I do?"

"Forget about Juilliard for now. Get some acting work. Go next year if you still want to. Mom can help you pay. I'll tell her it's a good idea. And stop asking him for approval!"

Cynthia had always transformed defeat into something else. When Cordelia was pudgy and unpopular in seventh grade, Cynthia had taken her to a Who concert and shown her how to wear eye liner. She was the only one who made horrible events appear to be funny and unimportant. Her love had been unconditional.

The waves of missing her hit Cordelia full in the face, filling her lungs with the acrid taste of loss. She sat down in front of a Lincoln Center poster advertising Zubin Mehta conducting the Philharmonic, and she wailed. Musicians hurrying to their mid-afternoon rehearsals averted their faces as they walked past her. They would think she was some pathetic reject from Juilliard. She could not stop crying. Eleven blocks from home, and it was impossible for her to move.

"I hate you!" she wailed. "I hate you, you lying motherfucker!"

CHAPTER

22

SHE HAD SLEPT FOR TWO DAYS, WAKING TO DRINK WATER and use the bathroom but then returning to the silent darkness of her room, her cave, a place she found comforting for its familiarity. The phone was unplugged. At some point someone rang her buzzer. She did not know if it was day or night. Eventually the person left. She thought she heard her name being called, but she might have imagined it. She slept heavily, without dreams. Her body was empty of food, but the hunger pains were not very intense.

On Wednesday she signed the contract for the commercial. On Thursday her alarm went off at six. She started the coffee machine and then ran a bath, mixing oil in the water. A tray with a cucumber face mask, hair conditioner, and a razor was hung across the tub. She applied the mask while soaking in the water and then washed her hair, leaving on the deep conditioner. She shaved her legs and plucked any stray hairs she spotted and then took a long, hot shower, followed by a cold rinse. The silk shirt felt smooth and cool against her skin. The suit had been worn to an interview she had with NBC News when she had decided to try and get a "real" job. It was gray, the jacket cut like a man's tuxedo, with padded shoulders and the skirt pleated.

She looked hip, sexy, and corporate: the perfect spokesperson for a hotel trying to encourage young female executives to give them their business. Her hair and makeup would be styled on the set.

She left her apartment like a thief, carefully checking the street to be sure no one was waiting to grab her. She walked quickly but evenly, not wanting to draw the attention of strangers. Her control was a complete facade. If anyone had asked her a question she would have begun to scream.

The set was crowded. Cordelia was hurried off to makeup and given the opportunity to review her lines, which had been changed slightly from her script, while her hair was curled, straightened, put up, taken down, and argued over. Finally, they decided to brush back the crown and let the rest curl softly around her shoulders.

The third take was perfect. Her voice was pleasant, nicely modulated yet strong enough to project authority. She was meant to be a young woman with a future of gold American Express cards, and it was important that her demands were met, her needs satisfied. Automatically, she injected a subliminal warmth into her demeanor so that she did not become the sort of yuppie that one must hate. She addressed the camera without hesitation, but her straightforwardness was not challenging. Somehow she also had to indicate vulnerability. It was crucial that her eyes convey honesty and integrity and, for all the men watching, some sort of promise that underneath her wool suit there was a body barely concealed by satin and lace. At that moment she was completely fascinated by her own duplicity. Rage had given her the power to manipulate. The technicians applauded. Dervla hugged her.

"Very good," she said. "How do you feel?"

"Fine. Thank you."

"You hit every word exactly right. Something was new I can't put my finger on. I can't tell you how thrilled we are. I think it's time to quit your day job, Cordelia."

Dervla's lips kept moving, and she appeared to be extremely happy. Cordelia could only hear a dull sort of pounding, a roar that sounded like what you hear when you press a conch shell against your ear, the sound of surf crashing against the sand.

"Excuse me," she said loudly. "The ladies' room?"

It didn't occur to her that she needed to throw up until she was pushing open the bathroom door and the vomit filled her mouth. Doubled over, she reached the toilet just in time, and when her stomach stopped contracting she felt her hand flat against her belly and there was something different. Her body was changed. She looked into the mirror, and behind the makeup she saw how tired she looked and that she was pregnant. As the idea formed in her mind it became, instantly, a fact.

Dervla asked her if she had an agent.

"It's a matter of letting someone else sell your image so you can concentrate on your craft. Also, you need a friend reading your contracts." Dervla threw an arm across Cordelia's shoulders.

Cordelia didn't want to be touched. After a moment, she dropped her purse and was able to move away.

She had been pregnant once before. In college. It was during the period she'd slept with too many men, after Seth left for Colorado. Up until the time of the actual abortion, her denial of the fact that she was carrying a child was complete. Seconds before the anesthetic took hold, she grabbed the male nurse's hand and said, "Tell someone to come and get me. I'm not old enough to have a baby." She had called Seth's house the night before, after drinking a bottle of wine. It was very late. Seth answered the phone.

"I'm pregnant," she whispered. "Oh, God, I'm so sorry I didn't come with you."

"Cordelia?"

"Yes. Oh, Seth. Oh, God, did we really love each other?"

"Delia . . ."

"Just tell me. I'm afraid I dreamed it."

"Yes."

"Was I a nice person?"

"You were the most beautiful woman I ever saw in my life."

"No. You left me. I couldn't have been that beautiful."

"Babe . . ."

"I'm sorry I did this. I'm not really pregnant. I just wanted to upset you." She fell asleep with the phone against her ear.

She stopped at the corner drugstore to buy some syrup of ipecac. The pharmacist frowned at her.

"You a bulimic?" he inquired bluntly.

"No," Cordelia said, putting down her money.

"Someone get poisoned?"

"Maybe," she snapped. "Maybe my baby's sick."

Before she took off her coat, she drank half the bottle. Gagging, she followed it with half a glass of straight vodka. Her stomach lurched, contracted, and then emptied into the sink of the bathroom. She ran the water and then got under the shower, sitting in the tub, too weak to stand. Finally, she staggered into her room and lay down on the bed, nauseous, in pain, cold, and still pregnant.

She woke up to the sound of someone turning the key in her lock. The phone was next to her bed, but she thought it might not be such a bad thing to let someone bash her brains out. It was dark. The hall light was switched on, and she saw a tall figure blocking the door.

"She's in here. She seems all right. Thank you very much."

"Let me know if you need a doctor." It was the landlord's sister. "Or a priest."

"Fuck priests," Cordelia muttered, hunching the covers over her head.

"Cordelia?" Harrison leaned over the bed. His face was filled with concern.

"What?"

"Are you all right?"

"Why have you done this?"

"No one knew where you were. You missed work. You haven't answered the phone for three days."

"So what?"

"People get hurt in New York."

"People die in New York. Did you expect to find me decomposing, with rats gnawing on my flesh?"

"Not exactly. Are we feeling a trifle melodramatic?"

"I've poisoned myself."

"Are you sick?"

"No. You should leave me alone."

"What's the matter?"

"I can't tell you."

"Why not?"

"Because it's so terrible. I'm evil." She was shivering. Ice was forming on the inside of the windowpanes. Harrison began taking off his clothes. Climbing into bed, he took her in his arms and pressed his warm body against hers.

"Christ almighty! You're freezing!" He rubbed her legs and arms.

"I want to die!"

"You can't bloody die! Stop it!"

"I want to be with my sister!"

"You can't do that! She's not anywhere. There's no heaven, no reunion of nice little girls in white dresses. She isn't waiting for you, Cordelia! She went without you. Your sister's skin has left the bones, the bones are turning to dust. If she has a soul, it's gone somewhere else! There's nothing left."

"She hasn't turned to dust. It isn't possible! You never met her. If you knew my sister you'd understand she couldn't die like this! You didn't know her. I think she's just gone off somewhere, and if we give up on her, when she comes back it will be terrible. She'll think we didn't love her."

"But you were there. You saw her body, Cordelia. She was dead, darling."

"It was a mistake."

"Why are you doing this to yourself?"

"He's married. To a fucking shrink! I had lunch with her. She served me lobster salad and showed me pictures of their children!"

"You didn't know?"

"Of course I didn't!" She squirmed out of his arms, to glare at him.

"How should I know that?"

"I'm not that sort of a person. Can't you remember anything?"

"I remember getting yelled at."

"Oh, get out!"

"No. Tell me more."

"Just leave me alone. You think I knew he was married. That I fucked him to get work."

"Well, it worked, didn't it?"

She slapped him. She hit him hard enough to hurt her hand. She tried to hurt him, but her anger made her ineffectual. When he grabbed her wrists, she bit his shoulder. He let go of her hand and she hit him again. She kicked and she screamed and she tried to scratch his face. When she began to cry, her remaining strength left her body and she lay perfectly still in his arms, while he softly stroked her back and pulled her dirty, wet hair back from her forehead.

"I'm so sorry," she whispered. "I didn't mean to hurt you."

"You didn't. He's scum, Cordelia."

"He loves me."

"He's a lying bastard."

"I need him."

"He wants to see you beaten."

"I don't care. I need him. I miss my sister."

Sleep came like a blow to the head. It was dark when she woke up again. For a moment she thought she was dead, but Harrison seemed to sense her terror, and his arms tightened around her. He was not asleep. As she stretched he rubbed her shoulders. She felt as if she had been very far away.

"Shh," he whispered into her neck. "Gently." The air seemed heavy, and the dark made her feel as if she were on an island or a boat. She put her hand against the place on his face where she had hit him.

"I'm so sorry," she said. "I'm so sorry."

He kissed her hand. "Are you hungry?"

"I don't know."

189

"Baby, I think it would be good for you to eat. You feel so skinny."

She sat up and let the sheet fall away, and both of them saw that her ribs were very prominent and the veins in her legs seemed right next to the surface.

Harrison winced. "Shall we get up?"

"What day is it?"

"The same day. It's just late."

"Harrison . . ."

"Yes?"

"Nothing's the way it was meant to be."

"How's that?"

"When we were together in Dublin, I thought I understood the sort of things that could happen to people. My parents getting divorced, my not getting parts in plays, the way we kept hurting each other. I felt very prepared for real life. Like I was this person with experience. But nothing is like death. To be told that someone you love, someone you are meant to be close to for your whole entire life, is not going to be there, is, in fact, dying . . . When the doctor came out of the emergency room to tell us that Cynthia was going to die, I just assumed he was going to say something positive—like she'd lost lots of blood, but after all she was so young and she was supposed to have this life. . . . I mean, she was my fucking sister! And he took my hands. I tried to take them back because I got this feeling I wanted to run before he said anything, to run and get her and wake her up and tell her it was time for us to leave that fucking place, that I'd take care of her the way she'd always taken care of me. He gave me this really deep, desperately supportive look, and he said, 'Cordelia,' and I wondered how he knew my name. 'Your sister's condition is desperate.' And I wanted to scream at him, 'Then what the hell are you doing out here, you pig! Go back in there and save her!' But I saw from his eyes that she had died already but he was afraid to tell me all at once. I wanted to break his fingers for letting her go, for not making her live, but I smiled instead and I said, 'Thank you, Doctor.' Like a fucking Stepford wife. Everyone began to wail. My mother was crawling around on her hands and knees. The emergency room staff rushed at us with tiny paper cups and Tylenol. Tiny blue Dixie cups. I wanted to ask why the cups were so small. The doctor started giving us prescriptions for sedatives. An orderly tried to speak to me, and I put my hand over his mouth and I said, 'Don't.' I went outside, and I saw from my reflection that I was still smiling, except my face was just stuck. It was so cold out there. I wanted to take my clothes off and scream until something happened, but I just started scraping my knuckles across the bricks until my hands were covered with blood. I wanted to reach the bone. I wanted to feel something."

"Cordelia . . ."

"You asked me what happened. I'm telling you. The entire time this was going on, I had a voice in my head telling me my acting was going to be improved by the suffering, here was a rare opportunity to experience heartbreak. I'm a defective human being, Harrison. I don't love Philip; I don't think I even liked him very much. But when we made love I felt something. When he hit me I could feel I was still alive."

"How often did he hit you?"

"It doesn't matter. . . . Afterward I stopped eating in order to try and end my own life without doing something violent, since suicide is a sin. But it didn't work. Amelia wouldn't leave me alone, and then something would happen. I'd take a dance class, or I'd see something lovely, and I'd stop hurting for a second, and I'd realize I wasn't ready to die yet. It was terrible. The betrayal. How could I leave her alone in that cold place so easily? You can't get used to this. It's so hard every day. He hit me all the time. I thought that was the price I'd pay for protection. I thought he was trying to make me feel safe."

"That's all I want to do."

"I can't let you."

"Why not?"

"I'm not ready. I haven't forgiven you."

"I was wrong."

"Harrison, make me some coffee and then go home."

"How do you know it's not my baby?" He said this with his face pressed against her abdomen.

She forced him to look at her. "What baby?"

"This one." He gently tapped her belly.

"I'm not pregnant."

"Yes you are. You said that was why you tried to kill yourself. You were half asleep."

"I was lying."

"Fuck you, Cordelia!"

"It's not a baby! It's nothing yet."

"When did you have your last period?"

"It's his baby. You don't have anything to do with this. It's his fault. I know when it happened. You don't exist, Harrison. You're a memory, a ghost. I hardly know you."

CHAPTER

23

S HE CLOSED THE DOOR TO THE BATHROOM AND TURNED ON the shower. Sitting with her back against the toilet, her knees drawn up to her chin, she tried to stop the pain in her head. She felt the knobs of her spine against the porcelain, she saw that her knees were knobby, that her once strong, healthy body was beginning to become something else. She felt weak and close to falling asleep again, although she had done nothing but sleep for days.

I'm dying, she thought, tears spilling into her hands. *I'm dying after all*. A chill passed down her body. She recognized the fear and how badly she longed to be alive. *Cynthia must have felt this*, Cordelia thought. *She watched her own blood drain away, her life ebb, and no one came to save her.*

"Oh my God," she sobbed, the shower covering the noise. "My sister! My sister!"

Maybe Harrison would keep death away. He was strong, and he'd promised her that this time things would be different. He wouldn't leave her behind. He wouldn't persuade her to follow him and then go so far ahead she couldn't find the way. It had always been like that in Dublin, Cordelia stumbling after him or waiting for his return. Never sure if he was coming back or staying away. Too proud to ask.

The Dublin Farmers Market was open every Saturday morning. They shopped for vegetables together. Harrison carried a large wicker basket he had bought in Portugal. The Moore Street women thought he was divine.

"Such a fine thing," they said, winking at Cordelia, filling their basket with carrots and parsnips. "A real handful you got there, madam!"

She was trying desperately to be the sort of girl Harrison wanted. His friends were mostly English, all very snobbish and interested in watching cricket, smoking opium, and reading obscure English poets. She bought herself several Laura Ashley dresses and tried to check her Yankee exuberance. She attempted to be coolly detached and affected an air of bored intelligence, until her friend Oona called her a "fucking bitch" because she'd refused to help with a lunchtime theater program.

"You've turned into the most incredible pseudo-Cambridge American git," Oona screamed, her Dublin accent harsh in anger. "Why, in hell's name, would you want to be like one of those stupid cunts?"

On this Saturday she had dressed in old jeans, an ancient NYU T-shirt, and one of Harrison's Aran cardigans, unbuttoned. As they were crossing Grafton Street they ran into one of his former girlfriends, who was dressed for a breakfast party, in velvet and suede boots. She even had a hair ribbon wound carelessly through her auburn curls. Cordelia wandered away from them and pretended to be fascinated by a basket of very dirty turnips. After a few minutes they strolled over—she had taken his arm—and Cordelia nodded and smiled. She knew Cecily from her Irish Literature tutorial. She wasn't very smart. Harrison moved to stand next to Cordelia and put an arm across her shoulder.

"So, Harry," Cecily said, "do come to Cambridge this summer!"

Cordelia felt herself shrinking. She started to move away, but Harrison held her elbow tightly.

"I think Delia and I are going to rent some sort of cottage. In Connemara, most likely."

It was a lie. They had not discussed the future, and she was expecting to go back to America in August. She looked up, and he kissed her nose gently. The Moore Street women looked pleased when Cecily flounced off, hair ribbon flying. Later that evening, the phone in his landlady's flat rang, and Cordelia stood outside the door, her ear pressed against its surface, listening to him discussing Cambridge with someone, and although he said it was unlikely, his tone suggested something else.

When she came out of the bathroom, Harrison was dressed. He had made the bed and opened the window in the bedroom slightly to air it out. He set a plate full of scrambled eggs in front of her.

"I don't care whose child it is." Harrison put a cup of coffee by her plate. "We can live together on the farm in Mozambique and have some sort of life together."

"I have a life."

"This?" Harrison looked around her apartment in disbelief, his eyes resting on her dead plants and the unmade bed. He folded his arms and smiled slightly.

"Yes! This. There's nothing wrong with any of it. It's mine, and I like it. I'm not leaving to go off to some stupid country that you hate just because you're mad at your wife because she stole your son! I don't want someone else's husband! What happens when she decides to come back and you have this person and her child living with you? I can't take care of this thing inside me right now. I know it's not my fault my sister died. All I did was love her, and if I could have died for her, if I could have felt those knives, I—" She stopped speaking and tried to eat.

Harrison reached toward her, but she recoiled, put down her fork, and moved away from the table.

"You don't understand! I don't want anyone to come near me! I think I may be losing my mind. I have to get an abortion, and I can only do one thing at a time. If I could kill that man—that man who made my sister's blood run down the street—I would. But I can't. I'm afraid I'd stand there and be forced to accept the fact that I don't know how to end a human life, and yet my hatred for every living thing is choking me! You have no idea what it feels like to walk around like this. I wish I could be like Antigone and commit some act of infamy for which I'd be executed. Everyone keeps telling me this is temporary, that it's not going to last, but I know it will last forever. My sister will be dead for the rest of my life! And her body . . . what they did to her beautiful body. I wake up wondering if she knew she was dying, and I can't stop thinking how frightened she must have been. Wondering if anyone was there to comfort her. How long it took. How much she hurt. But I can't talk about that, or I'll go crazy. And I can't go to the jungle with you. I don't have anything to offer. I'm going to stay here and make lots of money, hundreds and thousands of dollars. I won't have to go out on the streets or look at other people. I'll build some sort of fortress, and I'll live there. I'll be safe. I can't make you happy anymore, Harrison. I just don't care enough."

"That's not what I expect."

"Oh, yes it is! You came here, you came here to New York hoping I'd make everything better. The way I always tried to in Dublin. You wanted me to help you. I don't know why she left like that. You thought I might still love you and that would take the sting out of your wife's betrayal. When my sister had just been murdered, you turn up here, saying, 'Help me!' You want me to get better so I can take care of you. I don't feel anything for you. I just want to work."

"You can work."

"Harrison, I don't love you anymore. It's all over. Our timing is very bad."

"You don't love him."

"No. But the money is good."

"Delia . . ."

"Never mind. I can't see him anymore anyway. He's got children."

"Cordelia, did you love me in Dublin?"

"Yes. More than anything. I just wanted you to love me. I'm not sure what you call that."

"You made me feel complete. When I was a child I'd always wondered what was wrong with me, what was missing. I thought

God had forgotten to give me something, a heart perhaps. I remember that day we drove down to Wicklow in Sean's car. It was very hot. You took off your dress and went swimming in the lake. I stood there on the bank holding your shoes, stiff as a tree. I felt like some sort of landlocked bear, watching this girl, this druid, my naiad, like a mythical goddess of spring. All I could do was wish I were a different sort of person and wonder what I'd done to deserve such magnificence."

"You thought I was magnificent?"

"Breathtaking. It hurt to look at you. Pink and pearly, gleaming in the sun. I wanted to tell you then, but I was sure I didn't stand a chance with someone who was so willing to stand before me naked. I was terrified."

Cordelia sat back down at the table and drank some coffee. "You threw my dress at me and told me I was a consummate exhibitionist. That I humiliated you. I cried in the car."

Harrison sighed deeply, and they both were silent. He was so like her father, she thought: all the best intentions, no thought for the results of his behavior.

Their family had appeared to be very happy until her father's departure. Three pretty girls, a brilliant and lovely mother, a creative and exciting father. They had been rather poor, but they dressed with flair, and the girls were given lots of loving attention by their energetic parents. Until he had left and their mother, forced to recognize the truth of her failed marriage, entered a deep depression. Cordelia could recall mornings when she had stood by the side of her mother's bed trying to make her open her eyes, trying to say something funny or interesting so her mother would want to get up. So her mother would look at her.

One morning she did open her eyes. She smiled weakly and said, "Don't you understand, sugarplum? I don't want to be alive."

Cynthia had found her crying in the corner, telling her stuffed koala bear to be very quiet because their mommy needed rest. Cynthia had made her breakfast, washed her face, and helped her dress. When Cordelia told her what their mother had said, her face had become very pink and she'd gone upstairs. She heard her sister telling their mother that she was taking them to live with their father in California unless she got out of bed. There was a terrible sound of crying, and then Cynthia came down and walked Cordelia to school.

"I'm sorry," Cordelia said. Her sister's face was very grim.

"Why are you sorry?" Cynthia asked, stooping over to wipe the tears off her face.

"For being so little," Cordelia wailed. "For making daddy leave."

Cynthia sat down on someone's steps and pulled her into her lap.

"You're supposed to be little," she said tenderly, stroking Cordelia's hair. "I love you being my little sister. Daddy left to do something in Hollywood. You didn't do anything."

"You won't leave too?"

"No! Of course not. Where would I go? I'm going to be your bossy older sister for the rest of your life!" she said. "Now, screw school! Let's go to the movies."

"We should stop talking about all the things we never told each other," Cordelia said, scraping her uneaten food into the garbage. "I think it's useless and morbid."

"Don't you ever wonder how it was possible to be happy?"

She laughed. "I can't remember being happy with you, Harrison."

"You aren't dealing with anything."

"I'm trying to survive!" she shrieked so loudly the coffee cups rattled. "You don't listen to me!"

"Survival isn't enough."

"It's all I'm capable of. Now go away. Make some movies. Talk to pretty girls. Leave me alone."

When she heard the door lock behind him, she took out a mop, the broom, and a scrub brush. She took down the shelves and soaked them in bleach and vinegar. She wiped the walls and cupboards, the spice bottles and the tins filled with tea and sugar. Anger supplied energy. She scrubbed the floor, cleaned the bathroom, and then emptied and defrosted the refrigerator.

Later, standing in the bathroom, she stared at what was reflected in the mirror: a thin young woman with dilated pupils, gray circles under her eyes, and fading bruises scattered across her body. She pressed against her stomach, wondering how it was possible, how she had let things happen. It seemed like a pathetic waste of energy to struggle to the surface while the easier, sweeter choice would be to lie still and heavy on the bottom and let the light fade far away into the distance.

At the clinic, she was told to bring in a sample of her first morning urine.

"I know I'm pregnant," she told the receptionist. "Can't I just schedule an abortion?"

"Listen, dearie, I got no say about how things are done around here. It's clinic procedure." The woman snapped her gum and shrugged.

On the way back from the clinic, she saw Maxine standing in front of Lincoln Center, laughing with someone dressed in a tuxedo and holding a cello. She pressed the buzzer to stop the bus, but then she realized she couldn't tell her what had happened. Max had done too much. It wasn't fair. She was tired of ruining people's lives with her tragedies.

At home, still wearing her coat, she dialed Philip's number but then hung up as soon as the receiver was picked up. Immediately, the phone rang.

"Cordelia?" It was Philip.

She started to replace the receiver but stopped. What was the point? "Hello."

"I've been worried about you. Where have you been?"

"Sick."

"Are you all right? Did you miss the Marriott shoot?"

"No. I made it."

"Good girl. So . . ."

"Great. It was great. Everything's great."

"I bought that lot. The really pretty one that overlooks the harbor."

"Ah."

"I can't believe I actually paid that amount of cash for it! Jesus!" There was a long pause. "Delia?"

"Yes?"

"What's with you?"

"I met your wife." She said it flatly.

"Sasha?"

"Yes. She called me. We had lunch in her office. You have children."

"That fucking whore!"

"You're married. She said you spend five days a week in Stamford."

"She's lying. We're separated. She's a lying whore."

"You have children." A giggle rose in Cordelia's throat. "She said you don't have any friends." She roared with laughter.

"I'm coming over."

"I won't be home."

"I have to talk to you."

"I despise you."

"You don't understand."

"I'm pregnant." She hung up the phone, unplugged it from the wall.

CHAPTER

24

THE A TRAIN CONNECTED WITH THE IRT AT FIFTY-NINTH
Street. She had been out to the Rockaways once before,
during a summer when she was too poor to afford the train fare
to Jones Beach. Transported by subway to the beach—which was
covered with Puerto Rican families barbecuing pork—she and a
fellow actor drank rum and guava juice and passed out in the
sun. They woke with serious sunburns and late-afternoon hang-
overs.

This time she had left her apartment clutching her wallet and
a copy of *Moby Dick*. The sea was gray and rough, and the wind
cut across her cheeks, freezing tears against her skin. She was not
dressed properly for the cold, but the sharpness of the wind felt
good. She sat down on a piece of the pier that had washed up on
the beach. Way out on the jetty, two figures embraced. From a
distance it was impossible to identify the relationship: lovers,
mother and child, father and son? She looked down at her feet
and realized that her hand was gently protecting and cradling her
belly.

"I'm sorry," she muttered. "I can't take care of you."

She stayed on the beach until the sun set and the chill drove
her back to the train. A family bound for a night in Manhattan
sat down in the car. They were all dressed up, but the parents

were arguing in Spanish, while their son, a serious-eyed toddler, watched them, offering his bottle as a peace token. Cordelia wished she could pick him up and bury her face in his hair. She missed Tom. After a few minutes his father picked him up, drew his wife into the circle of his arm; all three fell asleep. As they crossed the bridge into Manhattan, Cordelia thought the city had never looked more beautiful. Lights reflected off the water, the buildings cut across the blue-black sky like silver mountains.

The clinic was crowded with young women. Most of them carried small packages, which the woman behind the desk was labeling.

"Cordelia Cavanagh." The counselor was Puerto Rican. She had three holes in her ears and lovely white teeth. She smiled as Cordelia sat down.

"That's a very pretty name," she said kindly.

"Thanks."

"Your test was positive, Cordelia."

"Thank you." She stood up.

"I'm here to discuss your options."

"There are no options."

"You want to abort?"

"Yes."

"Would you like me to schedule you for tomorrow morning?"

"Yes."

"Fine. We have all your information at the desk. It's a hard thing, but you're going to be fine. I'm sorry, Cordelia."

"Thank you."

"Do you want to call anyone? You look very pale."

"No. I'm fine. Thank you. I'll see you tomorrow."

Her appointment was for nine o'clock. She was given a set of directions, which included the advice not to eat after midnight.

When she reached her corner she saw the limousine parked in front of the building. She began to turn around, but there was nowhere to go. In any case, she thought, what did it matter if she saw him or not?

"Cordelia?"

"Yes?"

"Will you let me in?" He followed closely enough for her to smell his familiar mixture of expensive leather and aftershave. He did not try to touch her.

"How are you feeling?"

"The test was positive." She stood with her back to him. The room was still dark.

He cleared his throat. "And?"

"I'm having an abortion tomorrow morning." She turned on the light and saw that he had been afraid that she would insist on having his baby.

"I can't have this child because I'm too poor and crazy, but I feel it's wrong."

"Wrong?" Philip unzipped his leather jacket, but he left it on.

"Wrong not to welcome life. Any life."

"Let me give you some money." He opened his wallet.

"Fine." She was sitting on the edge of the couch, rigid, her fingers interlaced so tightly the circulation stopped.

"How much?"

"It doesn't matter."

"A thousand?"

"Fine." Her throat was closed.

"Delia . . ."

"What?"

"This was a little too much at once."

"I'm sure it was." She was very tired.

"I could leave her." Philip sighed.

"Who?" she asked.

"Sasha. My wife."

"Why?"

"I don't love her."

"Oh." *I don't care,* Cordelia thought.

"We could get a place together." Philip seemed to be speaking very slowly.

"Who?" She was talking like a zombie.

"Us. I have the lease on a one-bedroom on Central Park and Eighty-sixth. East Side."

"I live here."

"We could trade it for something on the West Side."

"You live in Stamford with your wife. And your children."

"Stop being a bitch."

"I have to have an abortion tomorrow. I don't care where you live."

"What about South Africa?"

"It's your child, Philip."

"It could be his."

"No!" She raised her voice. "I know when this happened. The night I tried to put in my diaphragm and you hit me. I knew I was going to get pregnant. Harrison never raped me."

"Okay. Look, would you have gone out with me if I told you I was married? I know you wouldn't have given me a chance. I had to have you."

Cordelia stared at her hands. Her fingers were very white. They felt numb. She unbuttoned her coat, but she could not seem to pull her hands through the sleeves.

"What?" Philip had said something she couldn't hear.

"Would you have had dinner with me if you knew I was married?"

"No."

"So?" He waved his hand in a gesture of dismissal.

"So what? It's fine to lie to get something you want? What about me? How dare you put me in this position with your wife!"

"I wanted to know you."

"You wanted to fuck me."

"It's the same thing! To know you, Delia, is to fuck you!"

"You don't know me at all."

"And me? You don't really care about me, baby. I look in your eyes and I see middle distance. When you lose track of your thoughts they go perfectly blank; it's like staring into the eyes of a china doll. No woman has ever frozen me out like this. . . . And that South African. He's got some kinda hold over you. A lot of women would find it less difficult to make me feel good."

"You are very generous. I'm sure you'll find someone warmer to take care of."

The money he had given her was still clutched tightly in her fist. A chill rose from her lower spine to her neck. She shivered. Something in her stomach ached. "I have to go to bed now," she said, standing. "You should leave."

"I thought I'd take you tomorrow."

"No, thank you." She walked toward the door.

"Let me send the car, then."

"No." Cordelia opened the door. Philip rested his hand on her cheek.

"There's no reason for us to stop making each other happy."

"Goodbye."

"Please, Delia . . ."

"Goodbye."

It was not yet midnight. She found a box of chocolate-covered yogurt bars in the freezer that would have to do. She turned on the phone machine and piled towels on top of the phone. She slept with her knees pulled up to her chest, her hand between her legs, the other hand against her face, with the thumb in her mouth. The alarm went off at seven.

She wore another of Cynthia's sweaters, a faded and stretched cotton pullover with a rolled collar. It was sea green, and the elbows were ripped. Her body had already changed; her breasts were bigger and she felt heavy. It was difficult to wake up.

In the cab, she huddled into the corner wishing she could disappear into the cracks of the seat. When she was small, her parents had a metal bookend that was a miniature replica of a Greek temple. She had wished she could shrink until she was tiny enough to hide behind the pillars. Her father drove an ancient Volvo with a floor so rusted you could watch the road move beneath you. She wanted to be small enough to slip out through the rust cracks. When Cynthia had been in the operating room, Cordelia had gone into the bathroom and squinted at her reflection, squinted until her face disappeared in a blaze of light. Now she wished she could become a puff of smoke, smoke that would be blown away by the air sweeping through the cab as they hurtled toward the clinic.

"You want this corner?"

Cordelia paid the driver and took an elevator to the seventeenth floor. As she approached the reception desk her knees buckled.

"Whoa." Somebody's boyfriend caught her arm, a young man with rosy cheeks, whose hand was held by a small woman with red hair.

"It's the not eating," she said, smiling at Cordelia. "I feel kinda shaky too."

She was told her name would be called. She started to read a *New Yorker* short story about a group of friends who were all feeling disconnected. One of them kills himself. After a few minutes she dialed Harrison's number on the pay phone in the waiting room.

"Hello?" He sounded sleepy.

"Hi." She had attempted cheerfulness, but her voice came out in a strangled shriek, and she coughed slightly.

"Cordelia? What's wrong? Where are you?"

"Nowhere. I mean, I'm home, and I just wanted to hear your voice."

"Let me call you back, then."

"Why?"

"The connection's terrible."

"No. I'm about to leave."

"Where are you?" Harrison began to sound very awake.

"Harrison . . ." What did she want to say?

"Yes?"

The waiting room was now half filled with people. Two men sitting with their girlfriends looked self-conscious and responsible. Two women were whispering in the corner. Only she had come alone. "I'm sorry."

"Sorry for what?"

"Everything." It was a hopeless conversation, probably inspired by the *New Yorker* story. Her name was called over the loudspeaker.

"I have to go now."

"Are you in an airport?"

"No."

"Are you getting the abortion?"

"Yes."

"Alone?"

"Sort of."

"Jesus Christ! Goddamn you to hell, you fucking martyred bitch!"

She hung up. The anesthetist gave her a needle in the arm and crossed her hands on her chest. She felt like the Lady of Shalott, floating down the lake to her graceful death. Dying for the love of Lancelot. The orderly wiped the tears off her face and patted her hand.

In her dream, Cynthia was teaching her how to read. Carefully and patiently, her sister sounded out the syllables. The strange part was that Cordelia was an adult and knew how to read. She kept interrupting, but Cynthia would not listen, continuing to stress the vowels and the consonants, reading aloud in a monotone.

She woke up in a dimly lit room next to a moaning woman on a stretcher.

CHAPTER

25

THE FOLLOWING DAY SHE CALLED THE MANAGER OF THE squash club to resign. For the first time, she used the excuse of her sister's death to explain the suddenness of her decision.

"I've decided to go into therapy," she said. "I've made enough money from the commercial."

He was kind and understanding. "Please believe me when I say we'll miss you," he said.

Without a job, she found herself headed downtown to take a yoga class. The teacher had returned from Europe.

"Too much butter," he said, smiling at her. "Belgian linen, beer, and butter!"

The room was warm and quiet. During meditation, she found herself free of pain for a single second, and then, with blinding clarity, she saw the child, her child, the child she had been, the child her mother carried with such love, raised with hope, the child her sister had protected from harm, the child her sister would never bear.

"Cynthia," she murmured, her head heavy in her hands. "Tell me what you're thinking." She began to gasp. Arms came around her. She was heavy with it and unable to resist. The yoga teacher was rocking her back and forth in his arms like a sick baby. She struggled, but then she let him hold her.

"Accept it," he whispered. "You won't perish."

But she was afraid of the force of her anger and did not want to be exposed in the quiet of that room. She ran out, and as she walked down the street she was sure her heart was beating so hard passersby must hear. She could hear the sound of her pulse echoing through her head. It had struck her that this blackness, this horrible longing, was all that was left.

The acting scene with Maxine was a disaster. She went up on her lines and failed to find motives for her actions. The dialogue was flat, lacking truthfulness and energy. Maxine tried to connect with her, but Cordelia avoided her eyes, afraid that her own lack of focus would ruin her partner's concentration. On their last line Maxine exhaled deeply, turned her back to the class, and muttered, "Fuck." Cordelia saw that she was furious and confused.

During the discussion afterward the teacher addressed his comments exclusively to Maxine. He suggested alternate choices for her character, but he emphasized how pleased he was with her work. He did not allow the class to comment. When he switched his attention to Cordelia, she cringed, expecting angry criticism.

"What happened?" he asked gently. "Where were you?" She dissolved into tears.

After a moment he leaned forward and whispered into her ear. "Come and see me later. Go out and get some air."

In Washington Square, she sat and watched three black teenagers practicing their dance routine. It was an awesome display of graceful coordination. Instead of rap they were dancing to Marvin Gaye. She remembered that Marvin's father had shot him. She thought about Marvin and John Lennon. Their music had been so clearly about life: sex, love, and feeling good. Their bloody deaths had been very inappropriate. She began to sob again. Loudly. Martyred musicians. Aborted babies. Neglected children. Dead sisters. Treacherous fathers. People slowly drifted away from her section of the park. Even the drug dealers avoided looking at her.

I am a pariah, she thought, filled with bitter satisfaction. *I am tainted by death*.

When she returned to the studio the class was gone and her teacher was going over his notes. He offered her a cigarette, and they smoked together quietly. The silence was interrupted by his sigh.

"Cordelia," he asked quietly, "what is going on?"

The room was quite dark. She felt that she was being interrogated by a representative of the truth. She trusted this man. He had encouraged her to take risks in his class, and always she had felt his support and the safety of this studio. He had tried to make her work clearer. Clarity seemed like a ridiculous goal. She giggled.

"Is that a funny question?" he asked kindly.

"No. It's just my mind."

"Your mind?"

"I'm losing it."

"Are you?" He was paying very close attention to what she was doing with her fingers. So far she had ripped four matchbooks into tiny pieces. She sat on her hands.

"Of course not."

"Maxine's very worried about you."

"Maxine's very worried about everyone." Her tone was sharp. "She should lose weight."

"She cares."

"I know."

"We all care, Cordelia. I'm not sure you do know. When your sister died—"

"Was murdered."

"When she was murdered, everyone here felt how terrible it was for you—"

"Bullshit!" Cordelia stood and crossed the stage to face her teacher. "That's utter fucking tripe! No one has any idea what it was like! No one! Think of the worst horror in the world—think of Nazis torturing babies—then multiply that by ten! That's what it was like for me! My sister was the only person in the world I ever loved without fear. She took care of me when I was a child. My parents were useless! Completely self-absorbed and totally selfish. They didn't listen to me. They ignored the fact that they were responsible for my feeling like part of something. My sister loved me more than anyone will for the rest of my life! And they killed her for nothing. She didn't have any money. She didn't try to fight. He slaughtered her. Her body was covered with blood except for her hands! I told them, 'That's not my sister!' But then I saw her hands, and I knew it was her. That's what I keep seeing. Her neighbors thought they understood what this did to us, to our family. My mother. Can you imagine what my mother thought, looking down at her own dead child? No? Well, I understand all sorts of things now. All sorts of wonderful secrets have been revealed. How you can debase yourself and it doesn't really matter. It's like a cheap drug. It's some sort of parody of human intimacy . . . of love. I'm not making sense. I think if I had a submachine gun I'd walk outside and start mowing people down."

Her teacher nodded. "It's not getting any better, is it?"

"What?"

"The pain."

"No. I don't want it to. It's all I have left of her. All I can remember. It connects us. The doctor told me to let her go. To let her go because she was suffering so much. But I wouldn't. I didn't. She walked out of there without me, but I wouldn't accept that—"

"What?"

"The release of her spirit. I want her back."

"Ahh. Cordelia . . ."

"I'm sorry."

"You need to get some help. Therapy."

"Do you think I have any talent?"

"Cordelia . . ."

"Acting talent. Or do I have to fuck people or do you have to fuck people anyway? Or is it just me? Am I some sort of victim?

Will I die like my sister?" Her voice had risen to a scream. She stood. "Excuse me. I have to go."

"Let me take you home."

"No. I'm going to see a friend. Thank you. I didn't think I mattered very much."

"You matter."

She paused. Dug at the door with one foot like a horse. "I want to die," she whispered.

"Yes." Her teacher sighed.

"You believe me?" Her face lit up with a smile.

"Certainly."

"Thank you. I won't do it."

"Good." He held her for a moment and then let her go. "If you survive this, and you will, any defeat will come as nothing. Your courage is unfathomable."

She didn't believe him, but she pretended to think that therapy was a good idea, something she was considering seriously. It seemed most important to keep other people from sounding the depths of her misery. Otherwise they would be alert and demand explanations and attempt to keep her from getting away.

She found a pay phone at the entrance to the square and dialed Harrison's number. Expecting a machine, she began to leave a message, but Harrison interrupted her.

"Hello?"

"Oh, Harrison."

"Hi, Cordelia."

"It's Cordelia."

"Yes. Where are you?"

"By the studio."

"Why don't you come over?"

"Okay."

She hung up and then realized she didn't know his address. She sat down and began to think. Clearly she was failing in her attempt to have the sort of life her sister had expected for her. The humiliation of this was offset by the idea that it might serve as an excuse to finally let go and fall backward. She was tired of the ascent. She felt scratched and sore, and the summit was as far from her grasping fingers as it had been when she first stood at the bottom.

She searched through her bag for her address book. There were an amazing number of items: leotard, leg warmers, perfume, shampoo, books, brushes, hair clips, talcum powder, an apple. She heard a buzzing noise in her ear, and the ends of her fingers were tingling. She wondered if the bench was absorbing electricity from the street lamp. She felt her pulse accelerate and looked down to see that her hands were shaking so hard she had spilled the contents of her bag. A scream stopped in her throat. She knew public screaming was often interpreted as a symptom of insanity. She didn't want to be caught, apprehended before her final destination had been reached. A man seemed to be walking toward her from the far side of the park. She jumped off the bench and crossed to the central concrete fountain. The man had something in his hand. A blade glinted in the light from the setting sun. She dropped her bag, and the contents spilled again. A nun picked it up and put her hands on Cordelia's shoulder.

"My dear," she said, "you mustn't do this here."

Cordelia took her bag back and smiled. "Do you know what's happening to me?"

The nun beamed. "Trust in God," she said. "Trust in the healing power of Jesus."

"I hate God," Cordelia muttered as the nun sailed away. "God killed my sister. I hate God, and he hates me."

She looked up to see the man with the knife still staring at her. He had put it away, but she could see the handle protruding from his boot. Using her credit card, she dialed her father's house in California. Tibetan gong music was followed by a few bars of George Winston's piano. Then Sunflower's breathy whisper.

"Hey, the two of us are out doing something cosmic, but leave your name, sign, and purpose for existing, and we'll be in touch."

The silence after the tone was impossible to address. After a second she said, "I'm sorry," and hung up. The receiver was still in her hand. She dialed Philip's number. He answered.

"You hurt me. There was nothing left to hurt, but you found a way. What was the point? It must have felt like kicking a dying dog!"

"Cordelia?"

"I killed a baby." She walked away from the phone, but the man with the knife was waiting. Harrison answered the first ring.

"Hello?"

"I don't know where you live."

"Where are you now?"

"Help me."

"Where are you?"

"Here still."

"In the park by the studio?"

"Yes."

"Stay there. Don't talk to anyone. I'm coming."

The temperature was thirty-seven degrees and the humidity was sixty-four percent. Barometer rising. Snow flurries. During the fifteen minutes she sat, her hands between her knees, her knees pressed tightly together, her eyes on the ground, the temperature dropped two degrees. When Harrison touched her arm, she thought it was the knife man, finally come to cut her throat. It was a relief. Her face drained of blood, she closed her eyes and offered him her neck.

"Cordelia," he said, tenderly pulling her into his arms. "Bloody hell, it's only me."

The Avenue A sublet was in an area populated by dealers and their customers. A few artists. He lived on the fifth floor. She climbed the stairs slowly, feeling the gentle pressure of his hand on the small of her back when she faltered. The apartment was tiny but clean and painted white. The furnishings were so minimal the place actually appeared somewhat spacious. The room contained a loft bed, and underneath, a dining table with two chairs. One corner had a built-in bookcase and a stereo. There were bars on the windows, and a huge piece of steel was propped against the door. She could not settle but moved around the small space, pacing from the kitchenette to the ladder of the loft, commenting on how nice everything was, aware of his silence, his observation, his recognition of her condition.

She saw in his eyes fear mixed with awe and a terrible sadness. She thought, with a feeling of triumph, *I am finally released.* Looking into the mirror, she saw that her cheekbones were those of a high-fashion model and giggled with delight. She hugged herself and was fascinated by how little there was left. There was a photograph of her standing with Oona in front of the Trinity gates. She was twenty years old and had very long hair.

"How fat I used to be," she said, taking the picture out of the frame. "Did you think I was fat?"

"No."

She saw that he was miserable and decided to try and be still. The table was covered with photographs. As she unbuttoned her coat, she saw that the pictures were of a two-year-old child. Sam. In several of the pictures he was held by a pretty woman whose face was fine-featured and innocent. The setting suggested a hot climate.

"Is she coming back?" She sat down and picked up a picture.

"Evidently not. She's found some sort of job and the sort of people she likes. Rich hippies."

"Will she keep Sam?"

"I don't know. I have to go there."

"To Greece?"

"Yes."

"When?" She stared at the photograph. Sam wasn't a baby anymore. The boy in the picture had Harrison's face. He gently took it from her and held both her hands. She felt herself trembling in his grasp. Cordelia stared at her lap.

"What's going on, Delia?"

"Oh . . . well, I'm just . . ." Her voice died away. She saw dirty dishes in the sink and thought to wash them.

Harrison did not let her stand. "Just what? If I wasn't home, if I couldn't have come to the park, what would you have done?"

"There was a man with a knife."

"Really?"

"Across the park. Behind the fountain. If you couldn't have come he would have killed me."

"Cordelia . . ."

"I won't call next time."

"Look . . ."

"When you touched me, I thought it was him. I was glad. It was a relief."

"For God's sake!"

"When do you leave for Greece?"

"I don't know. It's just for Sam. If I thought you wanted me to stay, I wouldn't go now."

"Why?"

"I want to help you. I think you're in trouble."

"I'm fine. I killed the baby, but otherwise, I'm fine."

"You did what you had to do."

"No, I cleaned up the mess I made. It's a different thing. Anyway, you must go to Greece and get your son! He must wonder where you've been. You don't want me. I was never what you wanted."

"Goddamn it, Cordelia! Let go of the past! Ireland was so long ago. We're completely different people now. Why can't you be here with me in New York? You're an actress; you're supposed to be in the moment. Why can't you feel anything?"

"I don't think I'm supposed to, Harrison. If you only knew . . ."

"What?"

"Philip understood."

"That slimy fuck? What could he possibly understand? He was bashing you around."

"I deserved it."

"Oh, shut up! How can you talk about yourself this way? He's married. He treated you like a whore. He paid you. That's understanding?"

"He expected nothing. I could do nothing. That's what I liked. It's what he liked. That's why he paid me."

"I think you need help. You need serious psychiatric attention. Shock treatment or something. You should go home and see your mother."

216

"My mother? My mother just had her breast cut off. She's being zapped every day with radioactive poison. I don't want her to know how I feel."

"It's not your fault you feel like this. Your sister died so horribly . . ."

Cordelia was talking to herself. "If it was just my father I left I wouldn't care. He has that featherhead to take care of him. But Mummy and Amelia . . ."

"What about Tom?" Harrison raised his voice. "You want him growing up wondering what kind of world would murder one aunt and then take away another? How could anyone possibly explain to him why his beautiful aunt committed suicide? You think that's what Cynthia died for? . . . And Maxine? She'll eat herself to death. What about your acting teacher and the people at the club and people that still love you in Ireland? And your mother? You think she'd survive this? You aren't some fucking stranger, Cordelia! And what am I meant to think? It's an act of hatred, Cordelia. Hatred and supreme selfishness!"

"Tom wouldn't remember . . ."

"Yes he would. Children remember everything. You of all people know that! And it would kill your mother. And your father. You can't will us to stop loving you. You have to stop trying to alter reality. You have to start eating. Maybe good old understanding Philip would understand. He'd probably pull the trigger for you, honey. Out of love, no doubt!" Harrison pounded the table with his fist.

Cordelia looked down at the floor and saw that a roach was inching past her foot. She ignored it.

"When did you last eat?" he asked. Cordelia shrugged. "I'm going out to buy us some food." He pushed all the pictures into a neat pile.

"Will you be all right for twenty minutes?"

"Of course."

CHAPTER

26

A S SOON AS SHE HEARD HIS STEP ON THE STAIR SHE LOOKED at the letter that was buried under the pictures. "When you come here," his wife had written, "you'll understand why I felt it necessary to bring Sam. You'll love the house. There's plenty of construction work and lots of quiet for your writing. Sam says 'Hi, Daddy' to your picture every morning. I can't wait to see you."

The handwriting was loopy, with little circles drawn above the i's. Cordelia stared at the photograph again. The woman had slanty eyes like a Siamese cat's. Harrison was going back to his wife. She would probably betray him again, but he needed to see his son.

She left, slamming the door hard, hoping he would return soon. Without thinking, she gave the cabdriver Philip's address.

The building was dark, but there was a light on in his office. The doorman recognized her. She looked at her reflection in the elevator mirror. She was wearing black leggings, red high-top sneakers, and a black sweater that nearly touched her knees. Her face was very pale. There was black eye liner left from several days earlier. She pinched her cheeks and fluffed her hair. She had not eaten much for a long time, and she looked fragile. Her pupils were dilated.

"You're crazy," she whispered to her reflection. "You're crazy and you're going to die." When she opened the door to his reception area, a bell sounded.

"Who's there?" Philip called out. She walked down the hall and stopped in his doorway. He was hunched over a pile of papers. He wore a pale-pink shirt with blue suspenders. Suzanne Vega was singing softly in the background about how cold it was in Times Square. His tan was fading. When he saw Cordelia he leaned back and stretched. The lights of the Empire State Building had just been turned on. The tower gleamed yellow. Philip looked like a commercial for some kind of designer aftershave or sports watch. Behind his smile she noticed apprehension.

"Hey, stranger," he said softly.

"Hi." She stood balancing on one foot like an exotic bird, a flamingo or a stork, halfway across the threshold she would not cross. Something was missing. She could not remember what she wanted from this man.

"What's up?"

"Do you have a gun?" That was it.

"A what?"

"A gun. That I could borrow."

"You want to shoot me?"

"No."

"You gonna kill yourself?"

"Maybe. Or maybe I'll execute some strangers. Some New Yorkers. Innocent pedestrian bystanders."

"Why?"

"I can't do it."

"What?"

"Live. I can't do it. I've tried."

"Was it so bad?"

"It?"

"The abortion."

"No. Yes. You don't have any right to know."

"Okay. But you don't have the option—"

"Yes I do. Who spread this rumor that we don't decide when we've had enough?"

"You can't do that to your parents."

"My father's jealous of me. It will be easier for him."

"Your mother, then."

"She'd have to understand."

"No. That's not how it works, honey. You don't just decide the time's up and reach for the light switch. Some of us are forced to carry on."

"Don't give me that Catholic shit, you hypocrite!" She lowered her leg, wrapped her arms around herself. "I can't." She stretched out her hand like someone trying not to sink beneath icy water.

Philip started toward her, but he stopped when she held her palm up and flat, her hard eyes blank. He sat on his desk. "You just have to."

"How?"

"Look, I was in Vietnam. I had to run away from a building where four of my best buddies were burned alive. Four guys I loved more than my own family. Four guys screaming for help. Crying for their mothers. Crying for me. I couldn't get in. I had to save myself. When I got back to camp I kept telling this one guy, this one guy who survived a massacre, what had happened, and finally this guy hands me his pistol, loaded, and says, 'Asshole, blow your brains out.' "

"Why didn't you?"

"Would you have liked me better if I had?"

Cordelia nodded.

Philip shrugged. "It's not what was planned. I had to get back and have this chance to fuck up my life. Get rich so I could take lovely, neurotic actresses out for costly dinners."

"Fuck you!"

"Lighten up, Cordelia. Christ, you were well named. Melodrama and tragedy are your middle names. Put this behind you."

"What about my sister?"

"She got a lousy break. She deserved to live."

"Why wasn't it me?"

"Because it wasn't. That's like all those people asking why they didn't shoot Paul instead of John Lennon. . . . I mean, what's the point? Maybe you knew enough not to take a walk in that neighborhood. Your sister must have thought she was invincible. You're damn lucky to be alive, and you're doing everything you can to ruin that luck. I think you have a lot of courage, kid. That's what really attracted me to you. I like brave people."

"I hate you."

"Yeah. That's okay. You look pretty skinny there. You want some dinner?"

"No."

"Right. I forgot. Silly me. You want a gun. You still planning on snuffing yourself?"

"Why should I tell you? You . . . Catholic!" Philip laughed. "My acting teacher thinks I need a shrink. Someone else suggested shock therapy."

"A shrink couldn't hurt. Your father's a slime bucket. You want me to pay for a shrink?"

Cordelia stamped her foot. "Don't call my father names, and stop offering me money!"

"Sorry. Your father's a prince. Get him to pay for therapy. I really wish I weren't married."

"I don't. You deserve that pointy-nailed bitch. You are a selfish, lying, whoring, fucking creep! And you're a hypocrite! I'm sure you chewed the wafer! And you're old. Your hair's gray, and you look strange while you're sleeping! I saw your driver's license, and you're forty-two! Not thirty-eight! You're going bald. You're dying. Of meanness and lies!"

She ran for the elevator, the sound of his laughter ringing in her ears.

"Go get 'em, Cordelia!" he shouted as the doors closed. "Damn the torpedoes!"

The grave was in a cemetery outside Princeton. The plot had been purchased for their grandmother, who still lay in an old age home, playing house with a Barbie doll. On the day they had stood together watching Cynthia's coffin being lowered into the earth, Cordelia expected the sky to split and lightning to strike

New Jersey. Instead there was a gentle breeze, a few birds chirped, and it was warm enough to unbutton your coat. Her father strolled up, suggesting lunch. There was the mark of tears on his face, but Cordelia did not believe he cried for anyone but himself. She shook her head and folded her hands tightly across her body.

"You have to eat, honey," her father said tenderly. "You're getting too thin."

"That doesn't matter," she said. "You know, Daddy, she didn't forgive you for leaving us."

It was a lie. Cynthia had always defended his decision to go to California. She insisted he had a right to find happiness. Cordelia had been torn between loving her mother, hating her for not being able to keep her husband, hating her father for hurting her mother, hating them both for their weakness. On top of it all she missed him so much her entire body ached for the sight of him. It was too much. In absolute despair, she had turned to Cynthia, and her eldest sister patiently tried to reveal the truth.

"They can't live together, bumblebee. He's angry at her because he can't find any work, and she's mad at him because he isn't a good provider. Daddy needs someone who admires him."

"We admire him."

"Well, a grown-up lady admirer. It isn't that he doesn't love us."

"Does he love Mommy?"

"I don't think so."

"Poor Mommy."

Their father was such a handsome and charming man that Cordelia could not imagine surviving without his love. She thought it was even more important to love her mother twice as much, and she spent the weeks following his departure bringing home poems and presents: stolen flowers and construction-paper cards. Her mother would not turn away from the wall to accept her gifts. When she finally emerged from her depression, she packed Cordelia off to a child psychiatrist, as her sweetness had turned sour and she was violently angry at both her parents.

Before going to the cemetery, she decided to return to her

apartment to pick up the secret stash of drugs, major tranquilizers that she had been given or had stolen from her mother. The phone machine tape was full. Without listening, she depressed the erase/rewind button. Setting the alarm for seven, she swallowed one of the pills and fell asleep.

In her dreams she was speaking fluent French, with a great deal of expression and style. She was sunbathing with Cynthia on a white beach. A Greek beach. Near them was a small boy with a pail and shovel. He had huge blue eyes and blond hair. "I'm digging to China," he said. Cynthia was braiding flowers into Cordelia's hair. "The secret to happiness," Cynthia was saying in perfect French, "is never to question fate. Accept the cards as dealt. Refuse to throw them in unless you have some sort of strategy." Cordelia was wearing a white suit. She had turned perfectly brown, and her hair was nearly blond. She walked over to the child, who held his arms up to be carried. Balancing him on one hip, she turned back to watch Cynthia wading into the ocean, swimming gracefully toward the setting sun, disappearing into a blaze of rose and gold. The boy waved, laughing, at the circling gulls. She walked over to where Cynthia had been writing in a notebook. On the first page was written: "Never forget I was your sister." She sat down in the sand, shivering in the cold breeze, and wept.

She packed her suicide kit—the pills and a bottle of gin—with the feeling that this project would not be very effective. She wrote a note to her mother and Amelia, full of apologies and ridiculous reasons for her despair. A will next to her typewriter left the little she owned to Tom. She wrapped up a small wooden box with a piece of turquoise and left them for Harrison. She turned on her answering machine. Standing in the middle of her apartment, she tried to think of what she'd forgotten. Her father. She took down a framed picture of them standing outside his California cottage. They were both tan. Cordelia had her arm over his shoulder, and her dad was looking down at her with an expression of absolute delight. She wrote on a piece of yellow-lined paper: "I know you loved me, Daddy. I'm very sorry." She tried to leave her home without feeling the tug of what amounted to an endearing if tentative way of life. She whispered to her own empty rooms: "Bye-bye."

Her mother visited the grave several times a week. Amelia often drove out with Tom, picnic lunch packed, to weed. Cordelia had not returned since the funeral, when, given the choice, she would have simply remained at the grave until she died of exposure. It was difficult to locate the site, but she finally spotted a crooked willow tree to the east of the plot. She recognized the brilliant pink flowers her mother grew in huge baskets on her porch. There were bowls of dried lilacs and rose petals. Tom had left an aging teddy bear sitting on a little wicker stool. To the side was a glass vase containing a large bouquet of fresh spring flowers, which seemed strangely out of place. Her father must have sent them. Cordelia stood twisting her fingers together, wondering if she should start with the pills or the gin. "Where are you?" she muttered. "Where have you been?" From somewhere in her stomach came a huge wave of violent anger. She kicked over the bouquet of daffodils and tulips. The vase shattered against the tombstone.

"You stupid, careless bitch," she screamed, hurling rocks at the marble slab. "How dare you allow me to need you so much? You let him kill you, you stupid bitch! Did you think you were some sort of fairy princess no one would hurt? How can you expect me to keep going? I can't. I won't anymore."

She took a handful of pills and drank down half the bottle of gin. Picking up the broken pieces of the vase, she slashed each arm from elbow to wrist. Fearing the wounds were too shallow, she retraced the path and was pleased to see her veins opening. She drank some more gin with the rest of the pills and then lay face down in the dirt, on top of the flowers. Their scent made her sleepy, but as her mouth filled with soil she began to scream and was not quiet until the police arrived.

CHAPTER

27

HER HOSPITAL ROOMMATE WAS AN ALCOHOLIC. WHEN COR-delia awoke, she was no longer strapped down. Her arms were bandaged, and her hair was pulled back from her face. She watched as the girl sitting on the opposite bed spoke on the telephone.

"Because I'm an alcoholic, Mother," she said in an exasperated tone of voice, examining her cuticles. "I drove the car into that wall because I was in a blackout. A blackout. That's when you can't remember anything. No. No, it's not amnesia. It's like *Night of the Living Dead*—you know that movie, where the zombie child eats her father. It's important, because I wasn't trying to kill myself. I'm not that unhappy. I'm just a drunk! Ma! Oh, never mind. Stop crying. I've got to go—the nurses are calling me. Mom, this is the best thing that ever happened to me. I have to go to those terrible meetings, because they help me. Yes! I do belong with 'those people.' Oh, for fuck's sake, Mother! Goodbye!" She slammed down the phone.

"God grant me the serenity . . . Fuck you, fuck you, fuck you!"

She stared moodily at the wall. After a moment she picked up a pack of cigarettes, took one out, and lit it. She lay back on the bed and blew perfect smoke rings at the ceiling. When she glanced over at Cordelia, she jumped.

"Oh my God," she said. "You've woken up."

"Sorry," whispered Cordelia, her throat feeling as if she'd been screaming for days. "Those are very good." She nodded toward the drifting smoke rings.

"Don't be sorry. It's just you've been like totally asleep for days."

"Days?"

"At least two days."

"Two days?" Cordelia looked at her bandaged arms. "Oh, shit."

"I guess you tried to kill yourself."

"Yeah."

"On your sister's grave?"

"Kind of."

"Why she'd die?"

"Why? Uh, I don't know. Someone murdered her during a mugging. Stabbed her to death."

"Oh, dear. That's so tragic. I'm really sorry. All that happened to me was driving into a brick wall. They had to cut me out of the car, and I punched the cop. I'm an alcoholic."

"That's too bad."

"Well, it's better to know what's wrong. I'd been doing all sorts of stupid things. Like I flew out to Vegas with my building super and married him. In a blackout. I didn't even know the guy. He speaks Haitian Creole, and I can't understand anything he's telling me. Are you an alcoholic?"

"I don't think so."

"They brought you here because of the pills, I guess. And not eating. You could pretend to be one. The A.A. meetings here are really nice. You're depressed, aren't you?"

Cordelia nodded wordlessly, tears sliding down her cheeks.

"So, can you get up?"

"I'll try."

She swung her legs around to the floor like an elderly woman.

Every joint and muscle in her body ached, and she vaguely remembered being restrained by the ambulance attendants and orderlies. They had strapped her down to pack her arms with compresses. They had put something between her teeth to keep her from swallowing her own tongue.

When she put her weight forward, her knees buckled and she almost went down. The girl caught her under her shoulder.

"It's just you've been lying down for so long."

Cordelia looked at her feet. They seemed especially vulnerable and precious. There was something miraculous about her entire body. She could sense the blood flowing from her fingertips to her heart. There was a steady pulse beating. She could feel the muscle and the softer flesh of the girl's arm. The air smelled sweet. She was starving.

"I'm alive," she said to her roommate.

"I'm Angela," the girl said, hugging her.

"My name's Cordelia."

"You wanna get dressed for the meeting, Cordelia, or you want to wear a robe?"

"I don't think I have any clothes."

"Your mom brought some."

"My mother was here?"

"Oh, yeah. All day yesterday. All night. She just left this morning. One of her patients had an emergency. And your other sister. Amelia."

"How was my mother?"

"Okay. I mean, she cried a lot, but I think she was so relieved that you were safe. I talked to her a little. I told her some of the really disgusting things I did, and I think she felt better about you. She's really nice, and my God, how she loves you!"

"I know."

"Your sister's kind of intense, but she loves you too. She told me you were a wonderful actress. Your mom said you were too hard on yourself, and that you'd tried very hard to be okay since your sister died. She said you two had been really close because of the way she fell apart when your dad left. She said she couldn't go on if you didn't wake up—"

"Angela—stop."

A vision of her mother sitting at her bedside, holding her hand, telling a complete stranger their family history, filled her mind. Cordelia sat down heavily on the bed. She felt completely drained, ready to go back to sleep.

"Oh, I'm sorry. I was just so amazed by your mother. I don't think my mother even likes me. All she does is complain because I wouldn't go to Radcliffe. Everyone in my entire family went there. She's never said anything good about me, except I heard her tell my aunt once that I was lucky to be a natural blonde. So I dyed my hair black just to eliminate my only asset. And my sister's a fucking CPA! It's hard to believe we're from the same family. Your family is so open."

"No we aren't. But I think you're great."

"Thanks. Then again, you're someone who tried to slash her elbows. How much do *you* know? . . . I'm just kidding."

While Angela talked, she was pulling out a soft pair of cotton pants, underwear, socks, and a sweater from Cordelia's bedside cabinet. All the clothes looked new. She pulled off the hospital socks and rubbed Cordelia's feet until the blood began to circulate.

"There," she said, nodding happily. "Take a shower, and then we can go to the meeting."

Angela was gone when Cordelia came out of the bathroom, wrapped in a small towel. Her father was sitting on the bed, reading the *New York Times*. He looked up as the door opened, and she tried to cover herself more completely. His hair was longer than the last time she'd seen him.

"Hi, honey," he said, folding the paper. "How are you feeling?"

She had removed the bandages, careful not to wet the stitches in the shower. The slashes went straight from wrist to elbow. She looked like a doll repaired in a doll hospital. Spitefully, she turned her inner arms toward her father.

"Look what I've done," she said gleefully, like a little girl showing off painted nails. "Look what I did with that broken glass." Her father glanced at the stitches and looked directly into her eyes.

"They'll heal," he said hoarsely. "Skin is remarkably resilient. Lots of vitamin E. Hungry?"

"I'm not leaving here."

"This is a loony bin, Delia. You don't belong here."

"Yes I do. I'm a loony. I want to go to the A.A. meeting with Angela."

"Are you an alcoholic?"

"Maybe."

"Sunflower says I drink too much." Mr. Cavanagh leaned back against the pillow and sighed. He didn't look as though he wanted to leave. Cordelia perched on the edge of the visitor's chair. "She wants me to see her acupuncturist," her father continued. "I already went through crystal healing. She says if I can't stop completely, I belong in A.A."

"Do you think you drink too much?"

"Probably. There's lots of times I don't want to feel anything. It's just my own private brand of anesthesia. Except sometimes you stay away from it because you know it's going to turn on you and you can't afford to feel any worse. 'Cause you're ready to die already. I stayed away from it when Cindy was murdered, and I haven't had a drop since your mother called about you. For Christ's sake, Cordelia." He stopped and rubbed his eyes. "Sometimes you just don't want to feel a fucking thing."

She saw tears rolling down his cheeks, his hands still covering his eyes. "Daddy?"

"Yes?"

"I'm really sorry."

"Do you have any idea of how much I love you?"

Cordelia felt the coldness of her bare thighs against the metal chair. She crossed to the closet, but her father's hand stopped her.

"Delia . . ." She shrank from the touch of his skin. "Honey . . ."

"Let me get dressed." She wrapped herself in the terry-cloth robe she found hanging on the closet door. "I'm cold."

"You're angry at me."

"I was cold."

"You've been furious at me since you were seven years old. You never looked at me again. These shutters came down—"

"I was just a child! I thought I was meant to have a father!"

"I've always been your father!"

"You haven't. You told me you loved me, and then you left to start a new life with some woman named after a plant in a place I'd never been. A place so far away I could never touch you. And I never heard those words again from you until I called to tell you what happened to Cynthia. Like it was an appropriate fucking response to a terrible piece of news! I wondered what it meant for you to say that. Like, what's he afraid of? You haven't touched me since I was seven years old."

"I was living in California!"

"You could have asked me to visit when I was little! You could have moved to a closer state!"

"You wouldn't come!"

"Yes I would have! I kept a suitcase packed under my bed. My God, it's so humiliating not to be wanted."

"Your mother controlled all that. She said you girls suffered so much because of me that it would be better if I just stayed away."

"I forgot how to read! They sent me to a shrink because I was biting people. I thought you left because I was too boring and little."

"My darling. You were my daisy! Oh, my poor baby. Cordelia . . ." Her father had his arms out, ready to hold her, but she wrapped herself more tightly in the robe and sat down on the chair.

"I really wanted to die," she whispered. "If you knew what it meant for me to lose her . . ."

"Tell me."

"I can't. Neither of you has ever really bothered with me. Mom was in this depression for nearly two years. Sometimes she was fine, but you could never count on her. Or she'd work so much it was as if she'd rather be at the hospital than with us. It was scary. I worried all the time. Cynthia made sure I felt safe.

She knew when something was going on at school, and she asked me questions about what I was doing. I keep having these dreams. She's always just about to tell me something that might change everything. Something that would stop the murder. I can't hear her properly, or she's speaking French, or there's too much noise. When I dream about her, it's like I can be with her. I just want to stay there with her. To stay there and touch her. And I keep thinking it was my fault, after all the care she took of me. I should have been there to save her. To keep those knives away from her. I want her to hold me like she did after you left and Mommy wouldn't get out of bed!" She was screaming.

Her father reached out, but she sat motionless on the chair, cocooned in the robe.

"I don't want anyone to touch me," she whispered. "I don't want you to touch me." She stared down at her lap, where her hands lay limp and pale, the fingers interlaced, the wrists thin.

She looked up to see her father's face contorted with pain, tears streaming down his cheeks.

"Daddy," she shrieked, "I'm so sorry!"

"There's nothing for you to be sorry about."

"Why did you leave us like that?"

"I couldn't make any money. It was humiliating. Your mother's practice was beginning to take off. It was different then. You were expected to bring home the bacon. People thought I was a bum. A bum with three little girls. I wanted to be a good provider."

"Remember our last Christmas? It was the last year I pretended to believe in Santa."

"You didn't believe in Santa?"

"Amelia told me about him, the Easter bunny, and the tooth fairy on my fifth birthday. She said it was a family tradition. Oh, Tinker Bell too."

"Tinker Bell? Why, that little brat!"

"Anyway, we had a real gingerbread house, and I got a blond doll dressed as an Indian princess, a blond Indian. She was so glamorous. You said she was the last doll because we were all getting so old. But she was my first doll too. All the rest were hand-me-downs. I woke up at five, and you were downstairs drinking a beer. I think you were putting something together, but you told me Santa had just left and we looked outside together and I pretended to hear the jingle bells, even though I knew that Santa was just this derelict hired for the Christmas season. You let me open up my doll. I had you all to myself. We made cocoa with marshmallows. I even remember my pajamas. They had little pictures of Batman all over them. You left the next day. I hated that doll. I put her back in the plastic box and I left her alone on the top of my closet. You called her the last doll. It was the last everything."

He had never listened to her like this. She looked up several times, expecting him to have returned to the newspaper or been getting ready to walk out. But he sat without moving. Listening.

"I thought I'd be bringing my babies to her. She'd sit there and tell me I was a great mother. We'd say mean things about our husbands and drink too much coffee. I thought she'd take care of my children. I thought she'd take care of me. I want to sit in her kitchen and watch her cook. But it isn't her kitchen anymore. It's like someone swept her life away, without a trace. How could something like this happen to us? We didn't do anything."

"I don't know, Delia."

"You didn't teach me anything about life. That guy I was seeing, the one who got me the commercials—he *is* married. He's got two children. I just had an abortion."

"Your mother told me."

"How did she know?"

"Amelia told her."

"Amelia?"

"The South African."

"Jesus!"

"He was worried sick about you. There're lots of people worried: your acting teacher, Maxine, your old boss at the club, some crazy Jewish doctor—"

"Dr. Schwartz?"

"He sent your mother a telegram, for God's sake. Wanted to

offer his services. He had a three-page list of shrinks for you—Freudian, Jungian, cognitive—a goddamned Chinese menu!"

"His parents died in a concentration camp."

"That's too bad."

"He thinks I have survivor guilt."

"Yeah, well, we've got enough guilt in the Cavanagh family to send a man to the Milky Way! Our guilt could fuel the city of Tokyo! The only guilt-free member of this clan is Sunflower."

"She's not in our family."

"Sunflower and I were married last week."

"You fucking bastard!"

"Delia . . ."

"You fraudulent swine! Get out of here! No wonder you bothered showing up. You had something to feel guilty about, and you thought I'd forgive you if you pulled this worried-daddy act! Don't you ever try to speak to me again. I despise you!"

Cordelia's father didn't move. She beat her heels into the floor, screaming into her bathrobe.

"I tried to call you," he said.

"Like hell you did!"

"You're never home. Never. I tried to reach you at the club, and they said you weren't working. I have to listen to that goddamned machine telling me to leave my message. What should I have said: 'Hi. This is Daddy. I got married'?"

"She is so stupid!"

"No she's not. You've never given her a chance, acting like a snobby little Ivy League bitch around her. She has a master's from Stanford in comparative lit, by the way, which is more school than you have! She has depth."

"Like a gopher. She's as deep and sensitive as a burrowing rodent!"

"I like gophers. They are industrious and patient creatures. However, that's not very nice."

"Go back to fucking California!"

"Shut up!" Mr. Cavanagh stood and crossed to where Cordelia sat, staring at the floor. He gently put his fingers under her chin and tilted her face up. "My feelings about Sunflower have absolutely nothing to do with the love I bear for my children. That love is unconditional. I respect you."

They sat in a silence that gradually became stony. Finally, she picked up her clothes and went into the bathroom. She stood in front of the mirror, attempting to see some sort of change in her face, some alteration caused by her recent suffering. There were no visible new lines. She squinted and succeeded in looking fifty.

CHAPTER

28

O N THE RIDE BACK TO MANHATTAN CORDELIA CHAIN-smoked, her window open to the cold air. Since Mr. Cavanagh was willing to sign her out, the hospital allowed her to leave. Her father's angry profile was painful to contemplate, so she stared at the side of the road, counting the exits on the New Jersey Turnpike. They stopped to stretch their legs, and Cordelia smoked while her father threw stones into an artificial lagoon built next to the gas station. The rest area was named after a famous football coach.

"I saw Seth at MOMA."

"Seth?"

"You know. The guy I met my freshman year. You said he was made up of equal parts of cheap sentiment and bad karma. The one who wanted me to move to Colorado."

"Did I say that?"

"Yes. You told me I'd die on the streets if I left school for him."

"Hmm. Oh, yeah. The Jewish kid. His mother wanted to gas herself because of you. The one with the hair."

"Yeah."

"Nice kid."

"You called him a loser and an arrogant puppy. You said we'd end up panhandling in some Mexican border town if I married him. You said he'd put me out on the streets like Charles Manson, and I'd end up with a cross carved on my forehead."

"You wanted to marry him?"

"He wanted to marry me. I didn't know what I wanted. I went to Ireland."

"Well, that was the right thing. I remember now. I was a little upset. What was he doing in MOMA?"

"Showing his wife and baby great art."

"Ah." Her father threw another rock in the water, greatly upsetting a duck. "You wish you'd married him?"

"I don't know."

"How come I disliked him so much?"

"Daddy, don't you remember?"

"I remember you being shell-shocked. It was like when Cindy was dating the Black Panther. She tried to convert to Muslimism. I mean, the guy was from Lawrenceville Prep, and she wants to become a Muslim! And he was an arrogant puppy. You were both a mess."

"You told me love didn't exist."

Her father paused, a rock held in midair. "Cordelia . . ."

"You don't pay any attention to me for ten years, and then all of a sudden I have this father who says that life is a lousy joke but you could avoid pain by not listening to the punch line."

"What did that mean?"

"How should I know? I just wanted to please you."

"Why did you listen to me?"

"You were my father!"

"Ah, God. Your father. So I knew the answers?"

"I thought so."

"My father was a jerk. I never listened to a thing he said. He hated everybody. Blacks, Jews, women, handicapped people. He never said a good thing about anyone except George Wallace. The jerk idolized George Wallace. He thought your mother was an 'uppity bitch' and advised me to slap her in the face every day for the first year of our marriage. Yup, good ol' Pop!"

He stopped in front of the apartment. "I'll call you tonight," he said, fiddling with the car lighter. "You'll be okay?"

"Oh, sure," she said, smiling at the bag lady who was counting bottles on the stoop. "I'm really sorry about all this." She waved her hand around, vaguely indicating her entire existence.

"There's nothing to be sorry for," he said, his hands twisting on the steering wheel. "You feel abandoned. I left, Cynthia died, your mother's sick, and Amelia's married."

"I should be more independent."

"You got away from us as fast as you could. You need to remember you have a family and we love you."

She put her arm around him awkwardly.

"You should have told us about the abortion, Delia," he whispered into her hair. "We could have helped you."

"I was humiliated," she whispered back, inhaling the scent of her father's wool coat. "How could I have let that happen?"

"Shh," her father crooned, stroking her hair. "Stop beating yourself up."

For a moment he held her tight. The bag lady was watching them, and Cordelia pulled away. His soothing voice reminded her of the last year he had lived with them. She could still fit into the space under his arm when he sat in his big leather chair and read Lewis Carroll to her. He had promised a chapter a night until they finished the book. He began with "The Hunting of the Snark," and his rendition was so wonderful she was unable to sleep afterward, remembering how deeply his voice had dropped when he cried, "Just the place for a Snark!" She had whispered that phrase to herself for weeks afterward. But he had left before finishing *Through the Looking Glass*, and when her mother picked up the book one night to read to her, Cordelia had had a tantrum and snatched it from her hands, to hide it under her bed in a box with her other fetish objects: one of his old shirts, a picture he had drawn of a funny fat man, and a cuff link she had stolen. It was her box of Daddy. When she woke up in the middle of the night and could not remember how he smelled or sounded, she took out these purloined objects and memorized his face.

"See you later, kiddo."

"Bye, Dad."

She stood on the front steps and watched him drive away. Then she sat down, leaning back, her face pointed toward the sun. The bag lady was figuring out her profit with a stumpy pencil. She glared at Cordelia, annoyed at having to share the stoop.

"Welcome home."

He blocked out the light completely. His hair had grown back, and there was an earring in his lobe. She could tell from the way he was smiling that he was very glad to see her.

"Hullo," he said. The bag lady gathered up her accounting and went off in a huff.

"I'm sorry," she replied, closing her eyes.

"What for?"

"Worrying you."

"Don't talk nonsense. I wasn't that worried. You quite often promised to kill yourself in Dublin." He sat down next to her and lit a cigarette. She noticed he had finally started smoking an American brand instead of Gauloises. "I don't think you really meant to do that."

"What?"

"That." He gestured toward her arms.

"You mean die."

"Umm."

"I did."

"No you didn't."

"Yes I did."

"Rubbish."

"Oh, yeah?"

"You'd never have fucked it up so badly. You would have gone somewhere slightly less exposed than a cemetery. You're too good at doing things."

"Just because I did it badly doesn't mean I didn't do it on purpose."

"For Christ's sake, Cordelia! Don't be so bloody . . . American!"

"What should I be? English? Cambridge English?"

"Stop it. I think you just wanted us to know how bad it was for you."

"No I didn't."

"I always knew."

"What?"

"How little you thought of yourself."

"How?"

"It was easy. You'd get drunk and say terrible things about your dad. The way he'd walked out on your mother and destroyed your first love. It was obvious you were very confused. You tried to make me happy, and I walked all over you. Then you begged me not to leave."

"I just loved you."

"Never mind."

"I don't anymore. This is stupid." She stood and stretched. Her back had begun to ache.

"Can I come up?"

"I guess so."

She was afraid to go into her apartment. It would not have seemed so strange were it not for Harrison standing there expecting her to open the door. She stared at her keys. He looked at the door, at her hand, which was trembling at her side, and then he took the keys and moved her gently behind him.

"Stand back," he said. "I'll get rid of the scary monsters."

She didn't care what he thought of her. She sat down on the stairs, her knees tight against her chest, her chin resting on her knees. She thought tiny. Tiny things were not deserving of being hurt.

"Come in, little Alice. It was a fierce battle, but the hobgoblins went back to Brooklyn."

Someone, probably her sister, had opened the windows, washed her dishes, dusted and vacuumed and polished all the surfaces. There were flowers in vases and a few new throw pillows on the couch. Her sheets were changed, the bathtub was scrubbed, and the kitchen was gleaming. All evidence of her

239

holing up like some sort of night-blind animal had been removed.

The apartment was somehow touching. It occurred to her that someone rather poor and hopeful lived here. If a picture of this place appeared in the Sunday *New York Times*, people would send money. They would finish their croissants and Jamaican Blue Mountain coffee and go right for their checkbooks. The tables were covered carefully with something, a piece of lace, an antique shawl, a yard of cheap India silk. Things had been accumulated or collected and arranged in little groups; small glass animals, shells, beads from European flea markets, feathers and polished wooden boxes. Her bed was covered by an antique quilt. Needlepoint pillows covered her futon sofa. She thought of the cruel, clean lines of Philip's rooms. She saw her apartment burning.

"It's so fucking pathetic," she said to Harrison. "How on earth could I have wanted to leave all this adorableness, all this . . . stuff?" Her sarcasm was ruined by the catch in her throat.

"Where's the stray cat?" she shrieked, tossing a pillow against a wall. "Where are the little talking turtledoves?"

"Delia . . ."

"I don't know this person."

"What person?"

"The person that lives here. Little Miss Muffet . . . Uncle Wiggily's retarded niece . . . Candyland."

"There's nothing wrong with your flat. It's like your flat in Dublin. You make lovely little nests."

"I want to be in a desert. Somewhere else. A desert with bleached bones and dirt. When my sister died I ate dirt."

"Look . . ."

"I'm sorry." She quieted down. "I really did something to myself, and it's very weird coming back to this." She started to giggle. "I have no taste," she said, almost gleefully. It wasn't so bad, really. It was almost a relief, since she was alive, to be home. "It just frightened me. All this effort."

"You're alive. She died. You didn't."

"I know. That's the rub. You're right. Anyway, it doesn't matter."

"Yes it does."

"I didn't expect to have to kill a baby."

"I know."

"And my mother. And my father. You're unhappy. Sam's gone. Amelia's full of rage and unwept tears. I had an affair with a sadomasochistic father of two."

"It's better than the soaps."

"Well, it has to stop. I want a normal life. I want control."

The doorbell rang. She picked up a pillow and stood in the middle of the living room, shaking from head to foot.

"Do you think I already had my nervous breakdown?" she asked Harrison brightly. "I mean a real one, where you get to be locked up and you're watched very closely. A lunatic asylum . . . do they still have those? Do I have to do anything special to be allowed in?"

The bell kept ringing.

"Shall I answer?" Harrison asked.

"I don't know. I'm going to take a Valium."

Harrison pressed the intercom. "Yes?"

"Is Cordelia there?"

"Who is this?"

"Philip."

"She doesn't want to see you," Harrison said. "Fuck off."

Cordelia came out of the bathroom, smoking a cigarette. She pressed the door release.

"I'll be right back," she told Harrison. "Let him in."

They were sitting across from each other, glaring, when she again emerged from the bathroom. She had applied teal-colored mascara. Without any other makeup, her green eyelashes were very striking. She had changed into a black T-shirt and blue jeans.

Philip was wearing stone-washed denims, lizard cowboy boots, a soft suede shirt, and a silver belt. His pupils were large, and he was chewing nervously on the inside of his cheek. Cordelia sat on a small stool. The apex of the triangle.

"You okay?" Philip mumbled, swallowing his words.

"She tried to commit suicide," Harrison snapped. "What's your definition of okay?"

"I'm fine," Cordelia said perkily, frowning at Harrison. The Valium had begun to round off the corners nicely. "I like your boots."

"Tony Lama," Philip remarked morosely, his hands drooping between his knees.

"For God's sake—" Harrison began, but he was stopped by her raised hand.

Philip noticed the bandages and groaned. "Sweetheart," he said tenderly, "how could you have done this to yourself? I thought you were just talking that way because of Sasha. I mean about the gun."

Harrison snorted. "You ever counted the bruises?" he asked Philip. "I think you loved hurting her. If violence gives you such a hard-on, you should check out the scars. They should be very sexy."

"Why don't you mind your own fucking business?"

"I'm fine," Cordelia said again, smiling at her company. "Could you stop talking about me as if I was some sort of violated zombie?"

"You aren't fine," Harrison said, pounding his fists on the table. "You almost died, and you're still completely fucked up."

"Who are you? Dr. Ruth? Honey, can we get rid of Stallone here? He's talking like a jerk."

"I'm not leaving her alone with you. In fact, she's coming to Mozambique with me."

"No she's not," Cordelia said, shaking her finger at Harrison. "I don't think that's what we decided." She turned back toward Philip. "But he's not leaving."

Harrison glared at Cordelia. Philip jiggled his foot and chewed his thumb. Cordelia tried to imagine something she might enjoy eating. It felt like years since her last meal. The phone rang. She answered.

"Honey?"

"Hi, Daddy."

"You okay?"

"Yup."

"Have you eaten?"

"Not yet. Harrison's here."

"Is that okay?"

"I guess so."

"What about the other one? The mob scumbag."

"He's here, too."

"Jesus Christ, Cordelia! What's going on over there? You need peace and quiet."

"It's quiet. He's leaving soon. The scumbag."

"Good. You want me to come over and throw him out?"

"No, Daddy."

"I was thinking about that little talk we had. About Seth. He wouldn't have let you shine. I saw him polishing up the birdcage, and I guess it really pissed me off."

"Daddy . . ."

"Did I ruin your life, honey?"

"I don't think so."

"Call if you need me."

"I will."

"Get the good one to make you an omelet or something."

"Sure."

"I love you, honey."

"I love you, too."

"Sweet dreams, bunny."

"Night, Daddy."

She returned to her stool. Philip had taken off one of his boots. Harrison was standing at the window, staring into the darkness.

"The abortion wasn't that bad," she said.

"They treated you well?" Philip asked.

Harrison had begun pounding his fist into the wall.

"Yes. I mean, they were kind, and the doctors there are very capable. But afterward I felt it was useless."

"You cut your wrists?" Philip was staring at her bandaged arms.

"My elbows. Someone told me it was faster. I slashed from my elbows to the wrists."

"Oh my God, baby—"

"Don't call her baby!" Harrison was standing with his back against the wall, his fists clenched.

"Fuck you!"

"Stop it! There's nothing more to be said here. Philip, I want you to go."

He stood and then sat down to pull on his boot. He reached into his back pocket and pulled out a large roll of bills. He put the money on the table. Harrison stomped into the kitchen.

"I just want you to have it," Philip whispered. "Buy something or go away somewhere nice. I can give you more."

"No! Maybe I'll go to Dublin for a while."

"Yeah. That's what I thought. Ireland. You can see your friends. That girl you told me about . . ."

"Oona."

"Yeah. It would be good to see her, wouldn't it?"

"Yes."

"It's been a long time since you've been back."

"Eight years."

"Your friends must have missed you."

"Yes. Also, it's Ireland. For some reason, I was very happy there. I was never that happy in America."

"With him?" Philip jerked his thumb in the direction of the kitchen.

"No. Harrison and I were miserable. Well, not all the time. It was just Ireland. I had this very simple existence. A three-speed bicycle and no supermarkets. I was never lonely there. You couldn't get lost so easily as you can in New York. People knew you. We did things. My friends had picnics and parties. Maybe it was just being away. . . ."

"I wish I could be your friend."

"Your wife said you didn't have any."

"I'm getting divorced."

"I don't care, Philip. You should take care of your children. I want you to go now." She stood up. "Thanks for the money."

"I'm so sorry, Delia."

"Goodbye."

When she heard the door click, she breathed deeply for a second and then turned on the radio to a classical music station. The money was piled on the table. Harrison came out of the kitchen with a tray.

"I've made us some tea."

There were toasted cheese sandwiches cut into quarters, a plate of banana-nut bread, apples and raisins cut up with orange sections, and a pot of tea. She recognized the bread as her mother's.

"Is my mother angry at me?"

"No. But she thought your father should bring you home. She thought you might want to talk to him." He poured the tea. "You won't come to Africa?"

"No."

"Why not?"

"I can't go that far away. My mother needs me. I think I have another Marriott commercial to shoot. I have to start therapy—"

"What for?"

"Harrison! You're the one who suggested shock treatment! I almost bled to death on my sister's grave. I allowed some man to tie me up and beat me black and blue. There's got to be years of stuff I can dredge up about my father. . . ."

"You've been depressed. This is a depressing city. Mozambique is beautiful. You can't be depressed there."

"I can be depressed anywhere. I want to be free."

"I'll make you happy."

"You never have."

"I've changed."

"Everything's changed, Harrison. I don't want to follow you to the jungle anymore. Eight years ago I would have walked on knives to hear you say this, but now I just want to find out why I'm so unhappy. I want a life."

"You've always been like this."

"So I'll change."

"When hell freezes over!"

"Thanks for the vote of confidence."

"I don't want you to change."

"That's no big surprise, considering my sole aim in life was to try and make you happy."

"Who asked you?" Harrison screamed. "I want my baby back!"

He had put down his mug and picked up a pillow. Tears streamed down his face. Cordelia put her arms around him, pulling him into her lap.

"Sam's coming back," she said. "Everything's going to be fine."

CHAPTER

29

THE AER LINGUS FLIGHT WAS PACKED WITH ROWDY IRISH-Americans. As cruising speed was reached, the attendants were run off their feet fetching drinks.

"Give me a Paddy, darlin'," the man sitting across the aisle from Cordelia said. "Better yet, give me two."

The stewardess bent over to whisper in Cordelia's ear. "They're going back to see their mums, and the poor dears are terrified of finding out how blissful Irish bachelorhood really is!'

Cordelia ordered a glass of wine and took a Valium. She wanted to sleep until she could see a tiny patch of emerald green between the clouds. As the plane flew through the darkness, she dreamed.

The two sisters sat in the garden. One, the older, was quite pregnant. The other was demonstrating how to do sit-ups without straining the lower-back muscles. She was wearing a white cotton sundress striped by grass stains. Her nephew ran out of the house and sat on her stomach. She lifted him high off the ground to fly, her feet flat against his belly. Her dress fell over her face, to reveal long tanned legs and blue cotton underpants. The insides of her arms were lightly striped by healing scars.

"For God's sake, Delia," her sister said peevishly. "You've been showing your panties like this since you were two!"

"Look, Mommy," Tom screamed, swimming through the air. "I can fly!"

"Look, Mommy," Cordelia yelled, "I can laugh!"

Amelia tilted her face toward the sun, closing her eyes and folding her hands across her stomach. Earlier that afternoon they were making tuna-fish sandwiches and Amelia had begun to weep.

"I don't want to have this baby without her," she sobbed. "I'm afraid."

Cordelia patted her sister on the shoulder until she was quiet. "I'll help you," she said. "I'll faint in the delivery room and make you forget the pain."

She woke with a start, rolling over to find herself face down in cat, a large Persian, whose fluffy body vibrated with purrs. There was a quiet knock on the door.

"Come in."

Oona was carrying a mug, which she put down on the table next to Cordelia's bed. She picked up the cat and flung her out the door.

"Disgusting creature," she said, "waking up our sleeping princess." She sat down on the edge of the bed. "Do you want to sleep in some more, Delia? You still look crippled."

Cordelia picked up Oona's hand and kissed it. "What time is it?"

"A quarter to three. You looked like you needed to be left in bed."

"It's the air."

"It's not the bloody air, Cordelia Cavanagh. You looked a thousand years old getting off that jumbo jet! Like you'd been through some sort of famine! Americans are meant to be fat!"

Oona pulled on one of Cordelia's fingers to illustrate, and the nightgown's sleeve fell back to reveal the long red scar from wrist to elbow.

"Mother of God," Oona gasped. "What have you done?"

When Cordelia tried to take back her hand, Oona took the other one and saw a similar mark.

"Oh, God," she gasped.

"It's not so bad."

"Not so bad? This is no feeble cry for attention! What's been going on over there since Cynthia died? Why didn't you call me?"

"I couldn't. I wanted to come here so badly, but my family . . . Well, my mother needed me. I was afraid if I got in touch it would just be worse. Anyway, I wasn't of much use. I stopped eating, and then . . . I can't explain."

"Try," Oona pleaded.

"The thing with Cynthia . . . I had this theory that if I scared her badly enough she might come back. I know it sounds completely cracked, but when we were little we played hide-and-seek, and I was always it. I used to get scared of the dark, and I'd scream until she got worried about me and came out."

"So you thought she'd run home and touch the tree if you did something terrible?"

Cordelia nodded.

"It makes perfect sense to me." Oona shuddered slightly and reached across Cordelia to light a cigarette. She hadn't changed very much except to grow prettier. She had the translucent skin and high color associated with the Irish, but her hair was honey blond and her eyes were an unusual shade of blue-gray. When Cordelia left after her year abroad, Harrison and Oona went camping in France. They had never been particularly close friends, but Oona wrote that they both missed her so much it helped to be together. At some point they fell in love. Cordelia tried in vain to reach Harrison on his landlady's phone, when finally one of the boarders answered and told her Harrison had moved in with his girlfriend. He gave her Oona's number.

She wanted to kill them both. At night she lay awake imagining conversations between them in which they said cruel things about her body. She, the exile, felt Oona profited from Cordelia's teaching Harrison how to feel. Her jealousy was a completely new experience. When she allowed herself to think of the two of them together, she would lose her vision, and her mouth would fill with something bitter-tasting.

When the affair ended, Oona wrote to her: "I could understand your never forgiving me, but try. He never loved me as much as you, and he couldn't love either of us as much as we deserved." She didn't believe that Harrison didn't love Oona, with her lovely cat eyes and her perfect Irish bones. The letter remained unanswered until, one night after drinking two bottles of wine by herself, she called Oona, waking her at five A.M.

"I just wanted to tell you I hate you," she said, slurring her words slightly.

"Cordelia? Oh, Cordelia, it's so good to hear your voice!"

Cordelia began to sob, and one hundred dollars later they were best friends again.

"How long can you stay?" Oona asked now.

"Ten days."

"Surely longer than that! It's been eight bloody years. Why do you have to get back so quickly?"

"I have things to do."

"What things? Don't be such a predictable Yank! Where's your fucking Filofax? I'm going to burn it!"

"Agents to see. Auditions. I've finally begun to get work. And my mom's starting a new chemo cycle. . . ."

"Ah, I'd forgotten. Sorry. How is she?"

"Pretty cheerful. But it's all denial, of course. Things have been very hard on her. She looks lovely, but all her hair went gray, almost overnight. It was as if her body was telling us what it couldn't manage to ignore. Also, Harrison: I think he's going back to Africa."

There was a brief silence. Both women lit cigarettes.

"For good?"

"I don't know. He's meeting his wife in Greece, and they'll decide what to do about Sam. Or maybe they'll work it all out." Cordelia put a pillow behind her back and stretched. "Or maybe he'll stay in New York."

"I doubt it." Oona was plucking apart a corner of the quilt with intense concentration.

"Why?"

"He belongs on a farm. Harrison loves dirt."

"There's masses of dirt in Manhattan."

"Fertile dirt. Family dirt. You know what I mean." Oona sighed. "His wife seems so cruel. . . ."

"Umm. But we only know his side." Cordelia looked at Oona, their eyes meeting for the first time since they had begun to speak of Harrison. "Do you think of him very often?"

"Harrison?"

"No. James Joyce! Of course Harrison. Don't play dumb with me, Oona McCafferty!"

"No. I don't allow myself to get caught in that trap. It's like a spider's web. I see his face and then a piece of his body: his shoulder—"

"His shoulder?" Cordelia laughed.

"Something. And then I'll have a flashback to some episode."

"For instance?"

"Oh, eating papayas in Swaziland." Oona put her head on Cordelia's stomach.

"I never went to Swaziland!" Cordelia pouted.

"You went back to America."

"I never ate papayas with Harrison."

"Oh, shut up!"

"He's a fuck!"

"A rotter!"

"A peasant!"

"A wanker!"

"A churlish son of a whore!" Oona was clutching her side and giggling.

"A silly bugger!"

"He misses his son," Oona said softly.

"He'll always miss something. 'Come to Africa,' he said to me. Like I'd give up everything to simply live in some sort of proximity to his perfection. No 'marry me' or 'live with me.' Just 'follow me,' 'trust me.' Blindly." Cordelia sat up angrily.

Oona laughed. "Ruby Tuesday, honey! When you change with every new day."

Cordelia groaned. "Still I'm gonna miss you."

"Exactly."

They sat in the kitchen drinking strong milky tea sweetened by honey that Oona's mother had taken from her own bees. The mug was Cordelia's, kept by Oona for eight years. It was hand-thrown porcelain, with a white glaze over blue clouds. They toasted brown bread and ate soft-boiled eggs in egg cups. A fire burned in the grate. Dublin was having a cool spring.

Before it grew dark, Cordelia borrowed Oona's bike and rode to Dun Laoghaire, through Blackrock, ending up in Sandycove. She sat across from James Joyce's tower and watched Irish children fish for crabs. Harrison had brought her here. They had stood looking over the "forty-foot" where the old men still swam naked in all seasons, as they did when Leopold Bloom strolled through his twenty-four hours. The spray from the waves covered them, and Harrison pushed her flat against the retaining wall and told her she was beautiful. She had thought he might finally say he loved her, but he didn't. Still, it was better than nothing.

"My beauty," he had whispered into her hair, "what have I done to deserve this?" Later, he had walked out very far on the pier, and she watched him stare into the sea and felt in her bones that they would never make each other happy. She wished she might look away and he would disappear.

Now she sat on the edge of the seawall, tossing shells into the waves, and gradually, inexplicably, the band of pain that had wrapped itself across her shoulders, like some sort of harness, relaxed, and she felt there was reason to hope.

They were playing Scrabble that evening in the living room, an uninspired, sleepy game. Mozart was on the radio, and rain was beating against the windows.

"Can I always come back here?"

"Of course," Oona said, spelling out the word INGRATE.

"Always?" Cordelia rolled on her back. She was losing.

"We love you, Cordelia," Oona said quietly, picking out new letters. "We didn't want you to leave. You can always come back here."

That night Cordelia dreamed she was on stage in front of a darkened audience, reciting a poem by Sylvia Plath in which she describes her father as being like a Nazi officer. Cynthia emerged from the shadows, and the two of them performed in absolute synchronization, hand to hand, face to face, a perfect mirror. The rules forbade her reaching forward through space to touch her sister. She could almost feel Cynthia's body at the very tip of her fingers, but it was as if she were Orpheus and by touching Cynthia she would condemn her to the same fate suffered by Eurydice. Despite her obedience, Cynthia slowly faded out of the light. Cordelia was left alone on the stage. She did not know her lines. The audience was filled now with members of her acting class, waiting for a performance. Her sister had left her alone without words. She sank to her knees in complete defeat, the spotlight a blinding pain.

After several days in Dublin, she borrowed a pack and a tent and hitched a ride to the west coast. She planned to camp on Inishbofin, a sparsely populated island where she had stayed with Harrison when they were vacationing in Connemara.

The mailboat to Inishbofin left at ten-thirty in the morning. It was filled with supplies from the mainland, as well as several German passengers. As they neared the island, she could see that Bofin was virtually unchanged, except for an increase in the number of power lines running out to the cottages.

"Cable television," the first mate told her. "They're all mad for it!" On the east end of the island she glimpsed an oddly designed house built to look out over one of the loveliest stretches of the beach.

"It's a geodesic dome," the first mate said. "The lunatic that designed it hung himself in Kerry last month. Too much cocaine, they said. It can't be made watertight. Too many seams. I hate the look of it myself. Reminds me of the Pentagon."

Birds were nesting on the high walls of the ruined monasteries where banished Catholic priests were sent by Cromwell. They used to escape, only to drown in the treacherous water. She recalled the mailboat's captain pointing out these monuments to the Irish troubles and whispering to Harrison: "The sea's loaded with dead priests! If Cromwell was mean enough to send them out here, he might have given the poor dears swimming lessons!"

While the boat docked, she gathered up her belongings, and refusing an offer of a "jar" in the pub from a crew member, she walked up the hill to a ruined farmhouse set above the island's only hotel and pitched her tent. It was the same site Harrison had chosen for them on their visit eight years before, and it had a nice view, as well as a spring nearby for fresh water. A few Germans were attemping to pitch their tent in the backyard of the pub, which was actually used as a privy. She hoped someone would be kind enough to advise them to move. After eating an apple and some cheese, she went down to the pub with writing paper and a book. She ordered a ginger beer and sat at a table against the wall to write a letter.

"Dear Harrison," it said. "Remember that weekend we came to Bofin because we couldn't stand to be alone together anymore?"

A shadow fell across the page. She looked up to see a bulky man wearing a dark-gray fisherman's sweater. He was bearded and middle-aged and had sharp blue eyes.

"So you've returned?"

"Yes."

"Eamon Downey."

"Cordelia Cavanagh."

"I know who you are. An American from New Jersey. Studied history at Trinity. Acted. Couldn't forget such a lovely name, the juxtaposition of that old fart Shakespeare with a good solid surname like Cavanagh."

She had ceased being surprised by the Irish ability to remember facts and recall faces.

"Where's your man, then?"

"Excuse me?"

"That giant of an African."

"Oh. Actually, he's in New York."

"So you got him after all? Ah, persistence is its own reward." Eamon sat down on the seat across from her with a sigh.

"Not exactly."

"Won't marry you, then?"

"He's married someone else."

"Someone else? Instead of you? The cheek of him! What a horse's behind! To be expected of an individual raised in a society where human beings are treated worse than animals! Cordelia! What a blind fool of a man! Still, you were already discouraged."

"When?"

"On your little trip here. You stuck to him like tar."

"No I didn't."

"You had a look of stark, raving terror in your eyes. Don't glare at me. I'm just having a joke. Happy, is he?"

"No."

"Ha! Good. Miserable?"

"His wife left him for his best friend and took their son."

"Terrible. Still, he made the wrong choice, didn't he? And what brings you back to the Emerald Isle during the worst depression since the famine?"

"I needed a vacation."

"A vacation, is it? In Bofin? I'd go to California for that. Palm Springs. My ex-wife lives there with some disgusting old man. What's here but cold rain and fish?"

"Peace." She had rolled up her sleeves absently. The scars were still very red against the pale skin of her inner arm.

Eamon whistled. "And what did you do to yourself here to cause such nasty-looking marks?" His hand held her fingers as he rotated her wrist back and forth. He was a very strong man. "You didn't do this over him, did you?"

"No."

"You've changed quite a bit, now that I look at you. It's hard to lay a finger on just what it is. I'd say you don't believe anymore."

"No." Cordelia had barely whispered. Eamon gently stroked her knuckles.

"What terrible event led to this bleakness?"

"They killed my sister."

"Who did?"

"Someone in New York. She didn't have any money, but she was raped and stabbed and left to die."

"Dear God—"

"There is no fucking God!"

"No. Not in that. Perhaps not in anything. So you tried to follow her?"

"Yes."

"But it wasn't your turn to die now, was it? You weren't meant to add to that terrible burden of grief your parents must bear. You were meant to do something fine."

"I can do nothing!"

"Nonsense! There's transformation in every woman. The power to conjure up something from nothing. My mother used to make feasts from an old cabbage and a few potatoes. Creation. Your bodies hold the secrets of the universe."

"Not mine." Cordelia choked. "I killed it!"

She began to cry, great wrenching sobs, while Eamon smoked his pipe and patted her hand. The pub was empty. No one stared. Perhaps the barkeep had seen hysterical American women before. After a few minutes she looked up and giggled.

"I can't believe I've done this."

"You're starting to heal. Feel better?"

"No. Yes. I don't know what that means. Better than what?"

"Never mind. Leave yourself alone. How long will you stay?"

"Just a few days. I have to go back to America pretty soon."

"Well, you're always welcome here. We don't always tell the Yanks that."

"Thank you."

The next day she walked the length of Bofin, stopping to sit in the weak spring sun, once stripping off her clothes to dive into a lagoon. There were no longer hands pushing her toward the edge of the cliff, and she saw that survival was, after all, an instinct. For the last time she apologized to her aborted child. She returned to Dublin feeling something that resembled happiness.

CHAPTER

30

"ARE YOU GOING TO MOZAMBIQUE?" OONA WAS UP TO HER elbows in water. They had cooked a complicated feast for Cordelia's last night in Ireland.

"I can't," Cordelia said dreamily, staring at her reflection in the bottom of the roasting pan. "The circles under my eyes have gone! I thought I'd have to have plastic surgery!"

Oona snorted. "Why can't you?"

"It's too far away from my mom. Amelia's going to have another baby. Anyway . . ." Cordelia sat down, still holding the pan.

"What?"

"I think it's all in the abstract. If I really had Harrison, if I was finally sure of him, I don't think I'd know what to do with him. He's too . . . distracting. I don't know where I'd put him."

"He isn't a coatrack, you silly cow!"

"Umm. I have a lot of work to do. . . . I look different."

Oona stripped off her rubber gloves and crossed the kitchen to kiss Cordelia's forehead. "You look human," she said quietly. "You look alive."

She was flying out of Shannon Airport, which meant leaving at dawn to get there in time for the flight. Oona wanted to come with her.

"We did that the last time," Cordelia said. "All I saw was your face completely puffed out by tears."

They said goodbye in the Busaras.

"Don't be so hard on yourself," Oona whispered, tears running down her face. "If it gets bad again, come back."

"I will."

"Come back anyway. Just come back and live with me. We can be unwed mothers together."

As the bus rolled out of the station, Oona ran along the pavement, Cordelia hung out the window, and they held hands until they were separated. As she sat back in her seat, Cordelia felt her chest aching and saw that the eyes of her fellow passengers were filled with a curious sympathy.

She had tried to call Harrison that morning to tell him when she would be arriving. There was no answer. The ring had sounded hollow and flat, and she thought it must have simply died somwehere over the Atlantic. She awoke from a nightmare in the darkened cabin of the plane. She had dreamed of an airplane crash, with people scattered across a hillside like fallen laundry. There was the headless doll always shown on news broadcasts of air disasaters. Was her panic a sign that she no longer wanted to die? She listened to the easy breathing of the people in the seats nearby and then raised the shade on her window. They were breaking through a cloud, which opened to reveal streaks of light. The sun was coming up.

Spring had arrived during her absence from New York. While she waited for the shuttle bus to the JFK Express, she was surprised by the soft warmth of the air. Winter had seemed like a permanent condition.

"You're the yogurt lady," a teenage girl said to her on the subway. "That's cool."

Cordelia smiled, unable to understand what the girl was talking about. Her eyes moved around the car and saw, next to a warning in Spanish about the dangers of drinking alcohol during pregnancy, an ad for a new yogurt. She saw herself, dressed in pink shorts, bending over a small boy, offering him a taste of her yogurt while the male actor beamed into the distance. She had completely forgotten about the print campaign. People on the train were smiling and whispering. She smiled back. A woman held up her baby. The baby, smartly turned out in a striped sailor outfit, beamed and clapped her hands together with a shout. Cordelia smiled at the laughing child.

A boy sitting next to her leaned over and tapped her knee. He was clutching a pile of He-Man comics. "You rich?" he asked.

"Nope."

"You that lady?" He was pointing at the poster of the smiling family.

"Sort of."

"You gonna be on 'Dynasty'?" He gave her a sly grin, knowing that Cordelia, with her knapsack and her ratty clothes, was not going to be a bad lady on TV.

"Maybe," she whispered, giving him a poke. "Maybe I'll be Alexis's long-lost sister!"

"Nah! They done that already. Blake had her kidnapped. You could be . . . her maid!"

It was her stop. Cordelia winked at the boy. "Watch out for me," she said. "I'll be the one in the white apron."

Seventy-second Street was crowded and smelled of Papaya King hot dogs. The smile on her face faded, and she felt her jaw grow tense, her lips pull back against her clenched teeth. The people on the street pressed against her. There didn't seem to be room to move. The air was close. As she passed the tall, skinny black man who panhandled in front of her building, he bowed from the waist and gave her a wink. He had on a new red tie. She put some money in his cup. Tulips were beginning to break the soil in the little squares of earth around the trees on Sixty-ninth Street. The landlord's sister was staring out her window, her chin propped on her hands. Cordelia felt very let down. She wanted to sit on the stoop until someone claimed her. Coming home seemed like a mistake.

Her front door opened to a dim, clean apartment. The mail

had been collected and piled neatly next to a vase filled with daisies. A note propped against the vase said: "Welcome home! It's not as bad as you think! Call me! Maxine." Next to the flowers was a giant Toblerone bar with a piece missing. She put down her bags and dialed Harrison's number. The computer told her that "at the request of the subscriber, this line has been disconnected." She hung up and began to sift through her mail. Most of it consisted of warnings that unless she responded immediately, she would not win incredible amounts of money. There was a large envelope postmarked New York. She recognized the strong italic script as belonging to Harrison. Before she opened the envelope, she ate a big piece of chocolate.

Darling Cordelia:

By the time you read this I should be in Greece with Matilda and Sam. From there we will slowly work our way back to Africa. I have decided to return to the farm and do what I am best at. Matilda says she's willing to give it a try, and she might like it. Probably not, but as you said: What have I got to lose? I shall miss you and hope that our time together will be remembered by you as something healing and lovely. At least we put some very weary phantoms to rest. Ever since I heard about your sister I'd wanted to tell you how I felt about us. I hope Ireland performed its magic. Oona had written to me in some sort of distress. She had felt your soul slipping away. We had feared losing you to that inconsolable sorrow. We have underestimated your bravery. Here are some little things I'd wanted to leave with you. I shall always love you in my very weak and stupid fashion.

She emptied out the contents of the envelope. There were two photographs from their winter in Ireland. In one, the two of them stood in a tiny snowfall, laughing, their arms around each other's shoulders. They were very drunk. The second picture was of Cordelia sitting outside the Connemara cottage, wearing one of his bulky sweaters and no pants. They had woken to a freakish heat wave. She was shelling peas, sunburned and smiling, her hair a wild tangle down her back. The girl in the picture had the gaze of a believer. The girl in the picture expected to be loved. The envelope had also contained a few shells, a piece of polished turquoise, a small ivory elephant, and a feather. She put the things in a handmade box that her father had once sent her from California. It was carved out of redwood. The letter was filed. Harrison had finally left.

She stood naked in the bathroom, holding her breasts, staring at her face. "I am almost thirty," she murmured to her pale, jet-lagged countenance. The bathroom mirror, ringed by fluorescent bulbs, provided her with sufficient proof that she was aging rapidly, totally without grace. She ran a short film through her mind of Harrison and Matilda, dressed in designer jungle outfits, looking perfect.

Cynthia had sworn to her that things got better as you grew older.

"Look at me," she said to Cordelia. "I've always been so much cooler than you, and it's just because I'm older."

They had been standing in Cynthia's tiny kitchen making Szechwan chicken, drinking wine from coffee cups. Her boyfriend, Bob, turned on the radio, and some old Aretha Franklin came pouring out. Cynthia began to shimmy.

"Remember when Daddy brought this record home and we all danced around the living room?" she asked Cordelia, pulling her into the hall, where the two girls swooped and swirled, ground their hips and shimmied, until Bob moved the couch and all three of them pretended to be contestants on *Soul Train*.

Cynthia had taught her how to do the pony, the twist, the hustle, and the bump. Each semester she came home from college with new information about the revolution that was sweeping the country, and she made sure her little sisters were kept properly informed about the Vietnam War and the status of women. She showed them pictures of boys who looked like the paintings of Jesus on black velvet. She referred to these men as her lovers. Cordelia found her birth control pills, and playing with the dial that recorded the day of the week you took your pill, she managed to snap the plastic.

"You idiot," Cynthia said, frowning at her. "How can I tell

which pill to take?" But that was the end of the incident. She never stopped trying to teach her sisters about the world as she saw it.

Cordelia hadn't spoken to Robert in months. None of them had been able to say very much to him. Secretly they believed he should have taken better care of her, despite their knowledge of Cynthia's obstinacy and their appreciation of his devotion to her.

"Hello?"

"Robert? It's Cordelia."

"Delia! Great. I'm really glad you called."

"I was just thinking about you."

"How are you feeling?"

"Okay. I was thinking about that night we were all dancing around to Aretha—"

"Yeah! Couple number two: Jerome and Adele . . . Szechwan chicken. I remember."

"She told me things could only get better."

Robert sighed. "Well, I guess she was right."

"I've been in some trouble."

"Amelia told me. I'm sorry, honey."

"I'm the one who should be sorry."

"For what? Feeling?"

"I don't know." Still naked, she was lying on her back on the bed, her head hanging over the edge.

"I miss her so much, Robert."

"I know. So do I."

"Is it any better?"

"Not really, Delia. It's just as it was. Every day I wake up, and for a second, before I remember what happened, I feel okay. Then I turn over in this fucking huge bed and my arms are empty and it's just a ton of bricks. I have to struggle to get up."

They were both quiet for nearly a minute.

"Robert, I think she liked me. I mean, not just because we were sisters. But as a friend. It matters to me, because I was so dependent on her taking care of us. I wanted to have something different than that."

"Sure. Of course she liked you. And she had such respect for

263

your work. She really thought your acting was terrific. Speaking of which, I caught your yogurt commercial. What a trip! You looked so real! I nearly fell out of my chair!"

"What do you mean by real?"

"Like a mommy. I mean, hey, I just never saw you like that."

"The kid's a monster." There was a long pause. "You want to go for a walk in the park or something soon?"

"Sure. Call me or I'll call you. Don't let things get so bad again, okay?"

"I'll try. Bye, Robert."

"Bye, kid."

He wouldn't call her. She looked too much like her sister. Before the funeral he had sobbed in her arms and told her he needed to forget that Cynthia ever existed. Otherwise, he said, he'd never stop grieving. Delia privately believed he should have died from the pain or thrown himself off a tall building, but she knew her judgments were too harsh.

She thought about Harrison and Matilda. She would probably hang back until he reached for her, and their child would help erase the shadow of her infidelity. He would allow Matilda into his magic circle, and she would be protected from harm. Why hadn't she held on to him? Why hadn't she simply agreed to go to Mozambique? She stared at her stomach. They would never have that perfect child, the link that would complete the circle, a circle that guaranteed absolute safety.

Maxine had written down a few messages: from her dentist, her new agent, and an actor who wanted to schedule a rehearsal with her. She had told most people she was leaving town. The signal on her answering machine was glowing red, which meant it was close to full again. While she found a clean T-shirt and some underwear, she listened to the messages, slowly finishing off the bar of chocolate.

"Hi. It's Amelia. Your sister. You were supposed to be home by now, but I don't think you've been kidnapped by Iranian extremists. Remember, we aren't Jewish. Ha, ha. I need you to take Tom for a day or two. We're having some problems. Don't freak out. Nobody's dying. That's all that really matters. Call me in the morning. Oh, I hope you had a nice time, and your yogurt commercial's on constantly. What a disgusting little boy! Tom should get an agent. You get paid every time? Anyway, you smile a little too much, but you're very cute. Bye."

"You aren't back from Ireland yet, I guess. You probably wouldn't talk to me anyway. I've left Sasha. We got a legal separation. I think we should talk. I'll marry you, Cordelia. Swear to God."

"Hello. This is Sasha Trelawn. I wanted you to know I just obtained an order of protection against Philip. He started beating me again. I don't know whether he did that to you, but I imagine he might turn up, trying to get you back. He's a very dangerous man. You don't deserve to be abused. Be careful."

She lay back on the bed again, her head hanging over the edge. The early-evening light filtered across the room, creating a lace pattern against the wall. She raised one arm high above her head and admired the grace of her own shadow. The bruises Philip had left on her shoulders were almost all faded. Oona had seen them, the marks on her buttocks, the finger bruises along her spine and neck. She had said very little, merely shook her head and muttered, "That fucker." The long scars that ran from elbow to wrist were growing less apparent. Her body seemed filled with possibilities. She resisted the impulse to pull on her sneakers and run until she dropped. It was easy to imagine the relief of that movement, the darkness that descended after a great enough physical challenge. She tried to listen to her own breathing, the inner pulse of her blood flowing through the veins. It was a miracle, life. Something not to be discarded.

Each time they made love he had hurt her. She was always in a position that afforded him the best access to every part of her. Her neck was twisted, her hair pulled, her back strained, and the fear of him had made it impossible to let go, so she was nearly always trembling on the brink. She had begun to welcome the possibility of death at his hands. It was humiliating to admit the depths of her degradation, that she would encourage a man who

265

so hated and feared women. She had refused to understand that, believing it was something different, something else. She imagined her will was powerful enough to bend steel, to transform this hatred into something like love. She had finally offered herself to him as a sacrifice to the force that had destroyed her sister. A force which severed bonds that had once appeared invulnerable. History was eliminated, burned beyond recognition. With Harrison gone, it would be easy to return to that flame. The obliteration of her past endangered the future. He would provide her with drugs and money and probably get her more jobs. And he would probably kill her. She did not want that anymore. She kissed her own inner arms and fell asleep.

She woke to the sound of the phone ringing. The clock radio said it was eleven-thirty.

"Cordelia?" It was Amelia.

"Yes? Hi. Hi, Amelia."

"Were you asleep? Sorry it's so late. Welcome back and all that. Did you have a good time? Don't answer that. I need you to take Tom for two days."

"Sure. What's wrong?"

"Golly gee, that's hard to say." Her sister's voice sounded high and thin, barely hiding hysteria.

"Amy, what's the matter?"

"Michael. He's screwing his assistant."

"Oh, God."

"I found this letter she wrote him about his amazing dick."

"Oh, Amy . . ."

"He came to me on his knees, begging forgiveness. He says he felt shut out—that's the fucking word he used—shut out since Cynthia was murdered. Since that man raped and stabbed my precious sister, my fucking husband has felt ignored. So he bangs his administrative assistant! Like I had any control over shutting him out. Like I was excluding him from something wonderful instead of keeping him away from my anger, my hatred for this whole goddamned world!" Amelia took a deep breath. "Like I didn't feel like dying too. Oh, God, Cordelia . . ."

"Amy . . ."

"Why did he slaughter her like that?"

"I don't know. I don't want you to feel like this. I love you."

"I have to feel like this. The bimbo may have AIDS."

"Michael would know, wouldn't he?"

"He knew nothing about her! She might have been sleeping with Liberace! She's so young. Anyway, we've all had blood tests. If there's anything wrong with this girl and it affects my baby, I'm going to kill him. Both of them. I'm warning you, Cordelia. I'll shoot him right between the eyes. I have to get away for a few days."

"Come here, you and Tom."

"Thanks, honey, but I need to be alone."

"Are you sure?"

"Yes. I'll be okay. I'm very strong. When you cut your wrists, Mom was ready to give up. She just decided it was going to be one thing after the other, like we were some doomed gothic family in a Poe story." Amelia laughed. The sound was hollow and thin. "I wouldn't let you die, Cordelia."

"I know. You're strong. What do you want to do?"

"Lie beneath clean linen sheets somewhere. I have Michael's gold card, and I'll spend some money. Then I'm calling a lawyer."

"What about marriage counseling?"

"I'm too angry. He should just be condemned to marry that yuppie little bitch! It's the meanness of this I can't believe. He's angry at me because I can't respond to his emotional needs because my sister's been brutally murdered, so he fucks his secretary! What sort of person is that? Yet I love him, Cordelia. I thought we'd married for life. But that doesn't seem possible anymore. It's horrible, loving people."

"I love you."

"You have to. I'm your sister."

"Amelia . . ."

"Don't say anything else. I'll fall apart, and I'm the one who doesn't do that. Are you okay?"

"Sure."

"You aren't seeing that pig anymore?"

"No."

"Harrison?"

"He's gone back to his wife and son in Africa."

Amelia sighed. "What a lovely man. You should have kept him."

"I couldn't."

"Ah, well. I'll see you tomorrow."

"Good. I'm sorry, Amy."

"Everything will work out for the best. Bye, ducky."

Tom arrived the following day with a bagful of He-Man toys, plastic creatures with snake heads and lizard bodies. He seemed elated by the prospect of spending the night with his aunt.

Amelia's pregnancy was more advanced, but her face seemed thin, with slashes of badly applied makeup on her cheeks and dark purple circles under her eyes.

"Have some coffee; it's decaf." Cordelia put down a plate of muffins she had bought in Zabar's that morning.

"How's the jet lag?" Amelia perched awkwardly on a chair, her purse in her lap. Cordelia wanted to take her in her arms, but she didn't know how. Amelia was always hard to comfort.

"Have some raspberry jam from Dublin." She put out the butter and filled a pitcher with cream.

Amelia stood up. "I can't eat any of this," she said apologetically. "Just let me go, and I'll see you tomorrow night." She kissed Cordelia and Tom and was gone.

Cordelia took her nephew to the planetarium. The space show was narrated by Charlton Heston, and Cordelia felt as if she were being lectured to by Moses. They had lunch at Tavern on the Green, where Tom was served a cheeseburger on fancy china. The waiter was very impressed with Tom's manners and got him a huge sundae topped by three cherries and a plastic palm tree. After a few bites Tom pushed the dish away; Cordelia finished it. She felt very full. People kept saying nice things about her handsome son. After lunch they walked down to the boat pond in

Central Park and watched grown men guide their expensive model boats across the water.

"Where's Harrison?" Tom asked her, running up to have his laces tied after helping a young man navigate his schooner into harbor.

"He went to Africa."

"With Aunt Cynthia?"

"What?"

"Is she in Africa?" Tom was bent over his sneakers, adjusting the Velcro tops with intense concentration.

"Is that what you think, honey?" She knew he had been told his aunt had died, but maybe something had changed.

"Sometimes. Sometimes I forget she's dead, and sometimes I think she's hiding in my closet." Tom giggled.

"Your closet?"

"Yup. And I'll open it and she'll jump out and we'll do something. Maybe I'll listen to my heart with her thingie. . . ."

"Stethoscope. Do you miss her?"

"No." Tom squinted up at her. "Is Mommy dead?"

"No!" Cordelia squatted down so they were facing each other. "She's just gone to visit some friends. She'll be back tomorrow."

"Did Aunt Cynthia go to visit friends?"

"Not exactly. She died."

"Was Aunt Cynthia your mommy?"

"No, sweetie. Grandma's my mommy. Cynthia's my sister."

"Is she going to be dead forever?"

"Yes, Tom."

"Are you sure?"

"Yes."

"How long is that?"

"I don't know. A long time."

"Why?"

"Dead people don't come back."

"I would," Tom said, spinning around like a top. "My mommy and I would." He stopped, wobbled. "Did Aunt Cynthia have a little boy?"

"No, darling."

"Maybe if she had a little boy she wouldn't have died." He finished tightening the Velcro. "Or she'd come back. That man said I could help him with his boat some more. Okay?"

"Sure."

Tom ran back to the captain, while Cordelia watched a group of expectant mothers comparing their bellies.

For dinner they had chicken noodle soup and grilled cheese on bagels. They watched a repeat of *Happy Days*, and then Cordelia read Tom nearly twenty pages of *Charlie and the Chocolate Factory* until his eyelids drooped. After she turned off the light, Tom pulled her down to whisper in her ear.

"Can she see us?"

"Who?"

"Aunt Cynthia."

"I think so."

"You think she's lonely for a little boy or something?"

"Not if she can see us."

"Will Mommy come back tomorrow?"

"Yes. And we'll make her a lovely supper. Go to sleep now, Tommy."

After a moment his breathing was regular and loud. She left the door ajar so he could see her sitting in the living room if he woke up. She wondered where Amelia was and whether Michael was sleeping with his girlfriend. She wanted to call him and scream at him for hurting her sister. Their family seemed like such a flimsy cloth, the threads unraveling, breaking with age.

CHAPTER

31

SHE AND TOM SHOPPED IN ZABAR'S THE NEXT DAY FOR A fancy supper for Amelia. The deli man gave them samples of caviar and smoked salmon. Tom had highly developed tastes for a little boy. They picked up a chocolate cake at the bakery and flowers from the Korean stand on the corner of Cordelia's street.

When Amelia arrived, Tom barely acknowledged her presence, continuing to piece together a massive Darth Vader puzzle while he chewed on a cinnamon raisin bagel.

"Nice puzzle," Amelia said. "Did Aunt Delia buy you that?" When Tom didn't answer she shrugged and sat down.

"We went to F.A.O. Schwarz," Cordelia said. "I don't know why he's so quiet. He was excited about seeing you."

Amelia sighed, spreading cream cheese on a bagel. "He's just angry at me. He knows there's something wrong."

"Well, he'll be fine. He was very good."

"Maybe he'll be fine. Maybe not. A new baby and a divorce is a one-two punch. It just might hurt."

"Oh, Amy . . ." Cordelia grabbed her sister's cold hand. "Don't you think . . ."

"I think it's best. I think it doesn't matter why. I think I can't sustain life with any more loss. Or anger. I have so much anger

I choke on it. I did a lot of screaming last night." Amelia's eyes were suddenly dull and hard. "I can't forgive him. I've tried. I don't think I can love anyone like that anymore, so it's probably better. He's done me a favor by giving me a way out." She put down the barely touched bagel. "I think it's time to go."

"Can't you stay?"

"No. Thank you. Come on, Tom."

"I don't want to go home!"

"Well, that's too bad."

"I hate you!"

"Yes, I know that. That's what mothers are for."

May was very hot. People grew angry waiting for subways and snapped at one another, their tempers strained by the heat. Those who owned air conditioners shut their windows and retreated. The rest sat on stoops or fire escapes and roofs, cold cans of beer or soda pressed against their foreheads, smiling weakly at their neighbors.

A young woman was murdered in Central Park, and the newspapers compared the circumstances of her death to those of Cynthia Cavanagh's. Cordelia opened the *Times* one morning to see a photograph of her sister sitting on the front steps of her new clinic, sandwiched between two smiling little girls. Her hair was pulled back from her face, and she was smiling. She would always be thirty-three years old and beautiful. Cordelia ran her hand across the picture, touched the hair and the face, her hands dark with newsprint. She tried to get away from the apartment, but the panic began on the street and she returned.

The phone was ringing.

"Come home," her mother said. "Please come home so I can see you're safe."

"Do you wish you'd had a better childhood?" Dr. Cavanagh was weeding a patch of arugula, while Cordelia lay in a pool of sweat, spread out in the sun on a chaise longue. She had fashioned a bathing suit from a scarf tied tightly across her breasts and an old pair of gym shorts that said ANDOVER. Her mother sported a gigantic straw hat anchored to her head by an Hermès scarf. She had on a huge pair of sunglasses and a faded sleeveless silk dress. She resembled the rich, eccentric aunt of an aristocratic family, one of the Beale sisters perhaps, a pillar of society fallen on hard times.

"Mother . . ."

"Really. I often wonder if you are able to forgive me for not sticking by your father."

"For Christ's sake."

"If I had, Amelia might have stayed with Michael."

"The scumbag was screwing his administrative assistant, for God's sake."

"And her baby gets born into a fatherless home and her son wonders what he did wrong. Maybe she could have forgiven him."

"What's the point?"

Her mother sat back on her heels and wiped the sweat off her face, leaving behind a long streak of dirt. She surveyed her lettuce patch. "Happiness. I want my girls to be happy."

"With scumbag men?"

"No, darling. You're right. Does your shrink think you had a terrible childhood?"

"Mother!"

"Never mind. I'm just sure we did something terrible to you."

"Why? Am I that much of a fuck-up?"

"No! You aren't anything but wonderful. It's just I feel so responsible."

"You aren't that powerful, Mother. Maybe you should get some therapy."

"Umm. Maybe." She stood and looked down at her sweating daughter. "Don't get too much sun. Do you have the PABA fifteen on?" Cordelia nodded. "You look so much better now. Not like some sort of Ethiopian famine victim. It's lovely."

"No it's not. I have to lose ten pounds by the end of the week."

"Cordelia!"

"Just kidding. But I have a TV audition, and you look much fatter on camera."

"Another commercial?"

"Nope. A series. Prime time."

"A series? Like Mary Tyler Moore?"

"It's just an audition, Mom. But my agent said they really want to cast an unknown."

"But you have all those commercials."

"Just the yogurt one. Marriott's paying me a holding fee for the other. I'm still completely unknown. Anyway, the series is about a woman who's still in love with her ex-husband. She's got a crummy job writing copy in an ad agency, no boyfriend, and terrible taste in men. She's worried about never having children, and she's addicted to sugar. She spends all her time going to the gym and zapping Lean Cuisine in her microwave."

"Don't you have a boyfriend?"

"No. I don't want to talk about it. The twist is she goes out at night and saves homeless children and pregnant teenagers. Like in bus terminals and stuff. So it's a comedy with a conscience."

"Oh, brother."

"It's pretty unbelievable, but who cares? I'd make an incredible amount of money. I could pay you back, and if I never meet a decent man I can have a baby by myself."

"Oh, Cordelia . . ."

"I'm not ruling out the possibility, Mom. I just want to know I have some control. It's important information, since the odds are so bad."

"You should be doing Chekhov."

"No I shouldn't. This series is about my life, except the noble part. And I don't have a microwave."

"You don't? Let's go buy one! K mart has a closeout sale."

"I'm not going to K mart. How's Daddy?"

"Fine. Except the bimbo's signed him up for some sort of horrible Tantric yoga class that's dedicated to showing how to produce orgasms that last twenty minutes."

"Yuck."

"That woman's a walking cliché of Malibu self-help. She's a parody of herself."

"She got him into A.A."

"Yes, but she'll drive him back to drink! She wears him out. Want some lemonade?"

"Why would anyone want to come for twenty minutes? It would get like everything else in life."

"What's that?"

"Boring."

"Oh, honey . . ."

"Mom, I'm kidding. I'm actually very uncomfortable discussing my father's sex life." Cordelia closed her eyes. "I'd like a Tab."

Her mom went into the house, and Cordelia stretched like a cat on the chaise. Her belly was no longer concave, and when she lay flat her hipbones were less prominent. She could hear Philip whispering in her ear, his fingertips tracing the path of her spine. "Never get fat," he said. "I want to feel each and every bone, see the muscles, know where the blood is flowing."

She could still feel the edge of that glass slicing through her skin and the sadness of recognizing she had done that to herself. She leaned over and put on her sunglasses. Harrison had written to tell her that Matilda was pregnant and they were living on the farm in Mozambique. Sam had finally stopped trying to follow him to work, afraid he would disappear again. A week after she received his letter, the phone rang in the middle of the night. When she picked it up she heard lots of buzzes and clicks, an operator with a South African accent, and then the sound of a man crying.

"Hello?" The sobs sounded very far away.

"Cordelia?"

"Harrison? What's wrong?"

"I'm drunk."

"It's three in the morning."

"I don't care."

"Why are you crying?"

"I miss you."

"You're just being morbid. You shouldn't drink."

"I don't want her here."

"Harrison . . ."

"I love Sam, but I don't love her. And the baby . . ."

"What?"

"It's not mine. I know that. We haven't fucked enough. The timing's wrong. It's not my baby. Delia . . ."

"Yes?"

"Why'd you get rid of our child?"

"It was Philip's."

"No it wasn't. I'll kill that bastard."

"Yes. He wouldn't let me use anything one night. I knew when it happened."

"That son of a bitch!"

"It's all right."

"No it's not. Nothing's all right. You've had a hard time."

"It was a rough year."

"And I made it worse."

"No you didn't."

"Yes I did."

"Our timing's just lousy. This is costing you a fortune."

Harrison sighed and hiccuped. "Delia . . ."

"Yes?"

"If I can get back to you, will you let me?"

"I don't know."

"Will you think about it?"

"Maybe."

"I want you to think about it."

"I'll try."

"Are you happy?"

"No, Harrison. Not yet."

"Have you met anyone else?"

"No."

"Wait for me."

"I'll try."

"I love you, Delia."

"Thanks."

They held on to the silence for a moment, and then they both hung up.

She had seen Philip once, helping a very young, thin woman into his car. Cordelia, carrying a bag of groceries, started to turn around, but he looked up from closing the door and saw her. She put the bag down on a stoop and faced him. When he looked into her eyes, he halted, turned his palms upward and smiled. She shook her head. For a moment he hesitated, then he spat on the ground, returned to his car, and drove off, his tires screeching.

That evening the phone rang and her machine recorded a message made inaudible because of the lowness of the volume. She erased the message and unplugged her phone. Someone rang the door buzzer a few hours before dawn. She saw the limousine parked across the street, and she hid behind the drapes, watching him staring up at her window, his arms crossed in front of his chest, his face concealed by the shadows. She felt he could see her despite the fabric. She was afraid he'd break down her door. Finally, he walked back to his car.

After dinner she helped her mother load the dishwasher, and then they brought a tray of coffee out to the porch. Fireflies flickered across the lawn, blinking in scattered unison with the chirping grasshoppers. The air smelled of roses and freshly mown grass. Her mother's face looked soft and young in the moonlight.

"I think of her less now. Sometimes a whole day can pass and I don't see her the way I did. It was the same for so long. She'd be six years old in her cowboy suit, or a young woman lying on a table in the hospital, white, dead. I wonder, am I forgetting?"

"Of course not."

"I woke up the other day and I felt for my breast. I was so happy to find it missing, because I had dreamed that and I thought: *My daughter isn't dead! I just had my breast cut off! Thank God!*"

Her mother's face was tilted toward the moon. Her eyes were shiny. "Somehow it has become normal. We can have Thanksgiving. Her birthday will arrive, and we'll get through it. What was once utterly inconceivable is perfectly acceptable. It makes me angry, but I know we couldn't go on with that violent denial. What it was doing to us."

"How can it be so short?" Cordelia leaned forward in her chair.

"What?"

"Life. It's so insubstantial."

"It seems so long to me. I feel like I've been alive for a very long time."

"No you haven't! God, Mother! No you haven't!"

"Baby . . ."

"I don't know how to let people go." Cordelia looked up at the sky and saw that the stars were all perfect. "I don't dream anymore."